Praise for Megan Kruse

Megan Kruse is a young writer of raw and fearless talent and *Call Me Home* showcases all she can do. She writes here of harrowing lives — of a family bent and broken by violence, where each person is desperately trying to somehow grow toward light and liberation. In the process, she offers a most unlikely tale of hardness and hustle, of grace and loss, of painful love and tough breaks and the unimaginable paths we must all eventually take toward survival.

ELIZABETH GILBERT, Author of *Eat, Pray, Love*

Call Me Home is an uncommonly powerful debut novel. Megan Kruse writes with great heart and intelligence as she crafts a gripping story from the shards of a broken family.

JESS WALTER, Author of *Beautiful Ruins*

I've been a big fan of Megan Kruse for a long time, but *Call Me Home* left me astonished by her talent. Beautifully written, deeply felt and utterly compelling, this story of a desperate family separated and on the run is full of unforgettable scenes and richly imagined characters and heady suspense. It's so vivid, it feels like my own memory. I recommend it with all my heart.

DAN CHAON, Author of *Await Your Reply*

Megan Kruse has written a tough, unflinching and very loving story about an isolated family trying to scrape by and find a way, one way or another, to survive. I was deeply moved by the lives of her characters and scared for them right up to the end. Just a wonderful book, in every way.

BEVERLY LOWRY, Author of *Crossed Over: A Murder, A Memoir*

An urgent, beautiful book about love and its consequences, set against a backdrop of the unglamorized West. These characters will lodge themselves in your imagination, stick with you long after you're done reading. A fine and original first novel.

KEVIN CANTY, Author of *Winslow in Love*

I'm not sure how Megan Kruse did it. Her first novel manages to be a swift yet contemplative story of how a family can love each other fiercely even when every heart involved gets broken. Through its cast of characters, she is able to focus on what makes a human life shine with joy or ache with conflict. Her writing is cinematic – going from intense close-ups to beautiful sweeping wide shots. *Call Me Home* is a multi-layered and deeply felt wonder.

KEVIN SAMPSELL, Author of *A Common Pornography*

I can't stop thinking about this book. The tension and suspense had me hooked on page one, and I didn't want the novel to end. Megan Kruse writes unflinchingly about the terror of domestic violence and its haunting effects on a family. She writes with compassion and grace about how humans fail and betray each other, and also how we find and take care of each other. *Call Me Home* is a harrowing, beautiful, and tender novel about the meaning of home, loneliness, and the endurance of love. Kruse creates characters so deeply drawn and compelling, they will stay with you long after you close the book, as will the novel's memorable settings, especially Kruse's vivid portrait of a dark, mysterious, and wild Pacific Northwest. Megan Kruse is a talented and fearless writer, and the prose is just stunning. *Call Me Home* is a tremendous accomplishment.

CARTER SICKELS, Author of *The Evening Hour*

Megan Kruse is a stunning and inspiring new voice in American literature. Her beautiful debut, *Call Me Home*, proves that even as the violence of our lives invents us, a story can do something like save us. Read it and stick it in your heart.

ARIEL GORE, *Author of The End of Eve*

For my mother, who taught me to love language;
my father, who taught me to love stories;
and my brother, who knew those woods even better than I did.

Call Me Home

A Novel

Megan Kruse

HAWTHORNE BOOKS & LITERARY ARTS
Portland, Oregon | MMXV

Introduction

Elizabeth Gilbert

WHEN I MET MEGAN KRUSE, SHE WAS TWENTY-ONE years old and sleeting across America like a storm. I was in Wyoming at an artist's residency, burrowed down to write a memoir, and Megan came blasting through our world, visiting a fellow artist-in-residence. She stayed for just the briefest moment, and then she sleeted out again, but I never forgot her. There was something both hard and bright about this young woman – something that impacted me greatly. She was brave (traveling alone, sleeping in her car, living without) and she gleamed with purpose. She was here to make things, to learn things, to see things, to write things. She was funny. She was bold. She was in a hurry. She would tolerate no obstacles. I got the feeling that fear – whenever it tried to hit Megan – probably just bounced off her and shattered into a million sparkling, harmless pieces.

For a while, we stayed in touch. Her emails were so smart and entertaining that I wished them to be published. Her writing was great – crazy great. Nobody should be able to write that well so young. She had such talent, such charisma, that I almost feared for her. I didn't want things to move too fast. I didn't want her to be swallowed up by the sheer force of herself. I felt matronly and protective toward her – toward her talents, really. I was always warning her to find her discipline, not to spin off on us, to keep at her labors, to steady herself down, to find her foothold. I was kind of bossy and stern about it. I wrote her long lectures about honoring her potential. I couldn't help myself; I had become invested in her.

Then I didn't hear from her for a long while. I didn't know where she had gone to, and I worried. I feared she might have quit writing. I feared she had not risen to meet her considerable gifts.

I needn't have been afraid.

Megan Kruse showed up in my life again just last year with the manuscript to *Call Me Home*, and suddenly it was very clear what she'd been doing during those vanished years: She'd been *working*.

What she has produced is this beautiful, haunting, elegiac novel. I happen to know that, in her travels and wanderings over her adult life, Megan has seen much of the world, but to tell this tale she returned home to her origins – to the raw, hard, stark, ravaged environment of rural Washington, where she had been raised. Kruse once described her homeland to me as "the country where the mudslides happen," which works as a descriptor on many levels. The landscape of this novel seems to be a mudslide in process – people slipping, lives slipping, whole towns on the brink of sliding away forever into poverty, despair, and violence. To return to that sort of world and to try to describe its dark power is to scramble for a handhold in the mud, but she has found that handhold, and her prose holds on for its dear life.

Call Me Home is not merely a story of place but also a story of family – particularly a story of siblings. I would say that, in a way, it is more about kinship than about family (two very different ideas when you break it down). It is almost about twinship, actually. The brother and sister in *Call Me Home* are not exactly twins but might as well be for all the power of connection that thrums between them. They might as well be conjoined twins for the ways their souls and fears and hopes are bound together. Certainly, nobody will ever understand anyone more than these two understand each other – for better or for worse. In the mudslide, in the miasma, in their own individual distractions of sexual desire and yearning, they reach for each other across the dark and grip tight. When they are separated, the grip still holds. The grip always holds. Their grip held on me, as well, long after I finished reading the manuscript. I can still feel their hands on my wrists.

In introducing her own manuscript to me, Megan wrote, "And so I think that in some ways the novel became a love letter and an apology. An acknowledgement that I am inextricably a part of where I came from, and that you can't actually weigh what is precious or ugly; it is itself, and so are we. What became important as I grew older was the inventory of what might be lost: the way my father would run backwards through the yard to make us laugh; the steep banks and creeks that filled in winter, where my brother always lost his shoes; my mother's jewelry strewn across a dresser."

That inventory is this novel, and it gleams with a dark radiance. It contains *everything*. Megan Kruse has met her promise, and I am glad.

ELIZABETH GILBERT
Frenchtown, NJ, 2014

CALL ME HOME

I.
The Pig

Lydia

Tulalip, Washington, 2006

THE SUMMER I WAS NINE, MY FATHER CAME HOME WITH a pig in the back of the truck. The pig was big, with thick bristles along his spine, and he scratched his back against the barbed wire. "We're going to fatten him up," my father said. He threw food into a long trough and then stood back and crossed his thick arms. I followed Jackson to the pen but I wouldn't touch the pig. Jackson was fourteen and braver than me. He let the pig eat from his bare hand, but I held tight to a long stick. That night I put a piece of bacon on the windowsill to warn the pig to stay away.

My mother had a broken arm that summer. Each day while my father went to work, she got up and cleaned the house, and I helped her until my hands were raw from Ajax. When I heard my father's car pull into the drive I would run to Jackson. We would wait to hear our father's voice, to know if he was angry. Sometimes, if they fought, my mother would come to my room at night, sit on the edge of my bed, and whisper. "You must be brave, Lydia," she would say. "You must trust me."

All summer long the pig kept rooting under the fence, and my father kept rebuilding it. I thought it must mean something that the pig kept escaping, that maybe it hated my father. That maybe it had powers. I tried to have powers, too. If I counted my steps in threes, I promised myself, if I saw two birds on the roof of the house, if the rain came by four, then my father would be kinder. My father would be new.

In June, while my father was at work, we put clothes into

bags and put them in the car. The pig watched us as we drove away. My mother took us to a hotel, but my father followed us and brought us back. He made dinner and danced my mother around the living room, but I felt afraid to let them be alone. I sat up late into the night with Jackson, listening, waiting. I held tight to his hand and he didn't let go. The next day, I took one of my father's beer bottles into the shed and smashed it to pieces with a rock until it was half dust. There was a dark empty hole in the wall behind my bed, down by the floor, where I kept secret things. I kept the bottle back there, or at least what had been the bottle, wrapped up in an old rag.

"You must be patient," my mother had told me. "You must believe in me." I was patient and I did, but every night when I was in bed I reached down to the floor, into the dark space, and felt for that rag.

There was quiet for the rest of June. It got to the point where I stopped reaching for the rag in the dark. I let the pig eat a slice of apple from my hand and wasn't scared at all. On the Fourth of July, we went to Marysville to watch the fireworks. My mother looked so beautiful, and the fireworks were bright blooms in the sky above the water tower. What happened between that hour and the next? My father drove the truck home over the rutted road too fast and when he pulled up to the house he pushed my mother out into the dirt. Jackson took my hand and we jumped out of the truck, ran to the edge of the pasture and crouched there. The pig came to us and pushed his head through the fence, and we all waited in the dark until it was over. I touched the pig's nose. "Shh," I said, and the pig stayed quiet.

The air was quiet and mean after that. The longer it lasted, the farther my brother and I ventured into the woods, across the property lines that were deep in fireweed and salal. At the end of July, when the brush was thick and dark, we followed the creek until it ended at a pile of trash. We opened one of the trash bags and things came spilling out – eggshells, torn paper, orange peels. Jackson held up a broken wicker basket. It had plastic eyes and was made to look like an owl. We brought it home, and I kept it hidden under my bed. I thought we might be caught, and so later I walked to the edge of the woods and threw it as far as I could.

We played with the pig every time our parents fought now. His bristled back scratched my palms. I fed him scraps from the table and wanted to be good, to do right. If I could be only be good enough, I thought, surely it would count for something. Surely things would change.

AT NIGHT I lay awake and listened to my parents talking. Not the words, just the sounds: "I love you, I hate you, I'm sorry." Jackson was in his room all the time, listening to music on his headphones and drawing in his notebook. Now that he was fourteen he kept his door shut all the time and wouldn't let me hear his music, but still he let me come in and sit by him. I stared into the snowy tunnels of the blankets. On weekends he'd take me with him to Randy's house, and while he and Randy smoked pot I would hold a lizard, let it crawl up my arms and around my shoulders.

In August, the pig escaped again and my father called the butcher. I was sad but didn't say it. I stared at the square white packages, lined up like coffins in the freezer. I held one in my hand until it burned with cold. I tried not to look at the empty place in the pasture where the pig had been.

When my father broke my mother's nose, I made his sandwich out of the bacon I would never eat myself. My hands were shaking to touch that bacon. I carried the sandwich to my bedroom and brought the rag out of the dark space behind my bed. I poured the glass dust into my hand and looked at it shining, and then I laid it between the mayonnaise and the meat. It was the perfect sandwich. It was the worst thing I'd ever done.

I stood in my bedroom and looked at the sandwich. I tried to pick up the plate, to carry it to my father. I counted to ten, and then I counted to ten again. The plate was heavy as the moon; I couldn't move. *Now*, I thought. *Do it now*.

When I heard my father's boots in the hall, I couldn't breathe.

He was coming toward me and all I had to do was hold it up. It was a gift for him to take, but I ruined it all. I ran past him with the plate in my hands, out the back door and into the woods behind the house, where I buried the sandwich in the dirt by the creek. I threw the plate into the underbrush and no one ever knew.

Now I think that if I had told Jackson it would have been different. He would have helped me be brave. He would have understood how badly I wanted my father to disappear, and what happened later might not have happened at all. But I thought Jackson already knew. ... He was the one beside me in the grass outside trying to keep me from hearing them. The pig was nowhere, but still he held me there in the grass, scratching the dirt, saying low, low, "Listen, you can hear the hooves, listen."

Amy
Tulalip, Washington, 2010

SHE KNELT BY THE OLD METAL STORAGE LOCKER IN THE torn-up garden plot, and the water soaked the knees of her jeans. She could see the house through the dark winter brush. She could hear the hard crack of the axe and the sound of the rain dripping from the trees, a soft and intermittent staccato. The storm last night had taken down a tree on the slick steep drive. The old winch had jammed months ago, and they hadn't replaced it, so Gary had gone to town and rented one to drag the tree up to the house, where he was splitting and stacking it for firewood.

He would have to return the winch by eight. She moved quickly, opening the storage locker, pushing aside the rusted trowels and feeling through the loose seed packets until she found the one she wanted. She slipped the cucumber packet deep into her pocket and started toward the house. Her ribs hurt and she held her arms tight at her sides. The wind was whipping her face, cold and wet, and she could smell chimney smoke. January. It had been nineteen years since she'd left Texas with Gary and moved out to Washington. Nineteen years that she had lived with him and raised their two children. She ran her fingers over the envelope in her pocket, emptied of seeds, and packed tight with the money she'd stolen from her husband.

Inside the house, she opened soup cans for dinner, stirred their contents together in a saucepan on the stove. She had put plastic over the window after he pushed her through the glass, and she could hear the rain tapping against it. The sound of it made her sick to her stomach, thinking of how her children had watched him push her.

Six o'clock. Half an hour for dinner, she thought, and then Gary would return the winch. She called down the hall for Jackson and Lydia to set the table, which they did, quietly, Jackson passing the plates to his little sister.

After the four of them had eaten, still quietly, and after Gary had pulled away in the truck, she turned to Jackson. "Get the things you and your sister need," she said. "Now." She handed them two garbage bags and took one to her bedroom. She pulled things out of drawers without really looking at them, and they put all of the bags in the backseat of the car – the shitty, unreliable one. She said a quick prayer to no one that it wouldn't break down before they made it to town.

They were all silent as she drove. Lydia ducked down in the backseat; Jackson looking out the window. She took the back road around Marine View Drive and then the freeway to Everett. Gary would be at the other end of town, turning in the winch, collecting his deposit. Everett wasn't far enough away, she thought, but that was the point. It was a shell game. He would think they'd try to get farther away, so she'd stay close. She drove the car up and down the dusky streets, not looking at where she was going, until she found a motel that looked abandoned. The parking lot was walled off from the street. A burnt-out sign read The Starlight.

Jackson and Lydia brought in their backpacks and the garbage bags of hastily packed clothes. She watched them, holding her arms against her broken ribs. Here were her children. Jackson at eighteen looked delicate and beautiful and older than the other boys his age, the ones she sometimes saw milling around the high school parking lot. Lydia was small for thirteen, always with a worried look on face. Her children, blinking dark and light in turns, striated with the things they let her know, what she inferred, what they kept from her. Never again, she thought, will they see Gary put his hands on me. Never again will they worry their days, stringing minutes into hours, listening for footsteps, for raised voices.

They locked the motel door and pulled the curtains. Jackson turned on the television and they sat in its blue light for a while: a news report she didn't hear, a sitcom, noise. She would talk to Jackson and Lydia more in the morning, but for now she just wanted them to rest. They'd done this all before, anyway: the constant television drone, the dim light, the uncertainty. When they had climbed into the flat, rough beds, she let herself imagine it. She allowed herself a faint, warm hope that she would never see her husband again. That he would not find them and they would be free. Nineteen years ago, she thought, and still she remembered it like it was yesterday. She and Gary had barely pulled off the interstate and bought a newspaper when they found the ad, a plot of land going cheap; they drove there the same day. It was on the edge of the Tulalip Reservation, five acres that needed a well, needed to be bulldozed again. It was a good half an hour from Marysville, the nearest town.

They'd pulled up in their pickup after driving the long days from Texas, where they had both grown up. The backseat was full of stuffed garbage bags and suitcases. The ninth of January 1991. It was a cold Wednesday, bone chill and damp, a dark little new year. Even now she could remember the day because of the way it felt like a beginning, like her whole life was about to start. Even in the dead of winter the brush was thick and green over the little plowed road. The owner had led them around, picking over the fallen blackberry, copses of alder, around stands of sword fern, and Amy had taken in the dark loam, the overgrown ghosts of the dozed paths, the flat area at the top of the hill, where the house should go. She wasn't sure what she was supposed to feel. It was so different from anything she had known – but it would be theirs, she thought. Surely it would not take long for it to begin to feel like her own.

When they'd seen the whole of the property, walked from corner to corner, sighted and nodded at the orange flagging tape, Gary had said, "We'd like it, sir," and the owner had smiled, and they knew he would sell it to them. It would be more than five years before Gary hit her for the first time, and ten before her love for him dissolved into a sharp bead of fear in her side, her stomach, her heart. They had stood together under a maple, beneath the dripping pavilion of its leaves.

And now, in the dim room at the Starlight, Amy thought of all the things her eighteen-year-old self had left behind all those years ago – her kind, worried mother; her father, who had come back from Vietnam when she was only an infant, but never really came back at all; her best friend, Jennifer, and her old dog, Sam; the streets of Fannin, Texas, the brisket smell, the bad bars and tire-ironed windows of the shops on the outskirts of town. Now, in the Starlight, her children were sleeping, and she tried to sleep herself, tried to dream her dreams into them, to dream a new life again, to will it to be coming for them even now.

Jackson

Portland, Oregon, 2010

THE LAST TIME HE SAW ERIC WAS A SUNDAY, AND BY THE time Jackson knocked on the door he felt like he might fall down or, worse, that Eric might send him away. He was thinking about that Greyhound bus to Silver, Idaho, and if he was going to do it. It was dancing around in the back of his mind. There's something to be said for starting over, Jackson thought.

He stood outside of Eric's top floor apartment, his boots crushing soft crescents in the white carpet in the foyer. There was a knocker shaped like a lion. He hung onto it for a second. He felt sick. His nose had been bleeding, off and on, and he hadn't been able to find an open bathroom to wash his face. "Come in," Eric called, and Jackson opened the door on the clean white hall with mirrored hangings on either wall. It reminded him of a woman's throat, her glittering earrings.

Jackson went to the bathroom; Eric had left a towel, a new pair of underwear in Jackson's size, and a white undershirt folded on the edge of the bath. This had become their routine, the comfortable confines that Eric had established for them. "Why don't you get ready for dinner?" he would ask, and Jackson would go. It seemed easier for Eric to pretend Jackson wasn't hustling, and maybe it was easier for Jackson, too. On the counter was a bar of French soap wrapped in the miller's ribbon.

He looked at himself in the mirror. He'd lost more weight, and his eyes were bloodshot. He looked like shit. His hair was dirty, hanging in his face. He tried to imagine that maybe he looked glamorous in a rough way. All those movie stars and musicians with long, stringy hair, ripped jeans falling off their hipbones, stubble. Stubble, he thought, that was a laugh. He could wait forever but that ship was not coming in. He didn't even have to shave. He looked at his chest, narrow and bare. He looked like a poor man's Kurt Cobain, he thought. A very poor man. He turned the water as hot as it would go and stood in the shower for a long time.

Eric was in the kitchen, as usual, when Jackson came out of the bathroom. He was pouring wine, and Randy Travis was playing. "On the Other Hand." Jackson had a memory of Travis on a record cover–his skinny sorrow, his melancholy eyes. All of Jackson's first loves were country singers or people he could imagine that way: wistful, tight jeans, drinking problems. Jackson's mother loved Randy Travis.

"For you," Eric said. He handed Jackson a glass of wine. Eric wasn't a county singer, or even close. He was nearly sixty, big in a way that seemed natural, not bad looking. But there was something about his money that made him ugly. In a restaurant Jackson imagined him sending the entrees back and talking loudly about the waiter.

"Tell me how you've been," Eric said, laying one hand on Jackson's knee. The routine was to pretend Jackson had been living somewhere, with roommates, maybe. That he wasn't sleeping in the gutted house on Forty-seventh, or in the park, or in one of the shelters if the temperature dipped too low. That he had money, and that Eric wasn't paying him.

It only bothered him when he really felt like shit–nights when he was eating gut rot dumpster food, listening to fifteen-year-old runaways tell their war stories. Then, he thought, it didn't seem right. He wanted Eric's money, but it still didn't seem right. Once, Eric had given him a twelve-hundred-dollar watch, a Movado. Jackson tried to pawn it, but no one bought watches for anything close to what they were worth. He kept it, but he couldn't stand to wear it. There was something terrible about that watch.

"I've been great," Jackson said, in his earnest voice, the

voice he used with Eric. He drank Eric's wine, sitting on the stool in those expensive boxer shorts and the clean white undershirt.

"Work has been hard," Eric said. "Busy. There's a new property I'm flying out to look at in Georgia, and we're hiring in the Clackamas office." Eric was the president of a real estate company that bailed out foreclosing apartment complexes, forcing the owners into high-interest loans. Jackson guessed he had been a fat and unpopular kid and that he had learned to covet all of the things he'd been excluded from. Eric wanted to buy a life, a personality, significance. It disgusted Jackson and turned him on, the idea of fucking this man who cared only about money.

At first, he'd taken what he could get. The men in the shadows downtown, up against a brick wall outside of a bar. Wandering around the video store up on Burnside, until someone asked him if he wanted to watch a video. The first time a man had asked, Jackson had nodded and followed the man downstairs and into one of the dark little booths. "Fifty," Jackson had said. The man nodded quickly. That was his first cock and he gagged on it. When the man came, Jackson spit the man's cum out onto the floor, took the money, and left.

That night, stepping out of the video store and into the soaking rain, someone tapped on his shoulder and he stood against the side of the building, the water dripping from the gutters down his neck, and jerked the man off, over and over, but the man didn't come. Finally, the man grabbed Jackson's hand. "Okay," he said, "okay." He handed Jackson what little cash he had. Fourteen dollars. He went to a bar and his face felt bruised and his eyes hurt. He had a drink, and then another. He made himself imagine that it hadn't happened at all.

With Eric, it was easier – the shower, the wine and dinner, easy sex, and then the envelope of cash that Eric left on the bureau. When Jackson took it, Eric would pour a glass of water or go to stand at the window, looking at anything else. It seemed like such a simple transaction. It had been two months – a short time in the world of houses, running water, and groceries on Friday. Here, two months was a little lifetime, and he didn't feel guilty. Most of the time, he didn't feel much of anything. Eric's bed was a soft shell to lie in. The stupid little luxuries, the wine, the soap, the heavy cotton sheets, tipped the scale after a week of otherwise scrounging in the cold, hungry and hung over. Sometimes he hated himself; sometimes he hated Eric. Often, though, it was enough.

IT HAD STARTED with the Starlight Motel, two months ago – February. Except it hadn't just started there; that was too simple. A broken window, tire ruts crossing an empty road, the stale smell of his own dirty clothes. It had all been set in motion a long time ago. The Starlight was only one of the louder notes of that song.

At the Starlight, his mother didn't look like his mother. She looked cheap and sad and old, dying her hair in the little motel sink. She'd always been a brunette, pretty but not in a prominent way. She was tall and she had broad shoulders. A crooked front tooth that she tried to hide, pulling her top lip down when she smiled. As a blonde she looked like someone else. Like someone playing dress-up, trying too hard.

She combed her hair out in front of the mirror, watching herself. Jackson sat behind her on the arm of a chair. She caught his eyes above the sink. "Do you like it?" she'd asked. "Is it the new me? The new and improved Amy Holland?"

Lydia was on one of the double beds, on the paisley bedspread, vinyl-covered batting. "I like it," she said. "You look pretty, Mama."

Jackson didn't say anything. He stood up. "I'm going out," he said.

"Jackson – " She turned from the mirror and looked at him. There were narrow rows in her hair from the comb. She sighed. "You be careful."

"I am," he said.

The motel was on the ground floor, a shitty pay-by-the-week place. Jackson in one bed, Lydia and their mother in the other, watching daytime television and eating hamburgers from the Burger King across the parking lot. Jackson felt like he was losing his mind.

Jackson took a left on the street and began walking. He had half of a cigarette in his pocket and he lit it. Everett was bigger than Marysville or Tulalip, a real metropolis in comparison, stretched out along I-5. To the west was the Sound, and to the east the highway that led you out to Snohomish and then over the mountains. He stood for a minute on the gravel outside the Burger King watching the constellation of city lights until the cigarette burned out and there was nothing to do but go back to the motel.

They'd left four times already. Twice in cabs to motels paid for by Volunteers Of America, where a woman ten years younger than his mother came and spread her sheaves of paperwork on the desk for his mother to sign: *I will not disclose my location. I will join a support group. I will eat Ramen noodles and Hot Pockets and stare at daytime television because there is nothing else to do.*

Every time, his father had found them. After a day, a week. But this time was different. He could feel it. After his father pushed his mother through the window she was wound tight as a wire, disappearing into the garden for long periods of time. It was three days before his father let them out of sight, and the moment he did, his mother's voice was quick and low in his ear: "Pack your things. Get in the car." He couldn't say exactly why this was different but he knew.

By the end of the first week in the motel, Lydia had painted her fingernails and toenails with magic marker. Their mother had filled out job applications for Shari's, the Royal Fork Buffet, the Fashion Bug. She wrote her name as Amy Merrick, her maiden name, instead of Holland. Their new life was going to be full of salad bar sneeze guards and ladies' fashion separates.

The caseworker was supposed to come out the next day to do another intake. Jackson hated the intakes. The woman would stay for hours, asking the same questions in a hushed tone, as though he and Lydia had no idea why they were vacationing at a roach motel. They left bags of holiday coloring books for Lydia, no matter what the season, and no matter that she was thirteen and hadn't colored in years, and something for Jackson–a dusty package of tube socks with yellow fade lines on them,or a Western novel with the cover torn off.

Jackson couldn't stand the idea of being there when the woman came this time. He already felt like he was going to crawl out of his skin. Lydia had one of his feet on her lap and was coloring his toenails with a purple marker.

"I think I'm going to take the bus back to Marysville tomorrow," Jackson said slowly. "I'm going to see Randy." He had some money of his own. Not a lot, but enough to get back north.

His mother looked at him. "Jackie," she said. She picked at the fleece pills on the hotel blanket.

"And Chris," Jackson added. If she didn't know, she guessed. Chris was the star of the high school swim team, and someone had seen them leaving the pool together once, long past closing. People talked.

"What if your dad sees you?"

"Mom–he's not going to."

She pulled at the hem of her shirt, touched her new blonde hair, watching herself in the mirror. "Just be careful," she said.

"Jack," Lydia said. She didn't say anything else, just leaned down to blow on his toes. Jackson sat up and put his arm around her. She was little for thirteen, with sharp elbows and knees, and her hair was cut in a blunt little bob. Her face was delicate, though. Her eyes were close-set but they made her look smart, he thought, like she was concentrating hard on something. If he got a job he'd help her get some new clothes. Cute things that would help her make friends in the new school. It was stupid, but it mattered.

"Please be careful," his mother said again, and he nodded.

RANDY HAD PICKED him up on Fourth Street in Marysville. Marysville was adjacent to Tulalip, "the big city," Jackson's mother called it. Home of the famous water tower, a dozen sluttish girls. Randy was a senior, the no-friends, pasty variety. He liked a radio call-in program – what was it called? It was local, AM radio with a temperamental bandwidth. Callers described weird occurrences, the paranormal. Things that happened right in their own homes. A ghostly fingerprint in the butter. A wife gone missing – all her clothes still in the closet, even her shoes. Jackson didn't mention that this was exactly what his mother had done the first time that they left his father. Randy was Jackson's best friend. In fact, if Jackson were to count the top three friends he'd ever had, Randy was first in a race that included a retarded boy from preschool and his middle school locker partner.

Randy had a car. He made money in some suspicious way, something with his computer. "Dude," he said. "Are there hot girls in Everett? I bet the school's fucking huge."

"I haven't been to school yet," Jackson said. "I guess I'm just going to skip for a while." Would he even graduate? Probably, if Sharon had anything to do with it. She was the kind of guidance counselor who looked at her delinquent charges with weepy, Precious Moments eyes. "Your potential," she would wail. "You could have it all." Jackson imagined his potential like a sickly man in the back of the room who coughed a little harder every time Jackson fucked up. Skipping school to sit in the chlorine smell of the pool watching Chris knife through the water? *Cough.* An eight ball of cocaine the weekend before the PSATs? *Cough cough.*

"Sick," Randy said. "Wish I could do that."

"Yeah," Jackson said. Jackson knew his friendship with Randy had something to do with Jackson being a fag and everyone assuming that Randy was, too, but he and Randy never talked about Chris, or about Jackson being a fag, for that matter. Randy talked about girls and seemed not to notice or care when Jackson didn't join in.

Randy brought Jackson from the bus station to his little house near the high school. The fields flipped by. It was still early spring but it might as well have been the dead of Washington winter. Still green, but dark green. Black-green. A living lake bottom, a mildewed constitution.

The house was boxy and collapsing, rain-beaten. Randy had the basement apartment to himself. It was cold like a tomb, damp and snaky. There was a brick and board shelf of books on the paranormal, and a radio with the antennae covered in tinfoil – presumably, Jackson thought, so he could catch the radio program even ten feet underground. Two milky fish tanks. "Looks good in here," Jackson said, and Randy grinned. The only lamp had a cloth thrown over it, making the whole place seem underwater.

Randy wanted to show him some computer game that Jackson didn't understand – didn't try to understand. They sat in the aquarium light of Randy's room until six or seven, and he watched Randy maneuver a guerrilla fighter through a dark forest. Randy bit his lip and pounded his fist on the desk when the guerrilla was ambushed. A saucer of ash and resin clattered to the floor. "They rig it," Randy said. "They rig the fucking thing so you can't actually get to the eighth level without paying somebody for a tip. There's a call line and everything." He wiped his hands on his pants, glanced at the clock, and stood up. "AM 530," he said. "Man." He went to the radio and flipped it on. Static, a distant, low voice. A woman was saying, "The refrigerator just keeps opening on its own."

Randy sat in a torn-up armchair and pulled out a bag of weed. He rolled some loose leaves into a crooked joint and lit it. "I don't know about the appliance stuff," Randy said, "I'm out on a limb about it." He took a long drag of the joint and held it, blew it out in a long trail of smoke. "Too many variables. Too many technological flaws." He handed the joint to Jackson.

The announcer was soothing. "How disturbing." How disturbing, thought Jackson. His head felt a little swimmy. The eggs are ruined again. The mayonnaise has turned. "Have you had any other problems in the house? Anything out of place?"

Randy leaned back in the armchair and crossed his arms. "That's the real test. It's like diagnosing a disease when you have to have a certain number of symptoms."

Jackson nodded. The woman said that the arms of her coat often appeared to wave at her from their hangers in the dark. The announcer made a low noise of interest. Jackson liked Randy's basement room. He always liked places where no one else came. The back of a warehouse, the cab of an abandoned pickup. Anyplace where no one would know. He thought of the empty locker room, of Chris.

Their whole thing – that was what it was, a *thing* – was muted in his memory. The bat sounds of swimmers underwater, interrupted with an occasional hand job. He wanted Chris to like him, desperately, but he couldn't say why. That was the bigger problem. Chris *didn't* like him desperately, but Jackson was willing to pour himself into whatever vessel it took to make himself wanted or wantable. He would lay everything out on the table in front of Chris – a desperate banquet of need. And now what did it even matter? Chris was out there, standing under the locker room shower, kicking off his Speedo, throwing it down against the tiles, the water beating against the broad of his back, running down the roads of muscle, and Jackson was going to be stuck in Everett, in secret, alone.

When the announcer faded off for the commercial break, Randy turned to Jackson. "What's going on with your dad, man?" He was looking very intently at crumbs of weed, trying to herd them onto another rolling paper. "I heard it was bad."

"What did you hear?" Jackson asked.

"Ah – nothing, really," Randy said. "Just that he ... you know. Hit her a bunch. Broke the windows."

Jackson picked up a paperclip from the table, bent it open, twisted it. "Yeah, well, don't believe everything you hear," he said.

The announcer came back on and they sat in silence for a while. "All of my sheep were gone, a man said. The whole farm, lifted up in the night." The announcer said gravely, "This is not as uncommon as you may think."

He ditched Randy at eight. "Dude," Randy said. "Are you sticking around? You staying with your old man?"

"Yeah," Jackson said. Later, he wouldn't know why he'd said

it, why he'd come to Marysville at all. His life – and his mother's life, and Lydia's – pivoting on that stupid "Yeah," accidental, inevitable.

"You want a ride?" Randy's eyes were bloodshot. His T-shirt was torn a little and a patch of his soft chest was showing.

"Yeah," Jackson said. "Thanks, man." Randy led him out of the cave of the room and followed him into the wet air.

The pool was a mile from Randy's, and it was seven miles after that to his father's house in Tulalip. His father's house, his mother's motel. Jackson hoped Lydia wasn't worried about him. Chris always practiced at the pool from four until seven. One night Jackson had shown up at the pool just around closing, and they'd hid in the locker room until the janitors had locked up. Chris lifted Jackson up onto his shoulders, naked, and threw him over and over again in the shallow end. It was dark and he had to keep clambering over Chris's head, clutching at his hair. They didn't talk about it, just kept laughing and doing it again. He could have done that forever. They hadn't even slept together – they never did, not really, but he didn't care. He would have done that for the rest of his life. The short flight through the air, the lukewarm water, again and again.

Randy slowed by the pool under the sodium lights as though he knew. There were no cars in the parking lot. Of course not. What had Jackson thought, that because he was there, the pool would suddenly stay open? That Chris would be slicing through the water or sitting on the pool deck waiting? He had the feeling of someone having come back to see an empty house, someplace he used to live. He wanted to feel what he used to feel, but there was nothing. His whole night was already mapped out – Randy's aquatic basement, the empty pool, his father. He knew he would go and he went.

His father's car was gone when he made it to the house. The mobile home. There was a trash bag taped over the window his mother had sprawled through, a week ago now. A sickening, slow fall that he had watched from the hallway, his throat tight so that he almost couldn't breathe. "Promise me you will never get involved," his mother had told him. "It will make it worse." She'd hung over the side of the frame, at the waist, where his father had thrown her, and then he came up behind her, kicked out the rest of the window, and watched her fall the four feet to the ground. Jackson had taken Lydia back to his room and held her there for the rest of the night. He'd gotten up once to throw up, hating everything, his father most of all.

That was their last fight, the one that had landed him and his mother and Lydia in Everett, and it had started with him. It made him angry at himself, and at his father, and at his mother. He'd said something about moving to Seattle for school, Seattle Central Community College. His mother had smiled. "There's queers up on Capitol Hill," his father said. "It's where the queers go." He looked at Jackson, a half smile on his face.

His mother put her hand on his father's arm. "It's a good school," she said. "And it's a little early to be talking about this, anyway." It was too early, Jackson had thought, thinking about the weepy guidance counselor and the column of shitty grades on his transcript.

"I'll go where I want," Jackson had said, and shrugged. And how had it gone from there? The loud confusion, his mother jumping to his defense. The window. Lydia in the back bedroom, chewing on her hands.

His mother sat in a deadly calm for a few days. She listened over and over to a Bellamy Brothers record, which only made Jackson feel more certain that they were about to leave. Let your love flow. Each time before there had been an uncomfortable incongruous quality to the days – "Don't forget your coat," he remembered her telling Lydia once at noon on a ninety-degree day before they loaded up the car and took off for three weeks in Carnation.

Jackson knew they were going to go, he could feel it, and so he went down to the pool one night and found Chris. "I might be gone for a while," he said. Chris had barely acknowledged him. Jackson gave him a round wooden box he'd turned on a lathe in shop class. Inside he'd slipped – he couldn't even believe this now–a lock of his hair. He hated to think about it. There was no way to make it not awful.

He took a beer from the fridge–empty otherwise, except for mayonnaise, a carton of eggs, and an open bag of chips that his dad probably put there when he was drunk. He sat down and turned on the television, trying to pretend he was someone else–a guy at home. Watching a little TV. Drinking a beer. The news was less and less interesting. Someone's tractor had slid into a ditch. There were too many animals for the local shelter. The key in the lock. "Hello?" His father.

"Jack," his father said. Jackson could see he was drunk. His pants were unbuckled–it used to drive his mother crazy that his father would piss in the yard–and he looked at Jackson and smiled. "My boy."

"Hi, Dad."

"Where you been?"

"Around. Came back to see you."

His father smiled. It was disarming, that smile. He had a shadowy face, eyes sunk deep under his brow, but then that hard, bright smile. One of his ears stuck out and when he smiled it made him seem goofy and disheveled. Jackson felt relieved. He wanted it to be normal, as though his mother and Lydia were just off somewhere shopping or at an appointment. No questions, just easy.

His father took a beer from the fridge and brought another to Jackson. He sat down and put his legs up on the coffee table. He wasn't a big man, but he was tall and strong. His arms were muscled and the table groaned under his heavy legs, his work boots. "Nothing on the news these days but shit," he said.

"Somebody put their tractor in a ditch," Jackson said.

His father laughed loudly. "This is good, Jack," he said. "I'm glad you're here."

He smelled like sawdust and beer. "How's your sister?"

"Fine."

"Your mother? How's she?"

"She's fine."

"Sorry you had to see that quarrel."

Quarrel, Jackson thought, was not a word he'd ever heard his father use before. He shrugged again and drained his beer. He felt a terrible guilt for a moment, thinking of his mother. Her new blonde hair. She was probably lying on the motel bed right then. Trusting him. Rain spattered against the plastic that covered the window.

"Where you been staying?" his father asked. "Someplace safe, right?"

"It's safe," Jackson said. He looked down into his beer.

"I hope your mother hurries up and heads home," his father said darkly. "You better leave her number here. We should chat, Amy and me."

"No, Dad." He looked at a spot on the wall, where a picture had been. A hazy not-there mark. The news had gone off and there was some crime show playing.

His father was quiet for a while, watching the fuzzy picture on the television. Jackson shook one of his father's cigarettes from the pack on the coffee table and lit it. L&Ms. His father raised an eyebrow but didn't say anything. The smoke curled up and then hung like a veil around the yellow lamp. The beer was making him sleepy, and he knew he shouldn't be here, but at the same time it felt like the only place in the world he knew. There had been times when they'd been happy. He and his father and his mother. Less when Lydia was born, but that was only because things were harder. Money was tighter. Where had it gone? To shoes and food, according to his father. To Christmas presents.

His father opened another beer and handed one to Jackson. There was something on the television – the crime show, the victim had been camping. "Do you remember when we went camping?" his father asked. "When we used to go?"

Jackson remembered a river, wide and brown, moving slowly. It couldn't have been Washington, or at least not the western half of the state. His father's shorts rolled up around his thighs, the languid air, the water warm and torpid. All evening the moon had wallowed in the oily water and his father had played the guitar while his mother sang, mournful, laughing. Jackson was small but still he was allowed to stand sunk to his neck in the river.

They had slept there on the bank, on camp mats, the mud bank strewn with crockery and beer cans. All night long mosquitos whined in his ears and bats swung across the sky. They had lost a suitcase in the water and found it days later, shored up in ragweed and briar. And there had been a motorbike – before? after? – and then a summer rain, and his father had driven, and his mother sat on the back, and Jackson fit between them so he could see only narrow lines of sky and ground above and below his mother's grasp. The water had come so quickly. He felt his mother's hands pulling him closer, and his cheek was against the soaked cloth of his father's shirt. He pulled his feet higher. He could see nothing, not the lights up ahead, not the trees washing free from their webbed roots, not the ground slipping away.

Jackson burrowed into the sunken couch cushion. He felt a relief that he'd spend the night in his own room, his tiny bed. His father had built bunks for him and Lydia, and then, four years ago, he'd taken a chainsaw and split them apart, shoved Lydia's half into the study. Jackson had carefully decorated his room, finally free of the schizophrenic décor: his music posters, her stuffed bear in its pink overalls. Not that his music choices weren't on the nelly side – at thirteen, he'd hung a poster of Reba McEntire, in her big hair days, and then that picture of Kenny Rogers from the cover of *The Gambler*, staring straight ahead, laying his money on the stacked poker table while a crowd of burlesque dancers and socialites crowd around him. There was something about that – the beard, the steely gaze, the vest. Jackson had nursed a long fantasy starring Kenny Rogers as a kind bachelor, a plane crash that tragically takes his parents' lives, his ultimate adoption by Rogers.

The adoption fantasy didn't start until the fighting did – or at least until he knew about the fighting. He didn't remember any problems until after Lydia was born, but maybe that was just because there was no one else to watch out for.

Jackson was aware, after a while, of his father looking at him. He felt uneasy. A few minutes later, his father flipped a beer cap across the room. It hit the wall and bounced off onto the carpet. "I saw that faggot friend of yours," he said. "What's-his-name."

Chris. Where had his father seen him? Had he said anything? Jackson felt a sick anger at himself, thinking of that lock of hair. Why would he do that? Then anger rose at his mother in the Starlight with that slutty haircut. Jesus Christ.

"Yep," his father said. "I saw him. Looked like shit."

Later, Jackson wouldn't understand why the idea of Chris and his father made him angry at his mother. And still – he'd sat on the sofa and thought about how she should be sorry for all of it – sorry that he was sitting here in the house they couldn't come back to, and why couldn't they just fix it up like adults, act like *grown-ups*, for Christ's sake, instead of his mother dragging him and Lydia off to another shitty one-star motel to start another shitty one-star life, when this one was bad enough already?

Had his father asked? The television was still on, but Jackson couldn't hear it and he only barely remembered saying it, but he had, exactly as though it was what he came to do: "Mom's in Everett," he said. "At the Starlight Motel. Room 121."

There was a long silence. Jackson stood up, walked to the fridge, and opened another beer. He wanted to drink it all, before his father could. His father turned from the sofa and looked at him. He smiled slowly, that boozy, friendly smile. "You're a good kid," he said.

That was it. His father went off to bed and Jackson sat staring around the house.

He did nothing – he didn't call the motel, he didn't change the story. He watched his father set out in the morning in the truck, heading south to the Starlight. Jackson milled around the house, waiting. There was a bitter taste in his mouth. He thought about his mother's new hair. The precise penmanship on the job applications, the way she'd said, "Well, that would be nice, a 10 percent discount for employees." She had looked out the window of the motel into the parking lot and smiled. Jackson looked out the window now–outside, the ruts that the truck had left in the yard were filling with rainwater. The house smelled of cigarettes and mold. There was nothing here, he thought. Nothing to show that this place was theirs. Just the scuffed-up walls, the broken spine of the couch, his watery reflection in the window. It was a shame, he thought, to have a face this ugly in a place with so little beauty already.

Now, two months later and two hundred miles south, in Portland, he couldn't piece together what he'd been thinking that night, why he'd done what he had. He and his mother and Lydia had almost been free. Instead, he'd ruined everything. His father brought his mother and sister back from the Starlight, and a week later, they left again without him, lighting out to anywhere, nowhere, leaving him in Tulalip with his father. ... He couldn't blame them; how could they trust him? He couldn't trust himself. He'd sold them out to the man he hated most in the world, and by the end of the month he was on the streets in Portland. His whole life, small as it was, and he'd fucked it up. His mistake.

Now, when he slept at Eric's on these precious Sunday nights, he curled himself into a ball, the sheets thick and slippery over his face. Tonight, though, he didn't sleep. He'd been thinking about Silver–about this idea of moving on–since he showed up.

Eric kept two thousand dollars in cash in a tin box on one of the polished wood tables. The box had a picture on the front in Technicolor–a row of peach trees, bright green leaves, blush cheeks of fruit. It was a test, Jackson knew. Eric knew that Jackson knew it was there, and if he were to take it the illusion would be broken; they would become the strangers they were. For now they could exist like this–in this world they'd made, where Jackson materialized once a week and then faded back to nowhere again. If the money was gone, it would all disappear.

He'd only taken one thing from Eric in the last two months, a necktie from a row of them that were looped over the closet rod. It was maroon and navy, striped diagonally. He put it in his pocket just to be able to take something from that world and carry it back to the other.

He must not have slept. He was awake when the alarm went off. The room was still dark because Eric had the kind of heavy, expensive curtains that could blot out the sun. Eric was in the shower, and Jackson opened the box so easily. In five minutes, or ten, Eric would step out of the shower, lie on the bed damp and flushed. There were hours still before Eric's afternoon meeting, and they would fuck and then eat breakfast in bed, chichi pastries that Eric had bought the day before and strong coffee.

Jackson slipped the twenty hundred-dollar bills into his boot. He knew what it meant – he couldn't see Eric again. He had an idea about his life, a way it was supposed to be. He imagined that somewhere else, if he was truly living in another life Eric and this part of himself might die off easily. The peaches like globes of perfect sunshine, smooth and covered in sun. Even the wood of the box felt warm. His mother had loved to drink peach nectar. She would buy a little carton of it and drink the whole thing alone. It saddened him, but he couldn't say just why.

The shower shut off, and Jackson could hear Eric humming to himself. "Turn on the espresso machine, would you, Jack?" he called. "I'll be right there."

"Sure." Eric's money was a hard wedge in his boot. Jackson walked to the kitchen and flipped on the shiny chrome espresso machine. He went down the hall quickly and quietly, let himself out the front door and was gone.

OF THE GREYHOUND ride he would remember the wet rock corridor of the Gorge, a long stretch of farmland, and a truck stop in Pasco, where a man was kicked off for buying a tall boy of dishwater beer. The camel color of Spokane and the slow climb toward Silver. Rocky hills, the stands of pines more regal than the ones he'd known, less stunted by washed-out roots. Lake Coeur d'Alene glittering, hiding something dark and sour. He thought of what he'd heard about the white supremacists out here, the queer bashers. Some kid at Marysville-Pilchuck had a butch sister who had gone to school out here and then dropped out after the windows of her car were smashed and her nose broken by a faceless group in the middle of the night.

The bus drove him fifty or sixty miles into the rocky panhandle. Signs for little towns, broke down saloons, a dirty rim of snow spitting up from the road. The bus let him off in a town called St. Regis, where he waited for several hours at the Travel Stop for his ride. He'd overshot Idaho, but that was what he'd been told to do. St. Regis was built around the Greyhound stop; there was a bar he wished he could drink in and a store full of Western novelties, antler coat racks, and cowboy bathroom fixtures. He spent most of the evening sitting on a wooden bench outside, smoking Camels. All evening, men wandered across the street from somewhere in the vague woods, where he guessed the houses were, headed for the bar. ATVs rolled up and down the road. At ten or eleven, a truck rattled up and stopped, and a man got out. He was broad-shouldered, wearing work boots, dusty jeans, and one of those canvas jackets made for the Rockies. He looked up and down the wooden walk that stretched around the Travel Stop. "You Jack?" he asked, looking Jackson over and lighting a cigarette.

"That's me." Jackson knew he must be a disappointment. He was a hundred and twenty pounds soaking wet, pale, his girlish hands.

"Mike Leary," he said, pushing back the sleeves on his sweatshirt.

"Listen," Leary said. "I'm beat. And nothing's open in Silver right now, so I can't get you set up. What do you say we just stay here tonight and then head over in the morning?" He gestured toward a dark motel across the street. One letter – T – flickered on and off, but mostly off.

This was something he hadn't bargained for. Was there anything worse than a long evening in close company with a stranger? Jackson looked around quickly. Was there booze? Anything? A restaurant? No, conversation over food was worse than the television.

In a motel room you could pretend to be tired. Jackson followed Leary through the gravel parking lot and toward the saddest motel. The door of each room was cracked plywood. The tiny windows had their plastic curtains pulled tight. It was April but still like winter. Jackson's bag was cutting into his shoulder.

Mike Leary was a generous man, it seemed. He paid for two rooms, side by side, shook Jackson's hand, and wished him goodnight. Jackson closed the door and sat down on the bed. Just another terrible motel – cigarette burns in the bedspread, a picture of a sailboat above the bed. He slid the drawer to the bedside table open and there was the Bible. Poor witness, he thought. Poor thing. He closed the drawer.

And so here he was. Idaho. Well, Montana, and then Idaho tomorrow. In the bottom of his duffel bag he'd shoved a pint of shitty whiskey and he brought it out. What else was there to do? He sat on the bed. Turned the television on, turned it off again.

His life looked more and more like a stranger's. They'd never said that at Marysville-Pilchuck High School, that it was possible to have a life you'd never imagined. One you'd never wanted. A quick prayer for Lydia to any God that might be listening – let her be happy, let her be at a slumber party, let her have friends – then he pushed the thought of her away before he felt sick and drank off of the whiskey instead.

He could hear the shower in Leary's room. He thought of Leary naked. It wasn't a bad thought. He was fifty-five or sixty, heavy around the middle but not fat. He looked like a guy who had a lot of friends. In any other world, Jackson would have been both terrified and aroused by Mike Leary. Correction, he thought, in this world he was both terrified and aroused by Mike Leary. Leary didn't seem at all put off by the fact that Jackson obviously looked like he hadn't held a hammer in his entire life. Jackson knew that Leary must know something about him; how much, he couldn't say. He'd landed here because of Ida, Leary's daughter, and this idea she'd had for him.

Ida was a street outreach worker, one of the young people

with yellow badges who'd waited in the parks at night, giving out food, clean needles, and advice. She was the only one who didn't annoy him. She was no different than the rest – young, mousy, with curly hair that she kept pinned up, a T-shirt that said Street Team on it. She didn't seem overly eager to make him talk about his life, but she remembered small things he'd asked for, and she was always where she said she'd be on certain nights. They'd sat one night in the wet grass and talked about country music. She liked all of the people you'd expect: Dolly Parton and Willie Nelson, the Dixie Chicks, and he told her about Robert Earl Keen and Randy Travis and George Strait. She would go home and listen to something and the next time he saw her she would be ready to talk about it. Jackson imagined her at home in some little apartment, boiling pasta on the stove and listening to those songs.

And that was why he was here, really – he'd done it for Ida. Her wet eyes, blinking fast. She didn't have to tell him about the job – hell, she might have lost her own job if anyone knew that she was extending personal favors. She had no real reason to believe in him. And Jackson did it for her because it seemed like there wasn't anyone left who wanted something from him, and that seemed rare and good. He'd disappointed everyone else, but he could do this one small thing.

The day that he went into her office. He could see already that he'd done something important, and it made him proud, in a silly way: Delinquent Pleases Social Worker! Woman Takes Leap, Does Not Regret It!

"I was wondering if your dad still needs help." He picked up a paperweight on her desk, put it back down. The wad of Eric's money in the bottom of his shoe – one more bridge he'd burned, and no telling yet whether that was a mistake.

"Nice to see you, too." Ida's cheeks were flushed. She was pretty, Jackson thought. He really did imagine her happy someday, with some nice, slightly faggy husband who would live in her shabby apartment with her and listen to her when she came home from work.

He smiled at her. “Sorry.”

“So what’s been going on?” she asked. She must have seen he was skinnier. He felt it even when he walked.

“I think I want to get out of here,” he said. “I’m tired of this.”

She nodded approvingly, but not in a bad way, not the guidance counselor way. Just like, I know. He saw how he was making her day, and instead of that old impulse – the part of his father he could sense in himself sometimes, which he hated and feared – to ruin it, to make her feel bad for thinking she knew him, it made him happy. “Do you think your dad still has work?” he asked again. “I’m free.” He shrugged his shoulders in that dirty coat. Of course he was free. A regular bird. He shrugged again. Four hours later he was gone, tunneling through the Gorge in the rattletrap Greyhound. “Riding the Dog,” a man next to him had said sorrowfully. “All my life I be riding the Dog.”

HE’D HAD JUST enough of the whiskey to make him good and drunk. It was a good feeling. It was snowing outside, and the heating unit was making a noise like it might give up, gravel in a tin can. He lay across the bed of the hotel room and put his feet against it. It burned when he touched it with his toes, but when he pulled them back it was cold again. He accidentally kicked the wall and then thought of Leary and tried to be quiet.

My new life, he thought. This is where I will be. Here. Thirty miles from here. Even the ceiling above him was stained. It floated on and off of its plane. The room turned ever so slightly and that comforted him.

He was cold all night. Did he sleep? He kept thinking of one day when he was younger, five, maybe. His mother took him shooting out on the back forty. The day was full of magic to him – he hadn’t known she could shoot or even that she owned a gun. She wore a dress and boots. Earplugs. He must have had earplugs, too, but he didn’t remember them. She was beautiful. She was pregnant with Lydia, buoyantly pregnant, the .38 steady in her slim hands, her dress, her bare brown knees above the tops of her scuffed brown boots. If there were problems between his parents then, he didn't know it. The house – the double-wide mobile with an addition built on – still seemed big enough; the woods outside were the dark green rim of his only world; he did not want or know yet what there was to want. Fragile egg of his naïve contentment. His mother, the gun, her hand on his tiny shoulder. That was all of it – his whole wide world.

Lydia
Interstate 84 East, 2010

WE DROVE AT NIGHT, AND THEN, WHEN WE WERE FAR from home, we drove into the day that grew brighter and brighter as we left the mountains behind. In Idaho, the only colors were the dark of the woods and the white of snow. On the highway I counted sixteen onions, spilled from the open beds of trucks. The snow was deep between the trees and I remembered a snowman I built once. I pushed rocks into his snow mouth and the snow closed back up. I pushed a stick right through him.

We kept driving south until the snow was just bright dust on the red rock hills, like snow on Mars, and the air was so cold it burned. All this time I'd thought that everywhere was as dark as where we came from, that the trees went on and on. The things we had were behind us in plastic sacks that rattled and snapped as we drove. I made lists of what I'd left behind. A closet of clothes. The toys I was too old for and my little bed. My big yellow tomcat, half wild. If I had known it was the last I would see of him, I would have been better. He clawed up my new jacket and I was mad all winter long.

I didn't speak my brother's name that whole long drive. My throat was a hard, hard stone. The things I said to my mother came out choked and thin. I thought again and again, I don't hate her. There was a fist in my stomach. In my chest.

In Utah, we stopped at a motel. In the parking lot two boys were smoking cigarettes, tapping the ash into empty cans. When she thought I was sleeping, I felt her sit beside me on the bed.

She touched my hair. Her hand was light on my face. "You are my home," she whispered, "and I am yours." Her voice stretched and lapped around me. When I woke up, my mother was in the chair and her tea had spilled in her lap. Her sweater was damp. Outside a bird sang in the gray snow of the parking lot.

We went to dinner that night in a restaurant across from the motel in the best clothes we had. There were thick plastic menus and the waitresses looked tired.

"It's nice to go out, isn't it?" my mother asked, and I said yes.

If my mother and father were going out, if we were left at home, Jackson would post me at the door like a soldier. I'd wait to see if the car raced up the drive, if my mother got out quickly and ran toward the back of the house or if the car idled in the driveway, if they kissed in the front seat. I remember it was always raining but I never felt a thing.

We left the restaurant in our good clothes, and in the car my mother took off her heels and put them on the backseat. She started the engine and drove us out of town. The highway pulled us forward like a long rope. When the sun spilled over I was always awake. I watched the gray fields and the shuttered towns. When we stopped I tried to look at no one, as if I had been made new, and if I were careful the regular world would not settle on me yet.

Those evenings, waiting for the car, I would become the same kind of nothing. "Listen for them," Jackson would always say, and I was only the sound of the gravel turning, the wheels that would beat up the road, the night ahead, and all the things that would happen but hadn't yet.

Jackson

Silver, Idaho, 2010

SILVER, IDAHO, FROM THE WINDOW OF MIKE LEARY'S truck, was about the ugliest place he'd ever seen. The buildings were squat and mildewing, roofs caved in. Storage containers, piles of junk. A dog picked over a pile of trash, his hide raw, no collar. There were shitty plastic toys in yards, in snowed-over dirt. Everything looked unarranged, things knocked from the shelves, bare foundations, the planks of new buildings.

Leary pulled up at a grocery store just inside of town. "Need some staples," he said. "We'll get you some things, too." There was a crate of squash in a sodden cardboard corral. A bulletin board of handmade signs–*HoneyDo Handyman. Wanted: Samoid Dog Hair for Spinning, Will Pay.* A cart, abandoned with one busted wheel. Of all his mistakes, he thought, this one was the biggest. In Portland he'd had it good, and only days away from it he was hit with nostalgia, a long corridor he could look down, each door a different scene: Eric's bed, the sheets with a thread count higher than he'd known existed; the Willamette dotted white with sailboats; the streets at night, wet with rain, when he was inexplicably happy to be alone, in the dark, just walking.

He didn't have any money. He'd put most of Eric's two thousand in his childhood savings account, but he didn't have a bankcard or checks. He'd kept a hundred dollars in cash, but he'd used that for the bus ticket. Stupid, he thought. Was there even a bank in Silver? He thought about his options and settled on saying it: "I don't have any money," and Leary winked at him. "Don't sweat it," he said. "You'll be able to pay me back soon enough."

Don't bet on it, Jackson thought. He'd never done any labor in his life, really. He'd never had a real job; he'd stolen money if he'd needed it, picked pockets when he was brave enough, or stolen money from his father, who blamed it on his mother. Once, when he was sixteen, he'd stolen a ten from his mother, and he hated himself for it even now. He'd watched her fight his father for it – "There's no food in this house, Gary," she'd said, and his father had taken out his wallet and peeled off two tens, saying "I should go with you, bitch, and see how you spend it," his eyes straight ahead on the television, a game, something just beyond that lit-up field. That same night, before she could spend it, Jackson had stolen half of it from her; he spent it on some pills the next day. His mother hadn't said a word about it. Half of the time, Jackson wanted to kill his father. The other half he wanted to kill his mother – for fucking up, for staying while he and Lydia got sick and stupid.

He followed Leary into the Bread Basket Grocery. What there was of produce was piled up and turning. Little blonde children in shopping carts steered by their mothers.

Up and down the fluorescent aisles and Leary bought him a block of cheese, a loaf of bread, sliced ham sweating in a plastic package. A half-dozen eggs in Styrofoam, some bacon. Man Groceries. A six-pack of Budweiser, apples. Thirty-two dollars total.

Leary drove him east down a road past a cluster of trailers and work trucks. Across a stretch of rocky grass was the lake. "That's all crew housing," he said. "But since you're late ..." He grinned. "You get the special." Beyond the little travelling circus of trailers was the lake. It was a steep drop from that pebbly grass to the water. "It's still filling," Leary said. "Everybody thinks a lake will fill overnight, but it takes a few months. Come summer, it'll look better."

The special, it seemed, was in the deep woods. They drove the rutted road around the edge of the lake, and the trees were all around them. About a mile in, Leary pulled the truck to the right, toward the water, and in a winter cul-de-sac of leaf mulch was the cab of an old semi truck without any freight. It looked abandoned. The trees beside it were scratching the windows, and the windshield was covered with leaf-fall, rotting and dark. Leary stopped the truck, and Jackson followed him out. Leary didn't say anything, and Jackson was glad.

Leary opened the door and Jackson stepped up and inside the cab to where the driver would sit. Behind the front seat was more room than he'd imagined; there was an entire living space hidden inside. It hadn't occurred to him to wonder where truckers slept. He felt a quick, sharp disappointment as his eyes adjusted to the dim light. The linoleum was coming up in ragged peaks. There was a propane stove propped on the counter, a few pots and pans stacked in the sink. On the counter, a handful of noodles floated in glutinous water. There was one bed to the left, framed with windows; it had been stripped of its bedding. The mattress was covered in a rubber sheet. The little dinette was missing one of its long cushions; the rest were laced with mildew.

Leary reached forward and picked up the pot, leaned back out of the door, and pitched the noodles into a nest of brush and weeds before returning the empty pot to the stove. "Listen," Leary said. "This is shit, I know it. But we don't have much out here right now. There's still some housing going up –"

"It's fine." Right on the back of the disappointment, a little thrill. It smelled like cigarettes but it was dry; someone had wiped the side windows and there were little blue cotton curtains that looked new and could be pulled shut. And it was his – that was something.

"I have a sleeping bag for you in the back of my truck," Leary said. "And a flashlight, and an alarm clock. There's matches and dishes in here. I hooked the water up, but you're gonna have to piss in the woods. There's a Porta-John around the corner, about a quarter mile. Later, you'll have to get to the site yourself, but tomorrow I'll pick you up. Five forty-five. Too early to piss straight,

I know." He looked up at Jackson. "You got questions?" It didn't sound unkind.

"I don't think so," Jackson said. "Anything I should do before tomorrow?"

Leary smiled. "Just get ready to work," he said. "Walk around. Town's close enough. A few bars. Start a tab if you want, with Mary, tell her I said it's okay."

"I'm eighteen," Jackson said. Lame, he thought. Exceptionally, zealously lame. At least everyone would assume that he'd graduated high school already. He had a late August birthday and somehow it worked out so he didn't make the cut and was older than everyone in his class. Everyone in his class who was still there, rotting in the dingy airplane hangar that was Marysville-Pilchuck High School.

Leary shrugged. "Suit yourself." He looked back into the gray dark of the semi cab. "Do whatever you want with this place. When we get more housing up, we'll try to move you. Pay's every Friday, and we've got a little bank in town that'll cash your checks." He pointed to the road. "You need me, just head to town and ask for me. Everyone here is crew or knows the crew, okay?" He reached into the pocket of his canvas jacket and pulled out a crushed pack of cigarettes. He fumbled one out of the pack and pointed to Jackson's steel toes, his street kid insurance. "Wear those boots, tomorrow, and something warm." Leary smiled again. "I'll be back in an hour or so with more supplies. You'll be all right?"

Jackson nodded. Leary brought him the sleeping bag and flashlight and a little battery-operated clock; he felt warm and grateful watching Leary drive away. His truck left narrow ruts in the soft dirt and birch bark around the parked truck cab. There were wolf's teeth of ice under the dirt.

The cab was in a pullout on a gravel road, a side road that ended in a clearing. He walked a little way up the main road and there was another clearing on the right. Two other semi cabs were pulled into the gravel there, but empty. Dark bosses, staring each other down. They reminded him of toys he'd had when he was little. Transformers, things like that. Machines that were beasts, too.

He'd never had a place of his own, just the little bedroom on Firetrail Hill, which he'd shared with Lydia until the eighth grade. Then, after his father sawed the beds apart and moved Lydia to the study, his father demanded the bedroom doors be left constantly open. Jackson was too much of a liability. Who knew what little faggots did in their rooms alone? His father would walk the hall knocking doors back open. He was suspicious of Jackson before Jackson was suspicious of himself.

The day his mother and sister fled without him, leaving him in Tulalip, he could not stand to stay with his father, to be his conspirator. He couldn't stand to look at what he'd done: the two of them, father and son, the drunk and the toady, alone in the house. Instead he hitched to Randy's and sunk down in the basement there, not going to class, just watching the fish tanks, the fish dull and shedding skin and the film of old food on the top of the water. He drank the cheap beer that Randy's father bought for Randy and smoked Randy's leafy dry weed. His stomach hurt him, either the beer or the guilt. Both.

Jackson had stayed there for a few days, even though he sensed that Randy was frustrated with him. He tried to be obedient, to get his thoughts together. Each night he sat like an attentive puppy while Randy tuned into the radio show. It was a terrible feeling, he thought, to have exhausted even the people who have always exhausted you, to need to lean on them so badly. And so, it was only a week after his mother and Lydia left without him that he left again, too, hitching his way to Portland, for no reason other than that was where his ride let him off.

And now. He walked back to his strange truck-house. There was a little Honda generator on the floor, with extension cords snaking to the hot plate and a little icebox. A bare bulb hung in a metal cage; there were little round lights on each of the walls, too, and Jackson pressed one and it emitted a weak battery-operated glow. There was a row of cabinets under a narrow counter, and he opened and shut the drawers–someone had left a box of plastic forks, half a dozen ketchup packets, and a porn magazine called *Creampie*. He opened his bag and took out his own meager housekeeping–a pair of good scissors and a knife; a photograph of himself with his mother and Lydia, on the beach, five years before; the watch and tie of Eric's; a little one-hitter that Randy had given him. He laid it all out and turned on the generator and watched the appliances come to life, and that was it, he supposed; he was home.

THEY WERE FINISHING up on his third day. It was a liar sun–or that was what they called in it Washington, in the late spring, when it seemed like maybe the long winter was over, and you could stand in the weak light in the afternoon and feel warm, until five or six when it was gone and the cold settled back in. Jackson sweated all afternoon and now his T-shirt was cold and stiff under the arms. He was dragging trash to piles, where later he'd burn it once the rest of the men moved on. That seemed to be the heart of it–they did all the work and then he took the scraps and the shit and burned it all down. He swept up, wishing he had something–anything–in front of him besides lying in the dark truck cab, blinking a flashlight off and on when he heard the mice down in the wheel well.

Dave Riley was putting his tools away across the lot. He slammed the truck closed and headed toward Jackson, wiping his face with a towel. He kicked out one of the footlights that were trained up behind the beams. "You coming to the Longhorn?" he asked.

"Is that the bar in town?"

"Sure. You coming?"

The men on the crew liked to spend the hours between five and eight in the bar in town, drinking Old Milwaukie and talking about their wives. Riley didn't seem to notice that Jackson was barely eighteen if he was a day, and so Jackson shrugged. It's not like he had any real pride to lose at being kicked out, anyway. Riley and half the rest of the North crew had seen him fumble through the back of the tool truck like the bonafide sissy he was, pulling out tools at random when they'd asked him for a Phillip's head. "Sure," Jackson said.

"You need a ride?" Riley nodded over at his truck, a monster of a Silverado, probably worth twice as much as the house Jackson had grown up in.

"Nah," Jackson said. It was a twenty or thirty minute walk to the main strip of Silver, but he liked the idea of having his moment of underage glory alone at the door, if the bartender kicked him out, without Dave Riley on hand. "I'm going to finish up. I'll see you there."

Jackson waited until Riley's truck had pulled away, with Slow Honey and Don Newlon following in Newlon's little Toyota. It was cold. The lake outside was turning a dark color in the evening light, swallowing up what heat was left of the day. He stood at the edge of the A-frame – where those picture windows would be. Where some other family would eat and go to bed and get up and keep their own secrets.

He felt a little jump of excitement thinking about the Longhorn – if he could get in. The summer that Lydia turned six she'd suddenly stopped being interesting to his father – too many questions, too much new strength. She'd lost some shine to their father, and he'd turned briefly to Jackson. It was, Jackson realized now, the last and only time his father had showed any real interest in him. He was trying to believe that Jackson was who he wanted him to be. It was that summer that he'd taken Jackson to the bar with his friends – the little bar down on Lake Goodwin, plastic picnic tables and an assortment of liquor bottles that looked like they'd been stolen from someone's parents. His father drank too much and Jackson ate two orders of French fries and watched everyone – the regulars, the couple in the back shooting pool, the bartender with the blouse that gapped between the buttons, showing her worn-out bra. He couldn't explain it, but there was something he loved about it. There was a bar for every loneliness, he suspected. A bar for every sad story, and one for every joy. All of those things, contained in the shifting glass, the water rings and finger-prints across old wood, the smell of sweat.

He'd been around and briefly inside the bars in Portland, but there he was someone else, a secret and a shame. All he'd wanted in those days with his father, sitting in the cigarette smoke that floated off a forgotten butt in an ashtray, was to belong to his father, to belong in that world and be held by it, and for a moment it had seemed like he did and he was. His father had gathered him up under his outstretched arm, rough wool against his cheek, and they'd gone back out to the car. All the way home, the painted lines weaved across the road.

He lost his way briefly on the way to the Longhorn, where the dozed roads met up with the strip of town; he walked too far around the lake and then had to walk back up through town. All of the little shops were closed, except for a little bar called Pete's – it looked smaller than the Longhorn and like if you needed to look at it twice you probably weren't invited. There were plenty of cars outside the Longhorn, though, and he could hear the jukebox.

Whatever scene he imagined – Minor Kicked Out of Local Bar, Loses Job He Was Never Qualified For! – faded away. Dave Riley called him over and made an invisible sign to the waitress and suddenly there was beer in front of him, and he was being introduced to some of the men who worked on the other sites, and it really was that bar dream, then. He took off his jacket and his arms had streaks of dust, and the guy everyone called Slow Honey clapped him hard on the back. He drank from the beer.

"You make any money today, Honey?" someone asked. "We've got a load of scrap and rebar down on eight."

Honey tipped the brim of his hat up. "Yup," he said.

Dave was sitting beside him and he put a hand on Jackson's shoulder. Jackson started from the warm weight of it. "Honey's our not-for-profit junkman. He makes his own little fortune picking off our scrap." Jackson had seen Honey in his pickup hauling a trailer of scrap metal, twisted parts. Honey didn't seem slow; but then, Jackson thought, it was hard to tell with the quiet ones. He hadn't spoken more than a few words in the last few days and they probably thought he was slow, too. Better to be a thought a fool than proved a fool, he thought.

Newlon, the crew boss, bought a round for everyone. The conversation dipped and swung, words like the tools themselves, the raw material of work. Rebar, scrap, plywood. Skill saw. Forms. The sturdy little blocks of names: Ed, Don, Dick, Joe – Jack, he thought, he would be Jack. Who had it good, who didn't. The concrete guys, who had it easy. All of their scrap settling down in the foundation, roughneck gypsies, backfilling dirt and moving on. The beer was dark and bitter and Jackson let it wash over him, conversation, the comfort of being unnoticed, of being part of a group of men who worked.

"I was driving one of the big old one tons, thirty-year-old dump truck things with the hydraulic lift – "

"She had tits like this – "

" – just hit the switch and dumped it all on that brand new Lexus – "

"You just couldn't believe she was his sister – "

He tried to name each man at the table and couldn't. Don Newlon was the boss, he knew that – olive-skinned, long and lean, that dark beard. He looked away. Dick, Ed, Eli – they were construction, still snowed with sawdust that fell from their clothes to the bar floor. Joe was the one next to him – lanky and mean looking. He had a scar over his left eye.

"My first summer," Joe was saying to Don, "that bastard was up on the roof and I was down below, cutting whatever he yelled out and handing it up to him. I was on the ground with the plywood and it had just rained – I'm standing in a pool of water and it's hell. I'm dying, and I'm scared as shit because it's my first job and he's such a bastard, and I keep fucking up because that saw is killing my hands, and finally he gets pissed and comes down and grabs the saw and nearly drops it, like *What the fuck?* There was a current running through that fucker. That was two hours I was getting electrocuted because I was so damn afraid of him."

Don laughed and shook his head. He turned toward the bartender and swept his hand in a circle. Another round. He was a good boss, Jackson thought. He could tell by the way the men talked in front of him. And Ed, the one at the end of the table. Ed was funny, but he was good, Jackson thought. He finished his beer and picked up the new one. He'd never had beer that tasted so good, just his father's cans of dishwater and whatever he could get on the street. Ed had strong arms and bowlegs, and Jackson liked him.

"I was driving a quad, two guys beside me," Ed was saying. "I just looked ahead of me and there was a killdeer in my path and she got up on her legs and wouldn't run, got up on her wings in my path, then, and one of the guys gets a rock. He says, 'I'll kill it,' and I say, 'I'll kill you.'" He took a long drink. "Can you imagine being that small, and something as big as us comes around, and standing your ground? Jesus."

Jackson felt a kind of humming in his chest, a tender relief, the beating of invisible wings. The bird in the path. The brave bird and the tender guard. "That was one of hell of a bird," Eli said, and the other men nodded in agreement. They weren't like his father, he thought. They weren't like his father at all.

Really, when he looked back on it, he had decided to get drunk. "Fuck it, let's get drunk," he said. And everyone had raised their glasses up like, *Of course*, but also like he had made a wonderful new suggestion, like he might in fact be their leader–or, if not their leader, he amended, in the bathroom, staring at the penis someone had carved into the wall above the urinal–at least one of them. One of the guys. He swayed a little at the urinal and laughed at himself. There was something he was supposed to be thinking–something he had been thinking–about the kind of person he was, the kind of person that he had been. All his life and none of it made sense together. He was a construction worker. A cleanup boy, but still. A construction cleanup boy. A construction cleanup boy out with the guys. And the Longhorn had such good music! And such good people! He shook and zipped and launched himself toward the table and this new fortune, his little family of outlaws, his friends.

Don Newlon was saying something about having been on a trip down in Mexico with some girls – "And they left!" he said, slamming down his beer, the foam spilling onto the stained table. "I had no food and a blown transmission, but hell, I was smiling!" He laughed loudly, and the rest of them joined in. Jackson laughed too. He was drunk. He was happy. He grinned.

A man from the East crew started to tell a story about getting drunk downtown – Seattle? Portland? – and passing out in his car. Somewhere where you couldn't do it, couldn't park. He'd woken up when the tow truck lifted the back end of his rig.

And Jackson must have said something – who was he talking to? – because then their faces were waiting – they wanted some kind of story from him, and small ideas were flipping through his drunk mind like a stack of cards. And he was talking, talking about a kid he'd known in Portland who had tried to steal his shoes – "I woke up," he said, "and he was unlacing my boots!"

Even at that moment, he knew it was a mistake. It wasn't funny in the same way. There were too many questions hanging in the air – where were they sleeping? Why was he wearing his shoes to bed? But someone – Don? Honey? – started laughing, "Your boots? Jesus, I'd kill him!" and the moment was saved, and the waitress brought another pitcher, and he filled his glass up. He was so fucking thirsty.

HE WOKE UP at four or five. He'd been having dreams that he'd wet the bed, he needed to piss so bad, and he pushed the door open and pissed a long stream out onto the dirt. He was drunk-dizzy, but steady enough that he knew it would be worse later. He didn't remember getting home, only a brief moment of his face against the cold glass of a car window.

He fumbled around in the cab until he found a gallon of water, opened it, drank half of it down without stopping for air. He had a terrible feeling. What had he said? Did they know he was queer? The end of the evening was a shadow of a shadow, just those moments – he'd been talking to one of the men. His face against the cool glass. His thankful, horizontal bed. The solid earth. His heart seemed to be beating funny. He thought of his father, who was half-drunk most of the time. Was every waking day like this? The dark lapped at him, and he thought he might throw up, and he wondered how his father had ever been able to stand himself. Jackson felt a nauseous self-loathing that began in his stomach and moved out his arms and legs. Suddenly, he needed air. He got up and walked out into the cold, feeling his way through the wood chips and snowmelt and dirt toward the lake.

He felt better almost immediately, in the dark, walking. In Portland he'd walked everywhere. Hungover or high or straight sober, he would walk those streets at night and feel like he could go anywhere because this was his body, these were his own two legs. The road was always stretching out in front of him, the bridges knitting across the river, one way, back the other. He could hear the soft lap of the lake water now, and he sat down near the slope to the water. The cold earth soaked his pants and he felt better.

In another month, the lake would be full. The old river had been washing the town out slowly, one ruinous winter at a time. Silver was full of sand and gravel deposits, holes where the river had eaten away the topsoil, streets where the concrete was crumbling. According to Leary and the rest of the crew, the river was a loss. Channelizing it would save what was left of that watery dump, and then the lake, instead of being a marshy sprawl with no clear borders, would instead be a carved-out bowl, perfect and shimmering, and the water would spill out of a narrow channel at one end and head down the mountains, neatly continuing on its way. An aerial view of Silver would show a neat dark stamp pressed into the ground, spilling out to the east to become a river again, snaking through the blue-black timber to eventually join the Lochsa.

The particulars of the project were uncertain to Jackson. Mike Leary was someone big on a project that was, in the scheme of things, small. Just a handful of speculators interested in a pretty jewel of a lake, a necklace of houses. And it was pretty. The A-frames were half-moon clusters at four points around the lake, banks of tall windows reflecting the water. It was summer camp for the six-digit circuit. It gave Jackson a thrill, even in the dark, to see the peaks of each A-frame like a cathedral, the faintest glow of the pale wood. Even as Spartan as it was, he could imagine the kind of high-end lives that would settle into the bare rooms. Stainless steel pans hanging in the kitchen; *New Yorker* copies on the coffee table; expensive shampoo in the bathroom. If the old heart of Silver was a craggy piece of rock, the new heart was a smooth pebble, a skipping stone. Cedar and glass, large porches that stretched, plank by plank, toward the edge of the lake.

He kept having little boy thoughts, his half-drunk mind – how do they make a town? Where do the families come from? But still how goddamn *weird* that you could take a patch of silt and stilt it up and hem it in, sew it like a glove – the lake's fingers, the palm of calm water, the wrist of the lake spilling down dark mountains.

Jackson imagined that in twenty years the cleared land where the new lake sat would be lush again, full of young timber. The old riverbank, now exposed to the tin cup of the sky, would no longer look ravaged. It would become land again, and everything that had surfaced when the water ebbed away would be carried off. The shell of the old pickup, the bottles, the nameless bags of sodden, decomposed trash. At some point, it would all be dragged away or the grass would grow over it.

But still, he thought now, sick all the way to his toes, sitting in the wet dark, there was something about it that wasn't quite right. To take something alive and change it completely.

He got to his feet, shaking his hands in the cold, kneading his numb fingers together. The deep woods here were not so different from the woods he'd grown up in. Idaho was drier, but it had the same density, the same feeling of roiling, tangled life. Thick bark, dense moss, roots that wrapped their arms around the earth. A moth at the window, a mouse at the door. In Washington, the double-wide they'd lived in on Firetrail Hill had been like a live thing. The cat left a squirrel twitching on the kitchen floor; mushrooms pushed up the carpet in the back room; a raccoon let himself in the front door. For a few years, the whole forest was a treasure chest. Even now his memories were flawed by fantasy–here, he remembered, a witch came out of the tangle of weeds. He and Lydia sitting in the old rowboat rocked by the hand of a giant. The forest floor moving beneath them, spinning them, a leaf trembling in his hand. He had that same feeling now, in the blue dark, dizzy and sick, but still the forest was all around him and he was glad for it. He took deep gulps of air. Scraps of last night were tossing in his foggy head–cigarette butts, spilled beer, the throaty laughter of the men. He'd followed them around the room, through the music and close heat, swinging his arms, pulling out his wallet. He turned back up into the woods, even as above the lake, the sky began to lighten.

Lydia

Women's Shelter, Alamogordo, New Mexico, 2010

FIRST, GATHER EVERYTHING. THE CREDIT CARDS AND your birth certificate. The bank statements. The social security cards. If they are gone, it's because he has taken them. This will make things harder, but not impossible. You will be lighter that way. You will make everything new. Go to a place where no one knows you. The closer you are to home, the more careful you will have to be. Close to home, you must walk quickly through the streets with your eyes on the ground. The world is big. It's best if you keep going.

We drove for four days to get to New Mexico, through the mountains, the red Utah canyons, the flat sand. I watched the lava fields and they were ghostly as the moon. At the shelter there was a room with a sink and a tall window I couldn't see out of. We sat for hours in a little room talking to the caseworkers.

"He could find us anywhere," my mother said. "He could always do that, track you down in seconds. We'd make these plans and it was like he knew before we'd even left."

It was a small town, they told us. He knew the car. He might have had surveillance equipment. They told us that it's different, now.

You will need to sell your car. Choose something that he wouldn't expect. Choose something that doesn't look like you. Try not to think about times you felt that you were being watched. Instead, think about the life you want. Imagine that soon you will have a new house, and all of your new friends will come to visit. They'll be the best friends you've ever had, even better than the ones you had before.

We would stay for two months at the shelter in New Mexico, before leaving again for our new life. "Texas," my mother said. "But not Fannin. That's where I met your father."

In the caseworker's office, we called my mother's mother, who I'd never met. Her voice through the receiver was as clear as if she were in the room.

"Amy?" The voice was scared. "Amy. Where are you?"

"Shh," my mother said. "Shh. Everything is all right."

"Amy, listen to me," the voice said. "You come here. You live with me."

"It's not safe. People know us there. People know G there." Even in the shelter, she wouldn't say his name.

"Exactly," the voice said. "If they see him in town, they'll kill him."

I looked at my mother and at the woman. "That's where I want to live," I said. It said it loud.

"Smart girl," the voice said.

Try not to think of the times when things were not what they seemed: when your mother carried in a bowl of yellow pears that had been eaten to lace by insects, and how you watched her from the kitchen window as she cried, wondering at her despair. Or the long week she stayed in bed and no one said why. You knocked and knocked, but your brother led you away. He fed you whatever you wanted, straight from the cupboards. Don't think of these things. Let them be over or they will break your heart.

It was as if I went to sleep and woke up in a dry and brittle country, and I was older, with a different name, and I had no brother. The dreams started, that my father was coming for us. On those nights I practiced everything I knew. *To truly disappear, you must change everything. Forget your habits. Choose a different life. Understand that who you have been is gone and will never come back*. I said it to myself over and over: My name is Lena Harris, I am thirteen years old, I've lived with my mother, right here, since the day I was born.

Jackson

Silver, Idaho, 2010

THE CREW BOSS WANTED TO SEE HIM. SLOW HONEY DELIVered the message to Jackson from the window of his pickup, just as Jackson had pulled up to the sawhorse to start in again, slowly splitting the beams the way he'd been taught. Shit, Jackson thought. He'd spent the whole afternoon praying he didn't fuck up, and now he'd fucked it up anyway. It had something to do with the night at the bar – he could feel it in his gut. What had he said – something about shoes. Too much innuendo for that crowd, that's for sure. He might as well have just told them he'd sucked cock for cash – that he'd do it for free! – and then let the chips fall. This was much worse, to have to answer for something he'd only insinuated. Where next? Who did he even know? Back to Portland? Back to Washington? His father in his armchair, the TV dinners he must be eating now. The new girlfriend he'd be fucking on the terrible worn mattresses.

He put all of the tools away, stacked the wood he'd been about to work with in a neat pile. Everything in its place. "You want a ride?" Honey asked.

To where? "Where's he at?" Jackson asked.

"East side," Honey said. It was worse than he thought. He was going to the rich side of town to be fired.

"Yeah."

Honey drove him in Riley's pickup, which made him think that maybe Honey wasn't as slow as they said, to be allowed to drive that shiny, expensive car. Everything's relative, sure, but Honey seemed just fine.

"Lots of metals out here," Honey said. He hauled metal from the sites to Kellogg on his own trailer. It saved Jackson and the rest some of the work, and Honey made enough to live on, selling the bulk for a few cents on the pound, dragging a magnet to separate the pure weight from what was more valuable – aluminum, copper.

"You make good money?" Jackson asked.

"Sure."

There was a long silence; Honey moved the truck around deep potholes, steering it expertly with one hand.

"Friend of mine," Honey said, "put siding on his whole house. Corrugated metal. Didn't spend a dime."

"Wow," Jackson said. Maybe he could haul junk with Honey when they kicked him off the crew. "Hey, do you know what he wants me for?"

"Nah." Honey bumped the truck over the potholes. "Bet yer scared, huh?"

"What did I say, Honey?" Jackson asked. Scrubby branches squeaked the windows. "Did I do anything really stupid?"

"What do you mean?" Honey asked, and Jackson began to understand why everyone called him Slow.

"I'm scared," Jackson said.

"Don't worry. They're just probably needing more help on this side."

"You asked if I was scared."

"Nah," Honey said.

The East side looked like a whole different game. The foundation had been set for a big house – a house that made the A-frames look like camp cabins, and apparently the whole crew was devoted to it. Jackson tried to imagine who might live in a house like that. A Senator? A business executive? Who, with that kind of money, would come out to this dark little corner of the bottleneck? There were a hundred things he didn't understand. The first being Honey's sad little smile as he let Jackson out of the cab.

Don Newlon was sitting on the edge of the foundation. Jackson had noticed him the other night. Don's skin was an olive color;

he had that dark hair and he'd just shaved his beard from the other night, so there was a shadow of stubble around his jaw; he was so beautiful that Jackson couldn't look at him full on; he just looked at Don's edges. Beautiful Don with his long legs out in front of him like a kid, eating a sandwich. Watching him with the sandwich pissed Jackson off, all of a sudden; how can you eat when you're about to fire someone? All the old adages of his father's – the way that the shift leaders would sell out their wives before they'd lose a profit. "Throw your beads at someone else's daughter." His father shouting at the Channel 5 news when everyone was protesting the union. That was one thing about his father – he was a union man. The union gave him health insurance and got him off in time for cheap domestics at the bar, and no matter how many times the pressure came for a union bust his father wouldn't budge.

"Hey," Jackson said. Don held out the hand that wasn't holding the sandwich and Jackson shook it. He had shaken more hands in the last few days than ever before in his life. Don's hands were strong with long fingers. His palms were warm and dry, not too soft. It was a good handshake.

"Hey, Jack. Can I call you Jack?"

"Sure."

"How's the work going?"

"It's all right."

"Do you know your way around yet?" Don asked. He was looking at Jackson with his blue eyes and the dark hair was falling into them and Jackson looked away.

Shotgun shacks around the mudflats, the dingy houses that used to be lakefront property. The shady dark arms of the ironworks. The row of failing businesses: Maxine's Shear Perfection; Gold Mine Pawn; the liquor store. The clear teardrop of the new lake.

"Oh, sure," Jackson said. What was this? "The whole damn bunker."

"Just like *M*A*S*H*!" Don said.

"Those were tents."

Don looked a little wounded. "Right," he said.

Jackson felt an immediate sense of remorse. He wanted to take it back so that Don would smile at him again. "I loved that show," Jackson said. *I loved that show?* He hadn't even watched that show, only when he and Lydia tried dressing the television antennae in tin foil and it had picked up the Trinity Broadcast Network and that – *M*A*S*H**, and neither were the forbidden treasures he'd been hoping for. Jackson had thought of *M*A*S*H** as an old person's show, he remembered now. Don must be twelve or fifteen years older than him – it hadn't occurred to him until now to wonder how old Don was, but he guessed he was in his early thirties. Older than himself, and younger than Eric. Don had faint lines at the corners of his eyes from the sun or laughter. Jackson looked at them and looked away again.

"Me, too," Don said, happily.

"Yep," Jackson said. "Me, too."

"Ha!"

Jackson fished for a cigarette. His hands were shaking as he lit it. He didn't understand what was going on. It didn't seem like Don was here to fire him, but why else? To try to be his friend? Don looked like the kind of person Jackson normally would have avoided – beautiful – too beautiful, he thought – and capable, too much of getting his way in the world filling up his chest. Jackson could imagine him in a sports bar or out on the street, harassing queers just for the hell of it. Throwing peanuts at a couple fags across the bar. He looked like the kind of guy Jackson hated the most – the kind who would play grab-ass with his douchebag friends and then beat some queer kid down on the street. But that was a lie, too – the truth was he hated them because he was afraid. A beautiful man might see desire on him, might catch a glimpse of something sparking in Jackson that the man felt the need to extinguish. And now Jackson could feel his whole body being pulled toward Don, a warm need in him that he could not let Don see. Please, Jackson thought, looking at Don's square shoulders, his easy smile, don't look at me.

"Where you from?" Don asked.

How to answer? "Portland," he said.

"Missoula," said Don.

Jackson nodded. He would die if he couldn't come up with something to say. His thoughts whirred and lit on words and then abandoned them again. "Montana," he said finally. Stupid.

"Yes."

Kill me, Jackson thought. Please God.

"You coming to the party?" Don asked.

"What party?"

"Saturday night. For Easter."

"Easter was two weeks ago."

"Well, it's a party, still."

"Sure," Jackson said.

"You ever shot a gun?"

"What?"

"A gun."

"No."

Don turned and grinned at him. "We'll fix that Saturday, then." He stood up, sandwich gone, and gestured toward his truck across the lot. "You want a ride back?"

They rode back in silence. Jackson wanted to throw up. What was there to say? Nothing. Don was the most beautiful man Jackson had ever seen and it had to be written all over his face. Why had Don called for him? Jackson fumbled for a cigarette, lit it, smoked it through the cracked window. If Don had wanted to tell him something he'd done wrong, then why hadn't Don brought it up? If Don had just wanted to see him ... Jackson sucked on the cigarette and watched the paper burn down.

Don pulled the truck up to the site and Jackson reached for the door handle.

"Hey," Don said, and caught Jackson's arm with one hand. Jackson looked down at Don's long fingers, the trimmed oval nails with a hairpin line of dirt under each one. They both did. There was a long beat and Jackson felt a flush come over him, the blood blooming through his body, electricity and fear. "If you need anything, let me know," Don said, and dropped his hand. "If anybody gives you a hard time."

Jackson was suddenly feverishly hot. He didn't know where to look, just nodded at Don and smiled in a way he hoped looked natural. He wasn't being fired. He wasn't being fired. Don had touched his arm. He watched the truck move off down the road, back toward the East side.

Finally, he walked back to the sawhorses to split the rest of the beams, moving mechanically, thinking about Don, his long fingers, his coltish limbs. It had been twenty terrible, wonderful minutes and now he felt ruined and obsessed. The whole of his experience: Chris, a half-dozen anonymous men in Portland, Eric. A certain dark Sunday afternoon in the high school pool, Chris lying across Jackson's lap while Jackson jerked him off, the damp warm chlorine, the wet trail of their footprints shrinking on the concrete. He'd looked down at Chris's half-closed eyes, his warm cock–Jackson had felt so sure he was in love then, with Chris in the cup of his hand. But in all of the too-quick weeks of their friendship Chris would never look at him, not really. He only let Jackson touch him, kiss him, and for a few weeks that had seemed like enough. Until it wasn't. A humiliating bitter taste in his mouth, the lock of hair. Chris looking past him. Later, the men in Portland, faceless, ghosts, numbers: fifty dollars, a hundred. A bottle, a meal. And then that first meeting with Eric, when he'd pulled out his billfold and reached across and touched Jackson's arm, and even sitting across from fat, despicable Eric he'd felt a flush of something. It felt like attraction but really it was something else. Flattery. Hope.

His arm was still warm where Don had touched it. He was nice, Jackson thought, or at least he'd seemed nice. But what did it matter? He was probably imagining that the hand on his arm meant anything. Even if it did, even if Don wanted something from him, Don would want him like Chris and Eric had wanted him. He was doomed.

"Jack!" yelled Ed. He had the air hose wrapped around him,

halfway up the ladder with the nail gun. "What the hell happened? You been taking a shit?" He grinned at Jackson and Jackson laughed. Ed was cool to him. Forget Don, he thought. He wasn't going to think about him anymore, if he could help it. He flipped Ed off, picked up his gloves, and went back to work.

THE BELATED EASTER party was to be held that Saturday night at A-frame A, the most complete of the new houses. Just a few beers, and then the Longhorn, according to the much-circulated plan.

Who had an Easter party? Jackson didn't care. He was going to see Don. He hadn't seen him since Honey brought him to the East side on Tuesday; each day that Don's truck didn't appear, Jackson tried to pretend he wasn't disappointed. Now he shaved in the pocket mirror, the one he'd stolen from Lydia, and put on a clean shirt. He did everything slowly, meticulously. He drank the rest of the bottle of wine. What a girl he was. He thought again about the lock of hair he'd given to Chris. In his imagined, more perfect life, he discarded sentimentalities. Into the trash with the birthday cards, faded photographs. A better Jackson would scorn them all.

It was a little past seven when he made the walk to A-frame A. Already the light was draining away; he hadn't remembered a flashlight. The lake was lapping against the shore, a dark, bright line that curved like a knife blade in the dim evening light. The clouds had lifted, and the faintest web of stars was beginning to stretch over the water. There were crushed cans along the path.

When he got to A-frame A, there was already a crowd. Jackson was a little late, because he hadn't wanted to be too early, but now it seemed like he shouldn't have worried. He could hear Jay Donahue and Bill inside, shouting and laughing, already drunk. The floor was still not sanded, but the windowpanes were up, the electrical wiring coursing through like veins. Someone had set up a card table and filled it with bags of chips, open plastic cartons of donuts, and cupcakes. There was a group of men sitting around it, drinking from a small cityscape of open bottles. Don was nowhere in sight. He had the feeling of walking onto a stage.

"Jack!" Bill flagged him over. "You gotta hear about this. Tell him, Jay."

The whole room smelled of men–a different smell from the high school cross-country locker room, which had appealed to Jackson in another way–wispy, ephemeral slips of running shorts, clean sweat, shampoo. The men in Silver smelled dirtier. Beer sweat, sawdust. No one had touched in the locker room–all of the runners were virginal, clean, and of themselves, communal only in their dedication to noble pursuits: a second shaved from the half mile, a lighter pair of running shoes. The Silver crew touched with beery, cheerful abandon, and Jackson was one of them. Their meaty hands palmed him. Was it possible they weren't thinking of sex? All of the things that had marked him in Tulalip, in Portland, evaporated. It seemed like no one saw. Then there was Don, he thought. Don saw or he didn't. Jackson looked around for him but he couldn't see him. Josh, the crew leader on the north side, was holding up a pen, one of those naked lady pens, and laughing loudly. Jackson laughed loudly, too, slapped his own skinny leg–*A broad! And her top falls off!* Was it really this simple? Men and their simple wants. Josh turned the pen and the woman's top slid down again.

Out of the corner of his eye, Jackson saw Don climb the steps to the open house, knocking his boots against the doorframe. Don was wearing a red sweater that pulled against his stomach, his round shoulders hunched forward. He was carrying a case of beer and smoking a cigarette.

Don didn't look at him. He gave a wide, encompassing smile to the room, and Jackson concentrated on an open fifth of Early Times. He took a long drink, and then another. One of the guys slapped him on the back. "Good man!" he said, knocking his own bottle against Jackson's.

"There was this one crew that I worked on," Jay was saying, "and I worked with this guy, his name was Cliff, and he had this freakish strength. I mean you don't mess with him, he'll kill you, he's got a full-blown psychopathic streak. And he's working with this kid, seventeen years old, who's trying to prove himself." The other men, Bill and Don, and someone Jackson hadn't met, nodded. "And the kid starts lipping off from a sixteen-foot scaffold, and Cliff grabs him by the throat, dangles him over the edge, says 'I'll fucking kill you.' And the kid says something smart and Cliff grabs him and throws him off and he broke his fucking ankle." Jay looked around, waiting. "You don't lip off at Cliff."

"So when the kid's ankle heals he comes back to work. It's hot again, a hundred degrees, and we're doing a roof on the barn, and it's hotter than hell up there. I mean, you can fry an egg. The kid finds a barn swallow nest and knocks it down. They're baby swallows and he just smashes them, and then he puts their bloody, crappy bodies in Cliff's water jug. He wants to show Cliff, you see. It's really fucking hot, three in the afternoon, and Cliff picks up the water jug and it reeks, and he opens it up and its full of dead birds." Jay opened his mouth wide and laughed.

Jackson glanced up quickly and Don was looking at him, smiling a little. He felt immediately grateful. It was the worst party he'd been to since he'd gone to one of the cross-country parties three years ago, where everyone had eaten pasta and talked about shin splints. In fact, this might be worse, Jackson thought, but at the same time he was enjoying it, watching the men, deciding who was good and who was bad, who was liked and who wasn't. Then men stood around the card table, putting their dirty hands into the chip bowls. A small group had gathered at the window and was looking out at the lake, talking about the eventual town, the new Silver. The rest slumped around, leaning against the raw wood walls. He kept thinking about the kid with his broken ankle. And those poor smashed birds. He drank the terrible whiskey as quickly as he could and hung around another young guy named Greg, listening to him talk about a band he was starting. There was some question about whether or not Jackson could play bass, which he couldn't. Finally, someone brought up the Longhorn.

The trip to the Longhorn was made in several pickups. Jackson found himself in the back of Bill McPhee's Toyota with two of the contractors, both drunk. He was drunk, too. He lit a cigarette and realized too late that the windows were closed; he kept smoking it. His father had done that, smoked with all the windows rolled up so that the smell stayed in all of their hair for the rest of the day.

Jackson didn't see what car Don had climbed into. Probably his own truck, weaving drunkenly down those dark wet roads. Jackson was glad; he didn't even want to think about how to talk when he was this drunk; everything he said was sure to be wrong.

There were a half-dozen cars in the Longhorn parking lot. Some of them looked to have been there for a long time, judging from the leaves on the windshields, the ruts under the wheels. The Longhorn, Riley explained to him, was for the working lonely, the tired. It was a bar full of men and the women they dated, but the conversation was about the town and the project. It was a drinker's bar, for people who held their liquor. On the other end of the strip was Mona's, for the heartsick, for people temporarily in trouble. The music at Mona's was slow and sorrowful, one sugar-sad ballad after another. Pete's was a little shanty of a place, shoehorned into the middle of the main block, and that was where you went if it was all you had, your life in a bottle.

He looked around the Longhorn more freely this time, since he was no longer worried about getting in. It was a squat building with a chicken-wire roof and a strand of perennially blinking Christmas lights. The walls were papered with B-grade bikini models, and the ceiling was festooned with lingerie – lingerie that might have been donated by patrons but that Jackson suspected had been placed there by the owner to make the Longhorn seem sexy and exciting, to make it feel wild, like you might just turn around from your game of darts to find the woman next to you unhooking her bra.

The owner was a stocky man who seemed to have been in Silver all of his life. The men who'd been in Silver back when the river was still creeping into basements told stories of the early days of the bar, when the owner had cared for most of the men of Silver like a mother, nursing their furies, phoning their wives. Before the rerouting, on hot nights, someone said, he would open the back door and the men would strip down to their underwear and swim, their beer glasses raised above their heads.

Jackson was conscious, the whole time, of Don next to him, of the occasional drunken, accidental touch of his thigh under the table. He wondered for a minute at how stupid it was, to like someone only because they paid you five minutes of attention. What did he know of Don, besides that black hair, that smile?

He sank into his beer, waiting out Don next to him, trying not to speak and not to be too quiet, listening, making little noises when he should, laughing. The conversation was tumbling around, over him: *The concrete guys aren't pulling their weight, they never do. They spend most of the morning in the bar, that is proven fact. That new bartender down at Mona's, Lori, is that her name? Have you seen that ass? Seems like she wants to talk, but it seems that way to everybody who goes in there. Levi on the East side quit. Levi's brother Mac on the West side got crabs, and not from Lori but someone else from Mona's, watch yourself there, you never know.*

Now out of the noise came Don's hand, heavy and warm, on Jackson's shoulder. "So you've never shot a gun," Don said.

"I've never shot a gun," Jackson said. That far-off day with his mother, the .38. "I'm showing you what this does," she'd said, "and I never want you to touch one again. Promise me." She'd sold it shortly after, and he suspected it was because she was afraid. Later, he'd grown to hate the idea of guns, had checked the house periodically. If his father had one – just one moment, he thought. Just one second that you couldn't take back. Any time his father left he prowled the house like a thief.

"Well, fuck, let's go," Don said. "I've got a .30-.30," Don said. "And an empty whiskey bottle. We're gonna shoot some whiskey skeet."

He followed Don to his truck and climbed in. The seatbelt was like a long loose rope he was trying to tie around his waist. He was squinting one eye and he felt embarrassed, wished he could hold his liquor – where was Don taking him? Then they were in a field and Don was handing him a gun, steely and cold. He held the barrel up and squinted again and couldn't see a thing. His hand on the trigger – suddenly Don was pressing into him – "Against your shoulder!" he yelled, his arms around Jackson from behind, pulling the butt of the gun into Jackson's shoulder, his chest. "Put it – It'll punch your shoulder right out – " and they were kissing. He let the gun fall down at his side.

They couldn't go to Don's trailer because it was directly in the thick of crew housing, and they couldn't go to Jackson's cab because it was just too sad and small. "Here," Don had said, "follow me," and led the way, the two of them crashing around the lake on foot, and then – from nowhere! – Don's pickup; Jackson made a move to say he shouldn't drive, but then laughed instead and climbed into the front seat. His neck felt loose on his shoulders. The truck lurched forward, narrow road between the trees, black against black sky. The headlights tossing against silver leaves; the branches whipped the windows; he reached his hand across the cab and rested it on Don's jeans, on his hard cock.

Don stopped the truck down the road from A-frame B and they climbed out into the cold night air. Don pulled a sleeping bag from the back of the cab and they were stumbling, half-drunk, up the stairs of A-frame B. When they made it inside, Jackson sat on the raw wooden floor. The ground was so comfortingly solid beneath him.

Don half-fell against him; Jackson unrolled the sleeping bag and pulled him back against it and they were kissing. Don's mouth was rough and hot and his tongue thick and powerful against Jackson's own; he could feel himself shaking with nerves and want. Don groaned and reached for Jackson's cock and Jackson tried to undo Don's jeans. It was dark, and he wished he could see Don better, wished that he wasn't fumbling with the button on Don's jeans. Don reached down to help him. Jackson jerked himself, waiting for Don to get the jeans off, and finally there were Don's warm, bare legs; Don reached out and touched him and gasped. "Oh fuck, Jackson," he said, his voice thin.

Jackson didn't have a condom – of course he didn't, but now it seemed so *stupid* – and so he grabbed for Don and took him in his mouth.

Don was gasping, bucking his hips, his cock sliding in and out of Jackson's mouth, hitting the back of his throat. Jackson was drunk and he wanted to cry, he was so happy. Here was this man he wanted so badly, and he was here, his bare skin, his clutching hands, and Don pulled out and shot across the bare wood floor and his cum was a silver shadow. Jackson's balls ached; he wanted to hold Don and kiss him; he buried his face in his neck – in all of the spinning dark, there was this steady place. "Oh, god, Jackson," Don said again, and reached for Jackson's cock. He stroked it slowly, lazily, then faster, and Jackson lay back and let himself come, and he wanted to tell himself something about sex and his life and how this was different than beating Chris off, or fucking Eric, or anything, but he let it go, and his own cum was hot on his bare stomach. A wind picked up and there was the sound of waves on the lakeshore, tiny spills over the rocks. Jackson's mouth was dry and he crawled up beside Don and pulled Don onto his own outstretched arm.

Even on the thin blanket, even with his arm beneath Don's heavy head, he must have slept the whole night through – already it was early morning. Don stirred beside him. His chest felt full, still aloft on what had happened the night before.

Still drunk, he thought, and closed his eyes, following the delicate spin behind them. Don stirred, snored, his eyes fluttered open. He cleared his throat and coughed raggedly once, twice. "Hey," he said.

"Hey."

He cleared his throat again and sat up, focused his eyes on Jackson. "I mean, hey. Good morning." He put one hand on Jackson's back, awkwardly. "What time is it?"

Jackson looked at his watch. "Nine thirty," he said.

"Shit. I'm late."

For what? he wanted to ask. It was Sunday, two weeks after

Easter, and they lived in a work camp. Still, he said, "Okay," and Don was smiling, gathering his clothes, pulling his jeans on over his lean, muscled legs.

And even after Don had left, when the truck had pulled out and there was nothing to do but lie back on the bare pine, he felt happy. What was there to do? A memory of an Easter with Lydia– "What is it for," she'd asked him, "Easter?" And he'd unwrapped a piece of chocolate for her and said, "God and rabbits."

Finally, he stood and began the slow walk to the construction site. No one would be there, and it was a chance to get ahead. No one had said anything, but Jackson knew he was a slow worker. He had left a pile of scrap, plywood ends and cardboard and wood chips, and he needed to burn it down. Besides, he wanted to work and let himself think of Don, to tease out what was just sex and what might be something, the way Don had sighed, the feeling of his mouth pressed tight to Jackson's own. *God and rabbits.* The sun was trying to burn its way through the clouds. And then he had left, Jackson thought. He had left him there in the morning on the bare wooden floor and hadn't said a word. The happiness was bleeding away from him, and in its place was a feeling he couldn't name, a feeling that meant being left alone in a still-warm bed by your boss, somewhere in the Idaho mountains, on the day after an Easter party, on a day that isn't Easter. Jackson pulled a jerry can from the back of the storage locker, then tipped it out over the scrap pile until all the trash was doused. He left a sopping trail and lit it and he waited.

Amy

Women's Shelter, Alamogordo, New Mexico, 2010

THE NEW MEXICO SUN WAS A FLAT DISK, THE CLOUDS high above in the hard blue sky. The house was the same as all of the others in town – a brown stucco box, bleached to a bone color in places. Inside was a long hallway with six doors and part of a family behind each one. The mailbox was always empty, and it bothered her the way the mail car drove right by. Wasn't it a give-away? It seemed like an obvious thing to overlook when you were trying to make a building look like a home, like a place that held any whole family instead of six or seven approximations: what was left of families, after. The backyard was a scrabble of dirt and rock, where Lydia sat with a little boy against the tall wooden fence while Amy was inside talking to the caseworker.

"You can't blame your son," the woman kept saying to her. "You can't blame him, and you can't blame yourself, but you were right, you needed to go without him. You couldn't take the chance that it would happen again." The woman's eyes were watering, in danger of spilling over. "This happens with teenagers," she said gently. "They get angry at their mothers. They want their fathers' love, and their fathers manipulate them just like they manipulated you. You had to make a decision for your safety and your other child's safety." She waited, but Amy didn't say anything. "Do you want to talk about it?" she asked.

Her head felt thick. The woman didn't understand. Who would? The idea of trying to explain made her feel like she was trying to walk through thick mud with aching, bone-tired legs. He was safe, she knew that. Jackson was always the self-sufficient one, the big brother. But that was the problem – he rarely seemed to need his mother, but he needed Lydia, and Lydia him. From the time Lydia was an infant he'd watched his sister, held her, fed her, protected her. Amy had at times almost resented their closeness, Jackson's hovering, for the way it implicated her, proved what Amy knew: that Gary was dangerous. In some ways, Amy thought, Jackson considered Lydia to be his, and she couldn't blame him for it.

She hadn't chosen one over the other, she told herself now; she had not. It was the right thing to do. Jackson had a life ahead of him that shabby Tulalip, Washington, could not give him, and she knew with as much certainty as she knew her own love for him that he would leave that town, that he would make his own life and see his father for what Gary was. And to take Jackson – to bring him to this new life, when he was supposed to be starting his own – wasn't right.

"He'll be better than the rest of us," Jackson's best friend Randy had said to her years before, and she'd been worrying it like a stone ever since, hoping it into existence.

It was a Saturday afternoon, and she had been driving the rain-slick road through town when she'd spotted Randy. He was wearing a man's black trench coat, and his hair was matted to his forehead so he looked like an ancient friar, a penitent shuffling through the ditch. She pulled the car over. "Randy!" she called, and he turned slowly and squinted, then shuffled slowly toward her.

"Hey, Mrs. Holland," he said.

"Cut the shit," she said. "You want a ride?"

Randy grinned and got in the car, shaking like a dog.

"Where are you going?" she asked. "Home?"

Randy nodded. He held up a paper bag. "I got a new game." He grinned. Adolescence was dealing Randy and Jackson strikingly different hands. Jackson was more beautiful than he'd ever been before or since. There was an angel cast to him, otherworldly, his skin like pearls over a scaffolding of fine bone, saucer eyes.

He'd stretched out, but not filled out; he had no acne, and his hair was downy and brown, ruffled in a way that she had coveted back in Fannin, and she knew full well the girls at Marysville-Pilchuck ached for now. But while Jackson had stretched delicately, Randy had lumped up like dough. There was rosacea on his cheeks and dirty-looking stubble on his chin. Looking at him in the passenger seat, she felt warm toward him, for all these things, and in spite of them.

"Is Jackson around this weekend?" he asked.

"He is," she said. "He's been locked up in his room all day. I'll see if I can get him out of there."

Randy laughed. "It's cool," he said.

They settled into silence for a moment, and then she felt the question coming. She wanted to stop it but she didn't.

"Randy–" She caught his arm, looked at him. "He's gay, isn't he?"

Randy didn't look surprised. He blinked. "Jackson," he said slowly, "doesn't really talk about it. But–" He smiled at her. It was a sweet, kind smile.

She felt such a deep relief–she had asked, and Randy knew. They both knew, and Randy had answered without answering. She had not been crazy, and nothing was terrible about it.

"He'll be fine," Randy said. "He'll be better than the rest of us."

It didn't mean anything, she thought. But she believed him.

She wanted to say something that Randy would take back to Jackson, something he could carry back like a present–your mother loves you, she wants you to know that, she loves you exactly as you are. But she knew that was useless. "Thanks, Randy," she said, and smiled back at him.

When she dropped him off and the car was empty again, the road stretching slick and wet toward home, she felt warm and light. She did not let herself consider what might be hard for Jackson, what dangers there might be. Instead she thought to herself, again and again, He is my son, and I know him.

"WELL, WHEN YOU do want to talk about it," the caseworker was saying, "my door is open. Meanwhile, you need to work on being kind to yourself. You need to work on you."

Ha, she thought. She understood that there were patterns, that she had everything in common with the other women at the shelter. It was comforting and eerie to hear the other women sit in group and say things she would have never spoken aloud: "He knew where to hit me, so it wouldn't leave a mark. He wanted to move out of town, and then I was stranded there." But when the caseworkers spoke to her she couldn't help feeling like it had nothing to do with her life. *Family violence*, the *cycle*, the *patterns* – no matter how many times they explained it and how much she understood, she still saw only Gary's face, his lopsided ear, the strange smile that nestled into the corner of his mouth when he was baiting her for a fight. Who could imagine what that was like? It was not possible for anyone to see the small, deep-set eyes that had tracked her, *hunted* her, she thought, that man who stayed a step ahead and would be a shadow that dogged her for the rest of her life. Stop, she wanted to tell the woman. *We're safe, just stop.*

Instead, she said, "I think I need to go find Lydia," and the woman gave her an empathic, tight-lipped smile. Amy felt a rush of anger and sweetness, a sudden need to cry. She left the room as soon as she could, and once she was in the hall she remembered a stack of paperwork she'd meant to take, but she only walked faster. She didn't want to look at the woman's face.

She walked quickly toward the back door to collect Lydia from the yard but stopped when she heard her daughter's voice. There were four bedrooms on this back hall, and the door to the first was ajar. The little boy, the one from the backyard, was unpacking a red leather suitcase, taking out his clothes and laying them in empty middle drawer of a cheap-looking dresser. Lydia was sitting cross-legged on the bed, picking at the rough wool blanket and watching him.

Amy stood outside the door, listening. "He takes us to the

lake," the boy was saying. "Sometimes," he says, "he can be really nice."

"My dad is the devil," Lydia said, and Amy felt an electric, snaking fear.

"Not," said the boy.

"He is."

"The devil has horns and a tail."

"So? So does my dad."

She thought about walking in but she stood there instead, a dark feeling in her.

"You lie."

"He'd kill you. He'd kill anybody. Don't believe me if you don't want to, I don't care."

Amy stepped out of the hall and into the room. Both of them looked up at her. The boy couldn't have been more than seven. His hair was damp on his forehead. His cheeks were flushed and he looked feverish. Lydia was scaring him. Lydia was scaring Amy. She'd hoped, all these long years, that she was shielding Lydia from the worst of Gary. He hadn't ever laid a hand on his daughter, Amy was sure of that, but she had been more and more terrified to leave Lydia alone with him. It's coming, she thought; how long until Lydia was no longer safe? And what did it do to a child, to see the things that Lydia had seen?

Amy cleared her throat and stepped into the doorway. Lydia and the little boy looked up. "Hi," Amy said. She stepped between them and knelt in front of the boy, putting one hand on his arm. "What's your name?" she asked.

"Sam."

"I love the name Sam," she said. There was an ache in her chest. "Sam, Lydia is just joking with you. Do you know any good jokes?"

"Like a knock-knock joke?"

"Yes," Amy said. "Like a knock-knock joke. Do you know any good ones?"

"No," the boy said shyly. "I don't know any jokes."

"Okay," Amy said. "Here's one: Knock, knock."

"Who's there?" the boy asked.

"Dwayne," said Amy.

"Dwayne who?"

"Dwayne the bath! I'm dwowning!"

The boy laughed and Amy touched his head. "Sam," she said, "do you want to go get a snack with us?" The boy nodded, and she led them all to the kitchen. She watched as Lydia took Sam's hand. She was so used to seeing Lydia as the young one, as a baby. Now, watching, she saw her daughter as suddenly older, as she would become. As she was – thirteen, a young thirteen, but still. Any minute now, she thought, Lydia will be grown up, and she will think of all of this. She will tell the story of this time, and of her father, and it will be her story. And what will she think of me? What, in her heart, will she think of the life I have given her?

When she thought of the years before Lydia, she remembered the steady rain, the vaulted ceiling of the forest behind the house. Jackson's hand in hers, pale and pink as the shells they slipped into their pockets, standing on the cold gray beach of the Sound. The house cold and damp or suffocatingly hot from the woodstove. The letters she'd written her mother for the first few years, sitting at the rickety kitchen table. They were ebullient, lavish with detail. A camping trip to central Oregon, to Bend, where they'd rented a motorbike, flying up over dirt hills with Jackson between them, and later she and Gary had made love on the edge of the river, her feet in the water, while Jackson slept in the tent.

They'd talked off and on about another baby. They'd stopped using any protection when Jackson was three, and it wasn't until two years later that she started to worry. It was only a small fear at first, a longing for a baby she hadn't known she wanted but who seemed more and more absent with each passing month. She pushed it away. Things were fine, she thought.

And then a night in February 1997. It was desolate, starless after a pewter-colored day, and they left Jackson with a babysitter to go out. "Come on," Gary said. "When was the last time we just went out and got drunk together? Before Jackie?" She felt guilty even so, imagining paying the babysitter who was just thirteen years old and already had a haughty little face, with boozy breath. "Ames," Gary said. "We need to have a little fun."

And he was right. She ordered stingers because supposedly they had been her father's favorite, and the drinks were strong and cheap, sloppy in big plastic cups. They ordered a pizza. They were less than eight miles from the house, down on Lake Goodwin, and it seemed novel that there was any place to go in the dark woods, as though someone had set the whole thing up for them and would tear it down when they left.

Sitting at a plastic table, chewing on the straw of her syrupy drink, she felt acutely aware of being happy in the moment. She was smoking her once-a-year cigarette and Gary was laughing, reaching across the table to touch her face and hands. It's not that she wasn't happy, usually – she had just been so tired, lately. Jackie was five now, almost six, and about to start school. He wanted to talk about everything, gravely, and she sometimes felt how close she was to the end of her knowledge, to being found out as someone who wasn't particularly smart, who had none of the answers he so baldly expected from her. And Gary had been tense. He was tired all the time from working, and days would go by when he didn't speak to her. She would watch him for signs of his moods and steer Jackson away from him. They needed this, she thought. A night for just the two of them, to remember what it felt like to have fun.

"You're beautiful, baby," Gary said, pushing another drink at her. "Why don't you dance with me?"

The Lake Goodwin Bar & Grill was not a place that saw much dancing. There was a jukebox in one corner, though, and a decent amount of space between the tables and the bar. There were five or six other people, drinking and eating fried mushrooms and hamburgers out of plastic baskets. The waitress, big-assed in her tight jeans – for a minute Amy felt a little jealous of her, being so big like that and still sexy, and brave enough to dress that way – sat and drank with two older men at the bar. "I can see your thoughts!" the waitress kept saying. "Look at that face. I can see just what you're thinking!" She pushed her chest up at him and laughed. Amy thought she was beautiful. Objectively, Amy was more attractive, but she had none of that casual sexiness to her. She drew her shoulders in like she was folding up wings, and her crooked tooth snagged her lip. Sometimes she imagined herself like a big fawning monster.

"Okay," Amy said. "Let's dance."

Someone had fed the jukebox with a long, loud line of music so different from what they had listened to in Texas – Nirvana, Pearl Jam, Alice in Chains, these bands she was beginning to like because of the way they seemed to have grown right out of cold rock, rain, and pine. Gary swayed her between the tables; she shut her eyes and the jukebox kept picking up the discs and shuffling them to the next song. No matter what, it was worth it, she thought, to have gone, to be somewhere else, and to be dancing in a bar and to feel exactly where you were.

They were both drunk when they left the bar, but Gary handed her the keys. She felt certain she could drive. In the parking lot she could hear the music trailing out of the bar. She wanted to stay longer, but they were drunk and they'd promised the babysitter. She started the engine and pulled the car onto the dark road, watching the needle carefully, keeping her speed exactly where it should be.

Gary was quiet, and she thought that he must be resting. "Don't pass out on me," she said. "You said you'd take Tina home." Tina lived a mile down the dirt road, and Amy was fairly certain her parents had been driving her drunk since she was in utero. Still, she chided herself. Next time, she thought, not so many drinks.

Gary said nothing, and she reached over and squeezed his knee. "Gary?" she asked.

He cleared his throat. "I hope that never happens again, what happened at the Legion that night," he said finally.

"Wait, what happened?" she asked. She thought he must

be talking about something he'd seen in the news. A local tragedy, some small-town shame.

"God, you hurt me that night," he said. "I just started thinking about it. It still hurts."

"What?" she asked. "Gary–what?"

But she knew what he was talking about. It had been a couple of nights before they left Texas for Washington, just before Christmas, and they'd gone to drink quarter beers at the American Legion. She was feeling a nagging loneliness, the anticipation of it, anyway, even in that cavernous building with its tacky murals of historic battles, flag-raising moments. All those soft-gutted, pockfaced boys she'd gone to school with. She'd kissed most of them at one point or another. Gary wasn't a Fannin boy and that was part of why she loved him, but for a minute she wished she'd gone to the Legion alone.

She was drinking her beer, holding its cool neck with her finger and thumb, talking to Scooter Jenkins. "Amy," Scooter said. "You feel like going down to Corpus with us next weekend?" He nudged his beer bottle against hers and clinked it softly. "It's too cold to swim, but we can party."

She looked at him. He was tall with a round moon face, a bobbing sunflower boy. She smiled. "Maybe," she said, even though she and Gary would be halfway to Washington by then. She'd hated the idea of going to the beach with anyone from Fannin in the days before Gary, when everyone piled into someone's car with cases of beer and three dirty sleeping bags, a half-dozen threadbare bath towels to share on the sand. Now, about to leave Fannin for what she imagined was for good, she felt a kind of loneliness for Scooter Jenkins and all of those boys who would spend the next sixty years right here at the Legion, marrying and divorcing one another's wives.

She was talking to Scooter for a while, maybe–the time wasn't clear, and she'd thought Gary was at the corner table, talking to someone he'd known from a junk salvage job he'd done in Luling. But when she stood up and looked for him, he had disappeared. She looked up and down the rows of card tables, toward the bathroom, out on the porch. "Have you seen Gary?" she asked the group of old-timers at the front, World War II veterans who took their posts very seriously. "That tall guy I was with? The dark hair and the beard?" They clucked at her and shook their heads; someone brought her another beer. The string of Christmas lights over the bar that hadn't been taken down yet burned out as she watched.

Gary's truck wasn't in the parking lot, so she'd given up. Maybe something had come up, or he'd run to the gas station for cigarettes. It was her last night in Fannin, and the worry slipped away. She danced with Lawrence, who'd known her father before Vietnam. He worked for the railroad. "Now, that's a pension," he said. "You want to be guaranteed your old age in peace, get a job for the railroad." He kept one hand on the small of her back and rested his rough cheek against hers. "I'm proud of you, Miss Amy. I'm sure your father's real proud, too. I never did travel much myself."

"Watch out for my dad, would you, Lawrence?" she asked. For a minute she thought she might cry, but instead she let Lawrence spin her, and when the song ended she fell into a folding chair, lit a cigarette, and listened to the laughter around her. She let it buoy her up like a wave, all of that simple happiness.

Walking home, her last night in the old house, she heard the truck before she saw the headlights. The engine sounded like a jet taking off. She stopped, listening, and then lights were coming toward her, fast. She jumped back from the street and tripped, falling on one knee in the ditch, scraping her leg in the scrabble of dirt and stiff grass.

Gary jumped out, lit up by the headlights. He'd roared out of the night like a god and he was manic, pacing back and forth.

"I drove my truck out to the bridge." His voice sounded strangled. "I stopped and I looked down at the water–Jesus, Amy, do you know what I was thinking about? That's how much you mean to me. That's how much I hated seeing you with that fucker."

He looked at her and let out a little cry. He slammed his fist against the side of his truck.

She didn't say anything for a long time; he paced, opened the truck door, slammed it closed again. "God, god," he kept saying. "God, I love you, how could you?" He ran toward her and put his hands on her arms and squeezed, as if to shake her. It didn't hurt but she let out a cry. She was drunk. Very drunk, actually, and she felt like she had been dropped into a movie at the climax with nothing to do now but wait for the pieces to come together, to pick up the beginning from the end. She had hurt him, badly; that thought was coming to rest inside her, becoming more real, and as she watched him storming up and down the road, she slowly began to wake up, to understand, and the sorrow, the regret, and the wanting to undo rushed toward her. She began to apologize, to beg him. "I didn't know," she said. "I'm so sorry. I'm so sorry." He raged at her and cried, and finally he quieted, covering his face with his hands. "Please, Gary," she said to him. She kept saying it. "Please."

When he moved his hands, he was calm again. He walked toward his truck and climbed back in. "I hope we can get through this," he said. "I really hope we can." He turned the key, started the truck, and left her there to finish walking home in the dark.

Long into that night, in her twin bed, she'd cried. What had she done? She felt sick with sorrow and frustration. She woke up the next morning and remembered and cried again. The feeling stayed with her for the next few days; she couldn't stop crying. She cried with relief when Gary's truck appeared the morning they left town, cried while she said goodbye to her mother, feeling a guilty relief for both the fact that her mother didn't know what had happened and that Amy appeared so convincingly heartbroken to leave.

After they'd loaded the truck and pulled out onto I-10, the tension had finally seemed to fall out of Gary. He squeezed her hand in his, pulling her close to him in the cab of the truck, kissing her head. And the relief she felt! Never again, she thought. Never again will I ignore this person who I love so much, and who loves me so fiercely in return. She'd let that night escape from her mind, existing there only as a quiet warning: do not forget your power, do not take for granted all that you have. Driving away from the Lake Goodwin bar, then, six years later, she was confused at first. Why? Why bring this up now? She watched the speedometer, the bright and comforting lights of the dashboard, and steered as carefully as she could. And then, slowly, it began to dawn on her what was happening. She thought, he's picking a fight.

"Gary," she said slowly, the headlights sweeping the undersides of leaves, "that was a long time ago. I said I was sorry." She felt too drunk. Don't do this now, she thought. She just wanted to get them home.

"You aren't, though," he said. "You *aren't.*" He was leaning toward her; she could smell the alcohol on his breath. His voice was soft but it was mean.

She *had* been sorry, she thought. And hadn't she paid for that? The way she'd spent the night crying, and her last hours with her mother were not about her mother at all but the storm of regret and fear still bearing down her.

"You aren't," he said again. It felt like he was poking her. All those days of being careful and quiet, of not wanting to piss him off, were swelling in her chest. She was so fucking careful all the time. She was so fucking *tired* of feeling like she was doing something wrong. She wanted to scream but instead she gripped the wheel tighter and made the turn onto Firetrail Hill. She just wanted to get home. She pressed her lips together and willed him to let it go, to not say anything. They were supposed to be having a fun night. They were supposed to be being in love.

He was quiet for a moment and then he leaned toward her again, one hand on the console. "You were never sorry," he said. He reached out and ran one finger across her cheek.

Her throat tightened. She was holding the wheel so tight her palms stung. "Fuck you," she said. She had never sworn at him before. "Fuck you, Gary." The lines on the road were weaving in front of her and his face was close to hers. "What is wrong with you?" he was saying, his breath hot and mean, and she leaned away from him and he grabbed for the wheel as it jumped her hands, but the branches were slamming up against the windshield, and then there was a long, loud crushing sound and the truck slammed back.

Her nose was bleeding, but where had she hit it? Gary was beside her, moaning. She needed to call an ambulance. Someone needed to call someone. Please, she thought. Please. The windshield, the slap of the leaves against it, the dark inside of the car, the silence. How long did they sit there? "I'm sorry," she kept saying. "I'm sorry. I'm sorry. I'm sorry." She opened the door and ran out onto the road, one of her shoes slipping off on the gravel. Later she would find little pitted cuts on the bottom of her foot. There were no cars. The bar was four miles one way, the house four miles another.

Gary followed her out, crashing through the bushes, looking at the truck where it had plowed through the underbrush and into a pine tree. He reached for her and held her by the arms, the same way he had that night on the Fannin road.

"Listen," Gary said, "you listen to me. You're going to get in the car and drive us home before the cops show up and take your drunk ass to jail. You understand me, Amy?"

She did understand. She nodded and picked her way over the brush and climbed back into the driver's seat. There were branches coming up off the grille and one of the headlights was busted out. The truck shuddered a little as she reversed it onto the road. She held her breath. She put it back in drive and she drove them home.

When she pulled the truck up the gravel drive she sat there in the dark while Gary went in and paid the babysitter, and then she went in and held Jackson beside her on the sofa while he drove the babysitter home. Thank god it was dark and no one would notice the banged-up truck. She didn't look at the girl and she didn't let herself think about how Gary was drunk, too. She kept holding Jackson long after Gary had come back in and gone silently to bed. She whispered into his hair and he slept slumped against her while the guilt washed over her hotly, the relief and the shame.

She was sick the next morning. The drinks, she thought, and the stress, but she was sick the next day, too, and then she was pregnant with Lydia all along.

It began after that, the change in Gary. Later, she would see how simply those events had fallen in line in her mind: her error at the Legion, so long before. The accident and everything that had happened beforehand – how cruel she had been to him. He looked at her differently now: she who cursed him when he was weak and wanting, who could have ended both their lives, orphaned their child. How simple it was for her to believe that these things were connected by the thread of her mistakes. How simple it was for him to make her believe she was to blame for the way he looked at her now, for what she began to believe was his hatred of her.

She never feared for Jackson, but holding Lydia, something stirred in her, a suspicion about that night. That they were complicit, in Gary's eyes: behind the wheel, her baby smaller than a seahorse and her own unsteady hands, and that for the rest of her life she would pay for it, and her little girl would possess for him a darkness that Amy would spend her life trying to hold at bay.

NOW, IN THE shelter, the bright New Mexico moon drove its light through the glass and wire windowpanes, through the wooden slats of the blinds. They would stay here for two months. An eternity, she thought. Long enough to make Gary believe they had disappeared completely. Long enough to change their names, to trade the little car in for something else before they went back to Texas, before they tried again to start a life without Gary. They would stay with Amy's mother, in the house Amy had grown up in, and Amy couldn't imagine what it would feel like to be back there. What would it be like, to go home? And her father was gone; when Jackson was eleven and Lydia five there had been the call that he was dead. The only call from Amy's mother she'd had in Washington – her mother didn't believe in long distance, in the same way she didn't believe in cabs or airplanes or designer clothes. The luxuries of the rich. Amy had answered the phone, and when she hung it up again she had been afraid to tell Gary because she was afraid to tell Gary anything then. He had been uncharacteristically kind when she did tell him. She wondered now if her mother would forgive her – for leaving, for never calling, for receiving the phone call that her own father had died and still not coming home. Amy wasn't sure if she deserved to be forgiven.

Amy lay on the hard, narrow bed in the shelter watching the rise and fall of her daughter's back, turned away from her in the bed across the room. She imagined her mother standing by the dusty windowsill in Texas looking out on her own small kingdom, that square of scraggled Fannin land. There was her mother, here was her sleeping daughter, and somewhere, far from her, was her beautiful son. She thought, Please. Please, this night, later, all your life, believe me that I've done what I can.

Lydia

Tulalip, Washington, 2005

WE BUILT FORTS. WE BUILT LITTLE HOMES FROM BLOWdowns in stands of alder. We sat crouched in nests of sword fern eating red huckleberries. We took off our shoes and wrapped maple leaves around our feet like moccasins until they tore, and then we walked barefoot through the black piney loam and leaffall. Our skin stung from nettles and the air smelled of skunk cabbage and rain.

We followed the creek and knew each of the ponds that pooled beside it. We ruined our shoes. We collected sticks and handfuls of dry pine needles from the pockets beneath roots and rocks, where they were shielded from the rain. We made rings of stones and tried to light fires with the sticks, the dry needles, the paper and lint in our pockets. The fires smoked and our old hall passes curled under the lick of flames and then went dead.

We used our thumbnails to split the blisters on the trunks of pine trees so the pitch spilled out and stained our palms. We told stories, about the wolfboy who lived in the woods and the Firetrail ghost who would run beside your car and grab you in the dark. We told secrets.

"Lydia," my brother told me, "the way that girls feel about boys is the way that I feel about them. Like I might marry a boy someday."

"Like gay?"

"Yes."

"You're a homo?" I asked.

"Yes," he said.

I thought for a minute. Jackson was looking at me. His hands were shaking, pulling an alder leaf into pieces and letting them drift to the ground.

"I understand," I said, and I did.

Between us, we knew everything already.

We practiced survival. We stripped the leaves from fireweed and chewed them to a bitter cud. We found tangles of blackberry and drank straight from the creek. We sat in an old rowboat that was abandoned in the woods. In heavy rain we turned it upside down, curled underneath it in the dirt and salal.

We lured a stray dog through the woods with pieces of stale bread and talked to him in low voices. He was skittish and thin and we named him Green for his eyes. When we whistled for him he would appear, a moving shadow between the trees. When we touched his fur with cold, careful hands we knew that he was meant for us.

When we heard voices from the house we went deeper into the woods and looked for bleeding hearts and trilliums on the mud-slick slopes on either side of the creek, and when we found them we did not pick them. We knew how rare they were, how beautiful, and how quickly they would wilt in our hands.

"I hate him," I told Jackson. "I wish that he would die. I wish he would go to jail. I wish he would move far away and never come back."

"Sometimes," Jackson said, "I still love him."

My brother could look so sad sometimes.

"But I don't think I should," he said.

I imagined that if our father disappeared then we would move into the forest, Jackson, my mother, and me. We would have the whole woods, and the creek, and the leaves would flash and spin around us. We would have everything.

In spring, when the brush was thick, we followed the creek for three miles, to an old trailer camp. The trailers were empty in the winter, and maybe all year round. Through the windows we saw the dirty kitchens, the stacks of books, the bare mattresses. I imagined that each one was a different life waiting for us. I imagined that somewhere in the woods I would find the right one. I imagined that it would find me. That it would call me home.

If it was a good day our mother would come into the woods and crawl into the fort. She would pour us invisible coffee from the curl of a leaf.

I was eight years old. Jackson was older, and I understood that all of this was for me, and that my brother was better than most brothers. I drank from my leaf, lying in the crooks of their warm arms. "You were born for just this," they whispered. They held me between them. "You were born for happiness, for great things. You were born so we could love you."

2.

The Dog

Jackson

Silver, Idaho, 2010

WHEN HE WOKE UP IN A-FRAME B, DON WAS ALREADY gone, due at a job site a mile down the road. Jackson lay there for a minute and then he made himself get up, find his clothes, roll up the sleeping bag, and stow it back in the tool locker. He walked to the dam and stood there smoking a cigarette, shaking out his arms and legs, rolling his neck. The new dam was fresh wood and steel, shivering against the bowl of the lake. He was so fucking tired. In his jeans pocket was a note Don had left him: "Dear Picklepuss, I want you little, I want you mighty, I wish my pajamas were next to your nighty. From, the squirt who is your pal and public enemy no. 1." He unfolded the note and folded it again, then put on his jeans and jacket and boots and started the walk around the lake to his site.

He had slept with Don three times now. The first time was after the Easter party, when they were both reeling drunk. After that there were four excruciating days of seeing Don at the job site, watching Don leaning against a sawhorse or chatting amiably with the carpenters while Jackson shuffled around the tool truck, his face burning. That was all it was, he kept thinking. Drunk sex. Except that it was drunk sex with his boss, whom he didn't know. Who knew he was a faggot. Don could tell on him, Jackson kept thinking through those four long days: He could tell he could tell he could tell. Jackson knew enough about fear to understand what men did to save themselves from suspicion.

Then, on the fourth day, and just about the time that Jackson was deciding he might want to quit the crew, Don had strode over to where he was piling wood scraps to burn later, and cuffed him lightly on the shoulder. "Jack," he said. "Come by the A-frame tonight. I need your help with something." And of course he'd gone, embarrassed at how excited he was, getting just a little drunk beforehand, and then waiting down the road in the dark so he wasn't too early. It was still drunk sex, but this second time felt important – Don still wanted him, right there on the floor of the same half-built cabin; Jackson himself was something worth repeating; he hadn't been a mistake.

The third time was last night, and after Don had begged him to come inside of him, and Jackson had, breathless, tears at the back of his throat, holding Don's hips, Don had told him that he was married.

Sex was still this giant mystery card, anyway, so what did it matter? All his life Jackson had been puzzling at it from afar. In elementary school, he hung out with girls and boys indiscriminately. He wasn't unpopular. That hadn't been decided yet. It was a poor town. Every kid's jacket was a little short in the sleeves. He touched the little penis of a boy named David and a girl named Martha's flat nipples. That was the sum of all the sex he knew.

And then middle school – those were the years he'd spent mostly with Lydia. He was a late bloomer and a weakling, and on top of that there was a year where he was both weak and chubby, somehow looking both frail and fat. He had a little girl's roll around his hips. He had noodly arms. He had a tiny wasteland of pubic hairs that grew as slow as old-growth.

And finally, high school. Or the first three years of it, at any rate. All of those kids were still there, sweating it out under the fluorescents. He'd gotten prettier. The fat disappeared and he was tall and bony, something girls liked. Did gay men like it? He didn't know. Sex was all wound up with a million other things to him, too – the Marysville roller rink. Licorice whips. A game of foosball with a pimply junior who everyone called Burger – later someone would shit on the foosball table, that was what kind of place it was.

Octopus legs, smooth linoleum. He wanted that boy who flipped the little soccer men around. He wanted to be in the middle of all of these small-town boys, these pale, asexual guys – Randy; the wormy little M-P tennis coach; his father's sketchy, nervous friend Larry. Feverish masturbation, cum spilled into pale petal hands, body against fish body. There was the thing with Chris, but Chris was just a confused opportunist who let Jackson jerk him off and who probably had a girlfriend by now anyway. Other than that crush, other than the chlorine smell and the trail of cum across the wet concrete pool deck, all he'd had was Eric, during what would have been his senior year. Jackson had sucked Eric off again and again, and then leaned his face into the pillow while Eric fucked him, but that was all – he was Eric's bottom; that's who he was paid to be. He had sometimes hated it, and mostly just endured it because he knew what it meant: cash. Equals food, equals pills, equals everything. And the truth was that some of the time it even felt good – there was a small, plain warmth, almost tender, to having Eric inside him that many times, week after week.

But now here was Don. Beautiful, married Don. Jackson had never fucked another man before – never been the top, and now he felt it electric inside of him: to have stood over this man, to have watched him beg, to have thrust inside of Don until the noises they both made were indecipherable from joy or sorrow or anger. In those moments Jackson could imagine that the road outside only curved back to the cabin, as though there was nowhere else in the world they might possibly go.

He made it to the site twenty minutes early, and one of the men gave him a hammer and had him pulling nails out of a stack of planks. He liked the feeling of knowing exactly what he had to do, of following orders. He had a job and he could follow orders. He had a place to sleep; it smelled like motor oil and there was sawdust and mud from his boots scattered across the metal floor, but it was a door and a room and bed, and it was free. What did it matter what happened with Don? He wasn't stupid enough to think that they were going to run off together. He wasn't stupid enough to believe that Don could just walk away from his wife. There were papers, furniture, trappings. Heavy things. He imagined a wedding ring alone could be heavy enough to hold you down.

He hadn't known what to say, last night, when Don told him. Jackson had been lying there on the floor of the A-frame, warmth still spreading through his arms and legs: "I'm married," Don said, and Jackson didn't say anything, just busied himself pulling off the used condom, setting it carefully next to the shadowy pile of his clothes and the sputtering candle with its flame drowning in its own wax. Jackson felt a burst of shame, thinking of how the candle seemed now–like he'd been trying to make things romantic–which he had.

"Are you angry?" Don had asked.

Jackson considered the question. It hadn't occurred to him to feel angry yet. "No," he'd said finally, because he didn't know what to say.

"Jack." Don looked at him, and Jackson nodded. That had seemed like reply enough, and they had gone to sleep.

But now, the nails clicking and screeching against the claw of the hammer, he felt a terrible nagging feeling. What did he want? If he figured it out, would he say it? He had all this guilt inside him all the time. The little things, the big things–they ate away at him with equal, excruciating measure. He'd stolen the candy from Lydia's Christmas stocking one year and that burned at him–what kind of terrible brother, what kind of brute, stole from a six year old? And then what he'd done to his mother and his sister in the end–he deserved nothing, he thought. No mercy, no love, no kindness. Don didn't owe him any explanations.

The site was stirring to life, the men shuffling in, coughing and clanking through the tool locker and someone turning the radio on, fiddling with the bandwidth. Jackson kept pulling nails, his arm a steady piston. He looked back around the curve of the lake toward A-frame B, a stirring in his dick. The man in the house, the man is the house. That rough wood floor was covered deep with scratches and cum and sweat stains, but not so anyone could see but him. It seemed to him sometimes that he was being carried on a wave that had been set in motion a long time ago, a wave of his father, his mother's fear, his own mistakes. He'd clung to his father's fist and just loped along, ready to push his mother and sister off a cliff, ready to pop open the next of his father's shit beers. Whiskey and beer, what his father drank. He had married Jackson's mother in a yellow suit. He'd given Jackson balsa wood models and then built them all himself while Jackson grew bored. Detail after detail that added up to nothing in particular; all of these things were tied together, and he didn't know where the string began or ended. The little buzz between his legs. The quiet cathedral of A-frame B. All of these things.

The sun was burning through the gray haze, and it was going to be a warm day. A good day. Something his mother used to say – "You get up, and you decide. Is this going to be a good day?" It didn't matter about Don, he thought again. He didn't have any control over it; they'd stay together or they wouldn't – get together or they wouldn't. He knew he didn't have much say in it. It gave him a lonely feeling.

Lydia

Fannin, Texas, 2010

WHEN JACKSON DIDN'T COME BACK TO THE STARLIGHT Motel, I guessed what he had done. It was as if I expected it all along, and so I waited at the window the next morning. My father's truck slid up like a shark. He waited in the parking lot, sitting on the hood of our car, smoking a cigarette. He had never laid a hand on me, but I looked at him then and I knew he could. He would, I thought. My mother drove the car home and he took me in the truck to make sure that she followed. All the way home, the truck rattled. I held tight to the cold cracked seats. His fists were on the wheel.

When we got to the house, Jackson was there. I'd never seen my brother look the way he did then, guilty and sad. I wanted to hate him, the way I hated my father, for what he had done. "Lydia," Jackson said to me, and I looked at him. I couldn't hate him even then, but it was like looking through him, or looking at someone I didn't know.

All that next week, my father was in the house. His ears were everywhere. His eyes. Out by the shed, my mother waved me over. She crouched close to the ground. "Lydia," she said in my ear. "I think that you and I should go."

"What do you mean?" I asked.

"Your brother is eighteen," she said. "It's time for him to go out in the world alone."

"He'll stay at home?"

"He won't," my mother said. "He'll stay with Randy, or he'll go somewhere. He'll know what to do."

I knew she was right, but there was more. "I need your help," she said, "to make sure Jackson doesn't notice. I need your help to make sure we get away." Once I'd agreed I knew that if there was a hell I'd burn in it. Once, I had told my brother everything. Now, I told myself, Jackson deserves this. He deserves this for what he did, and he deserves to be free from you.

In the car, driving away from my brother, leaving him behind, my mother said, "I'm sorry that you were the one who got less than. I'm sorry that you've had to be afraid." I remembered that dog. Green, we called him, for his eyes. I remembered how Jackson would always tell me, "If he loves you, he'll find you again."

The night before, I'd sat in front of the woodstove. I'd thought, if only they'd burned me when I was born. If only I hadn't been. I held my hands as close to the stove as I could. The pain was sharp and then it faded. I knew what I would do the next morning, how I would betray Jackson. He was beside me, watching me, and it was as though I was holding a gun. There's a bullet in there, I wanted to say. You just can't see it yet.

The bullet took us over the mountains in the dark. It took us across red hills to New Mexico, where for weeks there was no color at all, just the sad faces of the other women, the story we told again and again, the word *wait*. Finally, it took us down the bare highway again, to Fannin, where my grandmother opened the door.

The sink leaked, and the wind whipped off the field and right through the living room, and the screens were torn by secret claws in the night. Things from the outside kept trying to get in, and I had dreams of thieves at the windows. There were mice, but the traps we set only caught geckos. In the mornings and evenings there was a smell of rot, "of oil," my mother said, "of money," and pointed to the derricks like birds dipping their beaks to drink.

The first week, as we were sitting out in the dry heat, a man passed the house. He looked at us through the dark for a long minute, and I felt the fear like a hot knife in me. I didn't move. I tried to look like nothing at all.

He walked closer. I could feel my mother beside me. We

were two stones. "Gary could find us anywhere," my mother had said when we were still safe in the shelter. No, I thought now. No no no no.

"Amy Merrick?" the man called. We stayed still.

My grandmother banged out on the porch. "Jim," she called. "Get up here."

The man was short with a round belly. He was holding a can of beer in one hand and wearing work boots like my father wore. He put his big arms around my mother.

"Amy Merrick, you are just as beautiful as the day you left. I don't believe it."

"This is my daughter," my mother said. "Lena." She touched my hair. "And I go by Ann now," she said. "Ann Harris."

"You got a little girl? I don't believe it."

The man shook my hand. He sat down on the dusty wood of the porch beside my mother. She was laughing. She looked happy, I thought. She looked beautiful. She took one of his cigarettes and I watched it weave like a firefly through the dark.

She used to have a life here, I realized for the first time. Before the little house in Washington, before my father put his big hand against her cheek and promised her a hundred lies. Before they were driving west in the little pickup, my mother just eighteen and the sky white as a cup of an orange peel, the road a wire. My eyes were heavy and nothing mattered. I could hear an owl behind the house and above the field a dark cloud lifted like a wave and became a hundred birds, chattering.

"Girl, I haven't been out to the clubs in Austin since I stopped drinking that Crown."

"You don't look a day older. Not even a day. And this house is just the same. I can't believe it."

"Eva, Eva is working at Zarapes now. She has a little girl that age. *No conoces a tu abuela, queridita? Ah, esta cansada. Esta dormida.*"

I listened to the voices with my cheek against the rough nub of the chair's upholstery. The words were soft and round shapes in the dark, and I imagined this man young and my mother younger, a bright planet, their orbits. All of them hurtling through the dry air, circling this oceanless beach of a town.

"He tries to come here, he's a dead man. He is nothing."

"Don't talk about that. It's over now."

"Still. You'll be safe here."

I slept on and off in the chair on the porch and no one made me leave. The heat was like a blanket over my shoulders. The hot wind was in my mouth, and that moon. Here we are, I thought. There's nowhere left to go.

Amy
Fannin, Texas, 1990

HER BEST FRIEND'S BOYFRIEND HAD SEEN THE BAND before. In Houston, at Fitzgerald's, a month ago. He leaned into the cab of the truck pushing aside the empty cigarette packets and beer cans, the wax paper Coke cups, and shrugged. "They're legit," he said. "This is only the beginning."

Jennifer climbed in first, surrounded by the damp fruit cloud of her perfume. Amy slid in next to Jennifer on the creaking plastic seat. *Exclamation*, lilies and oranges. Jennifer shoplifted it from the Walgreens by putting the little black and white bottle deep between her breasts and tugging the zipper of her jacket half-way up her cleavage. Amy had watched her do it, right in front of the sales clerk, who was sixteen and covered in acne. He blushed beet red and was too embarrassed to say a word.

"That show was some shit," the boy said. "I hope this one isn't lame."

"Shut up, Scott," Jennifer said.

He gunned the truck through the main streets of town and southwest toward the highway, toward San Antonio. It was eight o'clock. There was a little clutch of cars outside of the American Legion and Amy ducked down. Every Saturday night her father's old friends went there to eat catfish and drink. They had their own table.

"Fuck this place," Jennifer said. She pulled mascara from a pocket inside her jacket and unscrewed it, leaning close to the rearview mirror and opening her eyes, expertly sweeping her lashes, leaning her head back, and shaking her hair.

Amy had spent all night getting ready for the show. Jennifer had loaned her a pair of blue pumps, and she tried on each of her outfits until she found one that was okay, a little skirt and a T-shirt with a plunging neckline. She had arms like a stevedore, she thought, but her legs looked good in heels and her ankles were narrow. Sometime in her freshman year of high school she'd suddenly come into D-cups, one of the better surprises of her life. Still, she was no fashion model. Her hair was the weak brown of burlap–the same color as Fannin, she thought, as though the town had already claimed her–and she had a crooked front tooth. When she was young she would press against it with a finger until her gums ached, but nothing had changed.

She sprayed her hair up, trying to make it look as full and untamed as Jennifer's. She didn't know anything about the band. "You heard them," Jennifer had said. "I play their tape like all the time." Jennifer liked them. Jennifer liked *her;* that was something in itself. Jennifer wore tight Palmettos that lifted her ass into a valentine and followed her long, thin legs to the deadly points of her stilettos. Jennifer led every boy at James R. Fannin High School on an invisible leash and had sucked off the student teacher in the teacher's lounge. "God," she'd said, "it wasn't like it took much. He was, like, ready to blow."

San Antonio was full of souped-up trucks. Drunks were weaving over the dusty streets, and Mexican workers were still sweating in long sleeves, working into the night. It was Fannin, she thought. It was a hundred times bigger but it had the same sad heart.

Scott threw the truck into park behind a warehouse and they picked their way across a gravel lot toward the club. Amy's ankles wobbled in Jennifer's pumps.

There wasn't any sign of Scott's friend–Amy's blind date, Jennifer's idea–when Scott pushed them through the double doors and paid the cover, when her eyes adjusted to the smoky dark. "He'll be here," Scott said. The band was on the plywood stage, pounding and tweaking their guitars. "That's not them," Scott said. "That's just some shitty opener." He pushed his way to the bar and came back with three plastic cups.

"Thanks," Amy said. She wanted Scott to like her. At least, she didn't want him to start wondering why she couldn't bring her own date. Not that Scott seemed to notice either way. When he looked at Jennifer it was like she was occurring to him all over each time; he would grin and throw a heavy arm around her and kiss her hungrily, and then one of the boys on stage would throw out a loud note on a guitar and he'd reel up from her lips and bounce toward the stage. Jennifer took a long drink from her plastic cup and rolled her eyes.

When the headlining band came on stage they were loud and angry as the tune-up had sounded. Death metal. It wasn't her thing. Amy loved Nelson, Bon Jovi, Warrant, Extreme. She had a crush on Gunner Nelson. She sang alone in her room to "More than Words" and Poison. Jennifer wouldn't approve, and neither would these murky, sinister boys.

She wandered from the front of the bar to the back, where it opened onto a cement floor, tacked-up plastic walls, beer signs. Jennifer was somewhere inside, dancing in an easy way, grinding her hips against Scott. The drink was syrup and it made her teeth ache. She tried to sway to the music, imagining the way that she looked: a girl alone in the back, half-dancing. She wanted to look graceful, but the music was loud and angry. She wasn't right for this place.

"Ames!" Jennifer pushed through a group of college kids who were laughing loudly, bobbing forward and back, straining to hear each other's shouted words. Jennifer's face was flushed and there was a shine of sweat on her upper lip. "Ames, Gary's here. You have to come meet him." She reached up and brushed Amy's hair with her fingers. "He's cute."

Amy followed her back through the crowd. Scott was standing with a tall boy with dark hair that curled around his neck. One of his ears stuck out. He was cute, she thought. "Amy!" Scott put an arm around her and pushed her toward the boy. He shouted over the music. "This is Gary!"

Gary smiled at her, and she smiled back. She stood next to him, but it was too loud to talk. Some of the boys in the front were throwing themselves back and forth in front of the stage, and the girls were behind them, looking perfect, dancing half-drunk, looking the way she'd imagined that she might look, in another world, another life.

She hadn't expected that he would talk to her much. It was loud, and wasn't a blind date to a place like this just an excuse to spend the night kissing someone you wouldn't have to see again? Still, Gary led her back out to the patio and they jumped the fence to the parking lot and his truck, which he presented to her proudly.

"You like Dead Horse?" Gary asked her, when they were settled on the tailgate.

"Dead Horse?" she asked.

"The band," he laughed.

She grinned. "They're my favorite," she said. "Can't you tell? I've been waiting for this for weeks."

"I don't like them, either," he said, laughing.

Gary *did* like Chris LeDoux. Dwight Yoakam and Vince Gill. He sat around the ranch where he worked for his father listening to George Jones and drinking Pearl. The things he liked were a holy list that he delivered to her as they sat in the back of his pickup: Pearl and his Remington hunting rifle and long days working when he could count the money he was making into triple digits. The West Coast, where the mountains and the ocean bridled up against each other, which he had seen in a *Reader's Digest* coffee table book called *America the Beautiful*. The things he disliked had even more gravity: people who didn't work enough, people with no ambition. School, which he had finished last spring, and which insulted his understanding of the world. His father was on both lists – he owned a ranch with two oil wells, where Gary had grown up and now worked and lived, and Gary admired him mightily, almost angrily. "He's done well for us," Gary said. "And no one, *no one* can tell me he hasn't." He knocked the ash of his cigarette into his open palm and then tossed it onto the ground. He turned to her suddenly. "God, you're beautiful."

Her face was hot. "You are," he said. "Beautiful." He reached into the back of the truck and pulled out a squat blue bottle of Mad Dog and took a long drink. "Where do you live? Fannin, right?"

She felt a sting of disappointment. He thought she was beautiful and interesting and now he was going to see her for what she was, another girl from a shitty town with nothing behind or ahead of her. "Oh, I hate Fannin," she said.

"I've been out there," he said. "There's not much."

"Exactly," Amy said. Fannin had been built on the old Sunset rail, but the railroad had given way to an oil boom in the twenties. Now it was an oil town, but a poor one. Everyone worked long hours and then drank it away.

"The ranch is in Geronimo," Gary said.

"That's nice," Amy said. "It must be nice to work with your family."

He turned quickly to look at her. "It's fucking not," he said. Everything about him seemed to darken. "My father's a fucking prick and I'd kill him if I could."

Amy felt stung. "I'm–I'm sorry," she said. "I didn't think–about how it might be hard."

Gary looked at her for a long minute and then his face relaxed and he laughed. "Ah, well," he said. "We just fight, you know how it goes."

"Sure," she said, and laughed lightly, though she still felt chilled. "I know how that goes." Amy didn't know, but she made herself try to imagine what it was to find yourself eighteen and working a ranch under the hand of your father, who held the key to everything you wanted, everything your father still, and absolutely, owned. She had never once fought with her own father. She kissed him on the cheek every time she left the house, and there were times when her throat tightened painfully in his presence, but even then it was a sorrow she couldn't dream of articulating. He was there and not there. She was conceived two weeks before her father shipped out for the forests near the Cambodian border. All of that year her mother waited for Amy to arrive, imagining the life they would lead when her father came home.

Her father came back when Amy was two months old, but he didn't come back in the way that he should have. He was home two months early, honorably discharged, his face carved up, slow as a baby. Traumatic brain injury, the doctors said, with severe aphasia, dysarthria, and cognitive deficits, and little hope for rehabilitation. The bleak prognosis was lost on Amy's mother. In the evenings she'd sit next to Amy's father, pumping the pedal of her Singer, the needle thundering over the alteration work she did. In between seams she would smile at him while his eyes drifted around and around the little bedroom, lighting on stacks of newspaper, the baby picture of Amy, the Purple Heart in its square glass case. "He's not in there, Ma," Amy wanted to say. She imagined that her real father – the part of him that had loved her mother, that would have loved Amy – had bled right out of him and was gone before they could fly him out of Da Nang. But it's true that there were moments when he seemed to surface, as though there was a break in the smooth waters behind his eyes, as though suddenly he was looking out again. Her mother lived for those hours when he would look at her, smile, hold her hand – when he was there. She believed – and this was what broke Amy's heart – that she could bring him back. That when he blinked at her and saw her, that it was her own will that had done it; when he didn't, that it must be something in her – or not in her, and that made it her fault.

The band was carrying their equipment out the back, and she could smell someone nearby smoking pot. Groups of people were making their way out of the club, milling on the lawn, the cherries of their cigarettes looping through the air. Gary put the palm of his hand against her cheek. "I'd like to see you again," he said.

IT WAS PAST three when Scott pulled the truck onto the lawn with the lights off. Jennifer was asleep with her head in his lap. Amy took the pumps off and left them on the seat next to Jennifer, then went barefoot up the dry scrub lawn and into the house. Sam was asleep on the floor and he lurched up, thumping his tail.

"Shhh, Sam." He was her dog. He listened to her. She put her hand out and he licked it but he didn't bark. She knelt down on the floor beside him and laid her head on his warm side. He wriggled with pleasure and she stayed there for a long while. She'd never had a brother or sister, just Sam. She couldn't think of a greater comfort in the world than his soft fur or coarse tongue against her hands.

She lay in her bed unable to sleep. She was drunk still, but barely. She closed her eyes and they drifted open again. There was a thumping ring in her ears. She put her own palm against her cheek and pressed it there.

She was awake in the morning before her mother, even though she usually slept late into the day. She put on her robe, made the bed, and walked quietly to the kitchen. The house was full of light and it looked pretty to her, the bare wood walls soaking up heat already. The painted concrete floor. You could have a house like this in Fannin because it was dusty and dry. When it rained, her mother swept water out with a broom and waited for the sun to dry it up again. It was someone's cheap old ranch house, but it looked nice to her today, in summer.

She knew there would have been other ways to live. Her father drew disability checks from the government and sat silently in the bedroom. Their life – her father's, her mother's, her own – had suspended the moment her mother drove her father home from the VA hospital. She tried sometimes to understand the life her mother had chosen or allowed, her implacable dreams, but it was as unreadable to her now as it had been in her childhood.

Her father was asleep, too. She stood, made the bed, went to the kitchen, gave Sam fresh water and some scraps. He thumped his tail against the floor, and she sang to him a little bit as she began the dishes, something tuneless she was making up as she went along. Her hands were shaking from too little sleep but her mind was clear. The sky outside the window was the color of bone. She could still feel Gary's thigh against her own, the warmth coming through his jeans. She thought about how he had looked at her, like he could see everything curled inside of her, all of her waiting hopes and dreams, like he wanted to reach in and bring them out into the light and make them real.

IT WAS MONDAY evening when Gary called her. Her mother picked up the phone. She was reading in the bedroom with her father while he watched television and she bolted from the room when she heard her name.

Her heart was beating hard when she took the phone from her mother. "Hello?"

"Hey," he said.

She sounded like an idiot on the phone. She had known this since sixth grade. As early as sixth grade, when girls from her math class would call her, she was already saying the wrong thing. "What are you doing?" they would ask. "Nothing." The conversation was supposed to go somewhere from there. She would hold the phone against her ear hard. "So, are you coming to school tomorrow?" she asked once, and the girl on the other end of line had laughed at her. She knew she was missing the point. Gary, however, did not seem to notice.

"What are you doing, Kitten?" he asked her.

"I'm just at home." Her voice was shaking. He'd called her Kitten. "Not really doing anything." She needed to fix that, soon. It had been two months since she graduated. She cleaned house for an older woman in town once a week, and she read copy at the *Fannin Herald* because the real copyeditor was having surgery. Amy was good at copyediting, but when Pat Morris came back she'd have nothing again. She'd thought about taking classes in Seguin, but that cost money, and she didn't know what she would want to study anyway. The girls in Fannin were either going to move to Seguin or Lockhart, or they had babies already and were staying here. Her mother hadn't graduated high school. Her father had, but who knew what he would have done if he hadn't been drafted. "He wanted to open a store," her mother said. "He was going to own a franchise, one of those gas stations."

"What are you doing tomorrow?" Gary asked her.

"Tomorrow?"

"No, come on, what are you doing?"

"I don't know," she said. "Nothing."

"You're not working at the paper?"

He'd remembered. "No," she said. "I did today. It's only three days a week."

"Come out with me then. I'll pick you up in the morning. Come out to the ranch."

"I guess I could." Her face was hot again. She wondered what it meant that he wanted to bring her there. He had seemed to hate the ranch and to love it all at once, his familiarity with the land and his enjoyment of the work at odds with his sometimes-anger at his father. Maybe seeing the ranch would explain things, she thought.

"Okay, tell me where to pick you up," he said, and she told him how to find the American Legion. Because it was easy to find, she said, right on the main drag, but to be honest she couldn't imagine introducing Gary, having him in. Or worse, running out to the car while her mother watched through the window. There wasn't anything wrong with Gary, or with her mother, really, but the idea of the two of them together made her squirmy. And her father – it wasn't time for that yet.

"I'll be there," he said.

When she hung up the phone, her mother called from the sofa. "Who was that?"

"Just this guy I met on Saturday."

"Where's he from?"

"Geronimo, I guess. He works on his dad's ranch."

Amy's mother didn't say anything, and Amy waited. She

opened the refrigerator and took out the milk. She poured a glass and stirred chocolate powder into it.

"Amy," her mother said finally.

"Yeah, Ma?"

"You need to be careful. You shouldn't go anywhere with him alone until you know him better."

"I know, Ma." She sighed. "Jennifer and Scott and I are going to go to his ranch tomorrow. We're all meeting at the Legion." Her mother liked Scott because she had gone to school with his uncle. Amy thought about the time that she'd watched Scott shotgun one beer after another and then take off his pants and shake his dick around at Seguin Bridge. Let her think that Scott was going to be there.

"Ride with Scott," her mother said. "Not–what's his name?"

The night of the dick shaking, Scott had passed out in the mud and Jennifer had gone home with Rick Pearson. "Gary," she said.

SHE WAS OUTSIDE of the Legion by ten thirty, a half an hour to spare. She went inside and Junior, the bartender, poured a bottle of Bud into a plastic cup and handed it to her, winking. "You gotta have breakfast, girl," he said. Junior knew her mother. He had spent some time in prison in Huntsville but now he worked here, washing glasses, stocking the coolers. He never talked about Huntsville and he was always sweet, and she liked him for that, for the way he could have two lives. She took the beer and went out to the front patio to wait.

It was Tuesday and the only people coming in and out of the Legion were old veterans, men who sat like kings at their card tables until the rush came in, when they went home to bed. She stood half-hidden behind the front pillars and watched the slow traffic on Main.

Gary was early, too. He pulled up in his yellow Chevy and got out, blinking in the sun. She watched him from the steps of the Legion for a moment before he saw her. He was handsome, she thought. He looked older than twenty. She stepped out of the shadows.

"There you are!" he called. He smiled at her broadly, and she laughed. The beer was warming her chest and she was already sweating in the heat. She threw her cup in the trash and ran down the steps to meet him.

The drive to the ranch took half an hour. Gary had a Styrofoam cooler on the floor of the truck. He opened a beer for her and one for himself, wedging the can between his thighs. "You'll like the ranch," he said.

"I can't wait," she said. She meant it. She'd been around ranches all her life, and they'd bored her – empty land dotted with sheds and rusted-out tractors. In Texas the land was everywhere and nowhere. It was too dry one year, and always too big, but mostly it was just flat and wide, hardly there at all. But Gary talked about it like it was a living thing, someone to visit. "Will you own it, one day?" she asked.

Gary laughed. He reached for the pack of cigarettes on the dash and handed it to her. "Will you light one of these?" he asked. When she did, he took a long drag and blew the smoke out the open window. She lit one for herself. "Hell, no," he said, finally. "I want to get out of here. I want this ranch to die out. I want it to go back to dirt while my father watches." It was that tone again, and she looked at him quick out of the corner of her eye. What had his father done? Gary caught her looking and a smile broke over his face, and just like that, the tone was gone. "I told you, Kitten," he said. "I want to go to Seattle."

She pushed back a pang of something at the idea of him leaving – she didn't know him at all; there was no reason to miss him. "What will you do there?" she asked.

"Shit, there's so much. There's logging jobs everywhere, and Boeing. I could work on planes. There's mountains, and the ocean is nothing like Galveston or Corpus. There's nothing in Texas, Amy."

I know it, she thought. But the idea of Seattle, of anywhere else, gave her that same blank feeling she had at school–what would a life somewhere else even look like?

Gary turned the truck down a dirt road, charging over potholes. The dust rose around them and Amy rolled up the window holding her beer out in front of her so it wouldn't spill. There was fencing on either side, and empty land covered with scrubby patches of grass and rutted dirt. Gary stopped in front of a metal gate and got out, opened it, pulled through, and shut it again. He was grinning and proud when he climbed back into the truck. "The house is down there a ways," he said. He put the truck in drive and started the opposite way, making no move to take her toward the house. He narrated as he drove, pointing to a pile of scrap metal towering across a ditch to the left. "I'm getting rid of that. I'll make a grand off of it." The truck rattled over a cattle guard. "I'm putting up a building over there, a shed, when I'm done hauling off that shit. Someplace where we can store tools or park a trailer or something." He looked at her. "It'll be the first building I've ever built completely alone from the ground up."

She could hear the pride in his voice again, and she smiled. "It's great," she said, and she meant it for his sake, even though to her it looked like every other boring ranch. "What was it like growing up here? You must have had a lot of room to run around."

Gary just shrugged and gunned the truck down the dirt road.

She lit a cigarette and handed it to him. It endeared him to her, the way he seemed to swing wildly between anger and warmth, happiness, and frustration. There was something childlike about it, and it made her want to protect him.

"Sure." Gary sucked on the cigarette angrily for a minute and then he turned to her and his face was bright again. She felt a rush of relief. He smiled widely and threw the truck into park. "Let's walk," he said. "I'll show you what I'm working on."

He led her down tire tracks in the dirt, pointing out where the new fencing was going to go, where there would be a new irrigation system, where the property line ended. It felt like they had walked forever.

"You're bored," he said, suddenly.

"No, I'm not."

"You are." He reached over and grabbed her hand. "It's okay, I have plans for us."

When they found the truck again he drove them to the edge of a pond and parked. The water was a wide, perfect circle of blue. "I thought you might want to swim."

Her blouse was damp through. She'd been pressing her arms to her sides, trying to hide the wet spots. "I don't have a swimsuit."

Gary raised his eyebrows. "Well ..." he said. "Neither do I."

The beer was making her brave. The grass around the pond was thick and green, gaining color as it sloped down to the water. She opened the door of the cab. "Well, then, I guess we're swimming," she said. Before she could reconsider, she unbuttoned her blouse and left it on the front seat. She stepped out of her shorts and ran toward the water in her underwear. She was a little drunk. The water was deep from the start and she fell forward, laughing. "Come on!" she yelled.

Gary tripped down the slope to the pond and sat in the grass, unlacing his shoes. "You're slow," she said.

He took off his shirt and jeans and waded to her, opening his arms. She put her cheek against his chest and he lifted her head and kissed her. "This is beautiful," she said.

"It's a goddamn cow tank," he said, and laughed.

IT WAS WELL into the afternoon when she followed Gary up to the truck, drying off with a thin blanket that he pulled out of the back of the cab. The sun was deep orange and low in the sky. She sat on the ground and used the blanket to dry her hair. She didn't want to worry her mother, to have her call Scott's uncle and try to track down Scott. "I should go home," she said.

"It would be a crime," he said, "to make me drive you out of here without promising me you'll let me take you to dinner tomorrow." He crawled on top of her, pinning her to the ground, and she started to laugh. He kissed her. The grass was rough against her bare arms and legs. His mouth was warm. It tasted like salt and beer.

She forgot to worry about being late. She was trying to remember each thing, even as it was happening. Gary's hand between her legs, the rough feeling of his chin against her cheek. His fingers were fumbling and then pushing inside her, hard and quick, and the other hand was on her shoulder, pressing her down. It hurt and she felt tears spring to her eyes. He pulled back and watched her, breathing heavily, and even as his hand was hurting her, she liked watching him want her.

He let go of her shoulder and pushed himself up over her. He pulled down his wet underwear with one hand and she struggled up to help, to see what was happening, but then he was inside her. She pressed her eyes closed. No one had told her, she thought. It was different than they made it sound. All the lies about roses and softness. This was more like hard need, the rocky dirt and Gary's rough breathing, her bruised hips and his sharp, painful want.

When it was over, she lay beside him not talking, shivering, and letting the sun warm her all at once. It was the first time she knew that her life had been lonely. That it had ached. And no one had told her, she thought again, how anything was supposed to be.

IN SEPTEMBER, WHEN she'd been seeing Gary for three weeks, he lifted himself over her, his strong arms on either side of her head. They were lying on a blanket by the San Marcos river, up from the waterline and hidden from sight by tall grass and a stand of sweetgum trees. He was deathly serious. "Amy, what would you say if I said we should go somewhere?" She thought he meant Port A, which was three hours away. She thought he meant calamari and po' boys.

"I would say yes," she said, and she meant it. The hours without him seemed empty, as though she couldn't imagine that she had spent eighteen years without this – that she hadn't felt hungry. But she had. Take me to Port A, she thought. Take me to Dallas. Let's go to New Orleans.

"I want to marry you first," he said. "I want to marry you, Amy, and I want us to move to Seattle."

She felt as though the wind had been knocked out of her and suddenly she wanted Gary to get off of her. She shifted but he didn't move.

"Say yes," he said.

"Gary–" She pushed at him and finally he rolled off her. "Gary, wait."

He was looking at her and his eyes were full of tears.

She did want to marry him. She wanted it more than anything. But Seattle–her mother, and Sam. Maybe it was silly, but she couldn't stand to leave Sam. When she thought about her old dog, her chest tightened. Sam loved South Texas. She couldn't imagine taking him away from this land, the only world he'd ever known. And how long did he have, anyway? A year? Six months? And her father. Even if no one had expected her to stay, *she* had expected she would. This was Fannin, Texas. This was what she was supposed to do. The person she should be.

"Gary," she said. "I want to marry you. Yes. Yes." She held his face, kissed his wet eyelids. "I want that so much," she said. "But Seattle–just give me a little time. My mother–and Sam. I just need to get used to the idea–and get my mother used to it. And Sam–" She was crying too, now. "I just need to wait until Sam goes," she said. "He's too old. I can't drag him across the country. He loves it here." It sounded silly, she thought, but it was true. Sam knew every path through town, every inch of the house, every smell. She felt like taking him away would break his heart.

"Baby," Gary said. He gathered her to him. "Baby." She breathed into his neck. Please, she thought. Please understand. "We'll wait," he said. "However long you need. Tomorrow, ten years, take your whole life, I'll be here." He reached above her and straightened the blanket they were lying on, made sure it was under her head. She pressed herself against him, touching his skin, his hair. "All of my life," he said softly. "This is what I want."

The sweetgum trees flashed the silvery undersides of their leaves in the dry wind. Her chest, her heart, felt ocean-full.

AT THE LEGION the next day, Jennifer squeezed both of Amy's hands in her own, in the gnarl of her silver rings. "You can't be serious," she said.

"I am," Amy said. "I love him. I want to marry him."

"But it's been like a month! You don't even know him. I mean, who is this guy?"

"What are you talking about? Scott's the one who knew him in the first place."

"He knows him, but he doesn't *know him* know him," Jennifer said. "They're like, acquaintances. They met like twice." She poured tomato juice into the mouth of her beer can. "It's not like I'm not happy for you, Ames," she said. "It's just, wow."

"Come on, Jen. He's perfect. I didn't even know guys like Gary existed."

"Amy–" Jennifer stopped.

"What?"

"I don't know–just–that night, he gave me a weird feeling. He seemed, like–I don't know, like anti-social or something. He kept you outside all night–I don't know. He gave me a weird look."

Amy pushed back a hurt feeling. Jennifer didn't know Gary, she reminded herself. "We were talking outside," she said. "And everyone was drunk anyway."

Jennifer reached for the saltshaker and salted the top of her beer can. She smiled. "All right, he is cute. Way cuter than Scott."

"How can you drink that?"

"It's like a Bloody Mary. Whatever, you eat pork rinds."

"Scott's cute."

Jennifer made a face. "Scott's got a pencil dick."

"Don't forget his monkey face."

"And he's hairy. What an asshole." Jennifer sighed. "Okay.

You're right. You totally 100 percent deserve to be happy. And to get out of this town." She drank from her beer. "Just don't go yet, okay? Wait a few months, maybe? I can't believe you're going to leave me here alone with *Scott*."

Walking home through the scrub grass and smell of oil, she tried the words: "I'm getting married," she said to herself. "I am going to be Gary's wife." Would it feel different, she wondered. She wanted to feel more of herself, more substantial. Significant to someone besides herself.

The house ahead of her seemed squatter than usual. It looked washed out. The screen was torn and the doorframe warped. She went into the kitchen and her mother was there wearing yellow dishwashing gloves and cutting peppers. "Look what Dolores gave me," she said, waving the knife. "She's got so many this year. I'm making jelly." She looked at Amy. "Where have you been?"

"Out. I went to the Legion with Jennifer."

"No Gary today?"

Amy smiled. "I saw him earlier. How's Dad?"

"He's okay. In his chair. So, when do I get to meet him?"

Amy picked up one of the rounds of chopped pepper and touched the edge to her tongue, feeling the burn spread across it. She had already waited too long, she realized. She should have introduced Gary to her mother earlier, given some signal of what was coming. "Soon," she promised.

"Gary's a Yankee name."

"Well, he was born here."

"His parents must be Yankees, then."

She didn't say anything. She didn't know, actually. She hadn't met his parents, and he didn't talk about them much, except for the occasional outbursts about his father, how controlling he was, how ungrateful. She hadn't seen the ranch house; they spent all of their time together in stolen places, the truck, on blankets spread in patches of sunlight between trees. Gary's work with his father seemed more and more sporadic, and he was often testy and frustrated. Her mother leaned toward her. "Get my hair out of my eyes, would you?" Amy reached up and brushed the hair back. There was an ache in her chest, as though she were already gone.

THAT FALL FELT long, nearly interminable. They were married in front of a justice of the peace on the first of October; she wore a cheap party dress from Beall's, and Jennifer signed as the witness. "I don't care if we don't have a place yet. I just want to know that you're my wife." She looked at Gary, tall and handsome and smart. I'm married, she thought, but it meant nothing, it was just words. She was still living with her mother. The ring was something cheap and she didn't wear it. It was as though they'd made a pact not to say anything. She and Jennifer didn't talk about it either; Jennifer still seemed distrustful of Gary. She'd done the witnessing and then left quickly afterward; Amy felt hurt and angry about it at first, but then she told herself it didn't matter. She and Gary didn't need a celebration; they were special enough just being together. It was their secret how powerful their love was.

Still, it was hard. *Seattle*, Gary kept saying. "In Seattle, God, we'll get a beautiful house, right in the city. Or maybe out by the coast and our kids can walk on the beach." He was unconcerned about telling his family. "It's my life," he said. "They're only interested in me if I'm working on the ranch."

She brought Gary home to dinner one night. My husband, she thought of saying. Meet my husband, Gary, but she didn't. Her mother made a roast, and they all sat at the little table. Gary's manners were good, but his aggressive compliments, his lavish kindness, embarrassed her.

"You're such a wonderful cook," he said to her mother. "I know that Amy must have inherited that from you." When had she cooked for him? Her mother eyed both of them suspiciously.

Amy liked the way he looked at her father, though. Her mother was cutting the meat in small pieces, helping him to hold the fork. Gary didn't stare, and he spoke to him like he was any father, and for that she loved him.

Later that night she stood at the screen, calling for Sam.

"I haven't seen him," her mother said.

She stepped back into the house but kept the screen cracked. "Sam!" she called.

Sam liked to lie in a scratch of dirt outside the tool shed and lazily watch the birds. He'd lift his head and groan, a sad little howl because he was too old and slow to hunt, or maybe to remind them that he was there. His paws like rough stones, his big old head.

She called around the block and no one had seen him. She remembered a time when he was barely older than a puppy and he'd wandered over the highway, all the way to the river. Amy had been five or six, and she'd driven up and down the streets with her mother for hours, her forehead pressed hard to the window, her heart breaking. When they found him, standing up to his hocks in the water, drinking lustily, panting from his journey, she'd stood and cried from the pure relief. It felt as though her life had just come flooding back to her.

She sat on the porch well into the night waiting, listening to the sounds of the town and the river shifting and settling in the dark. Please Sam, she thought. Come home to me.

EVERY DAY SAM was gone, she felt her own life in Fannin stretch thinner. The whole town seemed lousy with trenches and cellars, small, dark places where Sam might have gone to lie down. To die, she thought but wouldn't say.

In the end, it was better, she told herself. Sam was so old. She would not have to see him suffer. She tried to remind herself of that whenever her throat grew tight, whenever the grass rustled and she looked for him, her oldest friend, hoping against hope that Sam would come bounding toward her, mouth open, his body shaking with excitement, his tailing wagging madly in the warm breeze. But he didn't. And so, she told herself again, she would not have to see him suffer. And in some small way, she was set free.

Three weeks after Sam disappeared, she called Gary. "Tell me about Seattle," she said.

They made plans to leave after Christmas, before the New Year. When Amy told her mother, she didn't tell her that they were already married. "I'm thinking of going with Gary on a trip," she said. "To Seattle." She didn't say, "to stay," but her mother looked at her as though it was all already between them, the deceit, and everything Amy meant to do.

"You love him," her mother said. She looked so small.

On Christmas Day, the day before they would leave, Amy walked the neighborhood a last time, looking for Sam. When he didn't appear, she buried a soup bone near the steps and left the dirt in a tall pile so that he would know. At the last moment, she pulled a handful of purple and yellow johnny jump-ups from the pot on the steps and laid them there. "Oh Sam," she said aloud. "You were mine."

Jackson

Silver, Idaho, 2010

SILVER ITSELF WAS IN THE LOWER PANHANDLE, SOUTH-east of Kellogg and Wallace, still in the dark mountains. It was the river that had killed the mines; the river that killed what Jackson was beginning, even now, to think of as the *real* Silver, its rocky little heart. The way the men on the crew talked, and the way that the town bore its bad luck without complaint, with familiarity, made Jackson sure that even Silver's boom years hadn't been much, not in the way that you might imagine. Little bars, tired miners. Every penny had been pulled from the earth for more than it was worth. And the river – the creek – that sprawled its way down the mountains, just east of the town, kept flooding. It flooded with determined, manic consistency – no way to know when, just that it was inevitable.

In the mornings, when he didn't have to work, Jackson walked the channel of the old riverbed. The water was slowly disappearing, the ground turning back to flat hard dirt. It was an expanse of strange housekeeping, everything that over the years had been lost. The bright curve of a flip-flop, a muddy radio, scraps of torn fabric, garbage bags still full of waterlogged trash. An armchair, blooming with mud and leaves. There was an old man with shaky arms who was often there in the mornings, trolling the wide ditch with a metal detector in a pair of tall rubber boots. He stopped every few feet, digging in the mud, wearing a pair of yellow kitchen gloves.

A hundred, two hundred years of this town – what all had

sunk down in that sprawling river? Engagement rings, bottles, toys. He'd heard how police had been on hand when the river was diverted in case bodies showed up. Missing persons. But there were only the bones of dogs, cats, a cow, the shell of a 1931 convertible Cabriolet sunk deep in the mud. Jackson liked to watch the old man, plodding slowly along, his metal detector held in front of him like a dowsing rod. His mother would have found the man romantic, Jackson thought. "Oh," he could imagine her saying, "Look at that. He's digging up the past. Digging up bones. Like the Randy Travis song!" She had kept only a few things from her life before Jackson's father, things she'd brought across the country. Jackson liked to look at them, to try to add them up to something. A glass baby bottle with a thick rubber nipple, a cut china bowl, a yellow leather driving glove. Onto that stratum she added the sentimental detritus of his and Lydia's things. Report cards *(Jackson fulfills obligations but ultimately seems disinterested in engaging with his peers)*, drawings, the head of a baby doll that Lydia had made up with a Magic Marker–deep blue eyelids and a hideous pink grin. The dead walkie-talkie that Jackson had carried for years, intercepting messages from space aliens, benevolent imagined protectors, and Kenny Rogers.

That was one thing that bothered him about the new lake–on the surface, it seemed like a kind of forgiveness, to make newness and beauty out of the splintered wreckage of the old dam, the watermarked town. An offering of grace. But at the same time, wasn't it a falsehood, to think you could just move an entire river, make a new lake, and everything would fall into place? A litter of wild dogs, displaced by the flood, ran in and out of the woods, through the alleys in town. In the absence of more certain landmarks, birds flew woozily into the windows of the new houses. One morning, Jackson had stood in an empty house frame while the wind whipped through, watery and sharp smelling. One of the carpenters had left his lunch sitting in a paper sack on top of a sawhorse. When Jackson turned around one of the stray dogs was there, rangy and skittish, eating the sandwich in choking bites.

The dog finished the sandwich and stood there shaking, tonguing up crumbs. His fur was matted. He looked at Jackson with hungry, lost eyes.

AFTER DON TOLD him about his wife, Jackson didn't see him for three weeks. The work had picked up, and Don was back and forth to Spokane, to Missoula. Jackson was full of a sick uncertainty – was it over? Would he know if it was? Did it even matter? And then Don came to him on a Tuesday afternoon, when there hadn't been much to do and Mark Davis, someone Jackson understood to be in at least moderately in charge, told him to cut out early. Jackson had just finished taking a shower – five minutes in the narrow plastic stall, the trickle of cool water from the snaking showerhead, the curtain sticking to him and water spilling out onto the floor of the cab. Now he was trying to get warm again, half-reading a shitty thriller that had been left on the free shelf at Mary's. He heard sticks cracking outside the cab and froze, waiting. He had a knife, that was all, and he reached for it, wedged beside his mattress and the wooden frame. He held its cool weight and his breath. "Jack," Don whispered. "Let me in?"

Jackson swung open the creaking door and there was Don. Pretty, big-eyed Don with that shock of black hair and a shadow of stubble that raked Jackson's face when they kissed. Don was wearing jeans and a jean jacket – Jackson pictured Randy, stoned, delighted, *A Canadian tuxedo!* – but on Don it looked right, loose and easy. He had his arm threaded through two lawn chairs and a bottle of wine in his hand. "Hey," he said.

"Hey."

"I thought," Don said, setting everything down in the dirt and stepping up onto the first steep step into the cab, "that you might want some chairs. It's getting warmer out these days." He looked at Jackson. "You're wet," he said. "And so clean. I probably shouldn't kiss you, being so dirty myself."

"You're probably right," Jackson said, and he reached for Don, pulled him up and into the cab of the truck, onto his tiny bed, on top of him. God, Don's mouth. Jackson's skin was electric with wanting, all of the wanting of the last three weeks rising up in him, hard and nearly painful.

"Stop," Don said, sitting up, nearly hitting his head on the ceiling of the cab. "I wanted this to be romantic. I brought chairs."

"That *is* romantic," Jackson said. "Are they real plastic?"

"You're a brat."

"They're beautiful."

"And ungrateful."

"So well made."

"Shut up and help me." They climbed out into the five o'clock June light and carried the chairs – pink and green, made of clear plastic that reminded Jackson of Lydia's old jelly shoes – through the underbrush, to a break in the trees where a swath of the lake was visible, and the rusty blast furnace, the skeleton of an old factory. They planted the chairs in the dirt side-by-side, and sat. Jackson had the feeling that Don had brought him here for a reason, and he waited. When he was seeing Eric, Jackson had come to understand that this was how to talk to men – to pretend you weren't talking at all. Eric would move from talking about his lunch of scallion salad to his certainty that the other managers thought him a fool, his bitter jealousy of other men, his aching fear of death, while Jackson lobbed soft noises of interest at him from beneath the cloud of the feather duvet.

"So," Don said. "How have you been?"

"I've been working," Jackson said. "*Where* have you been?"

"Point taken." Don peeled the tin from the top of the wine and unscrewed the top. He passed it to Jackson. It was cheap and sweet.

Jackson wiped his mouth. "No," he said. "I mean it. I haven't seen you in a while, is all."

"There's been a lot to do." Don lifted his legs, in those dirty work boots, and set them on Jackson's lap. "I've been driving everywhere and, god, it's hell."

"Did you go home?" He tried to make his voice sound light, easy.

"Some. It was shit, actually."

"Why?" Clean laundry, Jackson imagined. The smell of detergent, the sports channel, Don's jizzed up socks in the back of the closet, his wife blow-drying her hair. He imagined they must have had a church wedding. Tastelessly expensive. Did she have any idea? Jackson wondered. Could she even imagine Don with him, here?

"Eliza is unhappy," Don said. "I'm unhappy." He raised his arms. "Is there anybody in the whole word who *is* happy? Are *you* happy?"

Jackson ignored the question. "Where is she now? Home?"

"Missoula. In our house."

"You miss her?"

"Yes. No. The idea of her." He sighed, shrugged, and adjusted his hands on the steering wheel. "This is not my beautiful house – remember that song? You're too young."

"So," Jackson said. What was there to say?

"So."

Over the empty last three weeks, he had imagined asking Don a dozen questions – Do you fuck her? Hold her? Spend all day in bed on Sundays? Do you love her? – but now they were ebbing out of him. He saw how he would sound, how pathetic he would seem. He took the wine and drank from it instead.

"This town was never meant to be a town," Don said. "It was Kellogg's dirty little barefoot mountain cousin." He looked at Jackson. "Where you from, Jack?"

He shrugged. He felt embarrassed at how little he and Don knew about each other, even after he'd been inside of Don, had pressed his hand against his broad chest, his heart. At the same time, he liked the idea that Don knew nothing about him, about what he was or what he had been. Just for a moment he imagined how Don saw him, untroubled and young. A blue-collar kid who probably had a hot girlfriend back in a small town, Superior maybe, and two parents who didn't make much money but kept a nice house.

"Come on," Don said.

Jackson picked at the top of the furnace and peeled off a rust-red sliver of corroded metal. "It's not a good story," he said. "It might make you sad." Did that sound interesting or pathetic? What, he thought, would make Don want to kiss him?

Don looked at him. "I've never in my life felt good," he said.

"Really?" Jackson asked. At five, with his mother – "Am I good?" he'd asked her, and she'd said, "The best in the world," and he'd whispered it to himself, "The best in the world," until its meaning was lost and only the warm comfort of it remained.

"Maybe when I was younger. A kid. A teenager."

Jackson felt a pinch of annoyance at Don, at his hound dog expression. Don had never had to suck an old man's cock for money, he thought. Don had surely never watched his father kick his mother in the ribs. What was Don, thirty? Thirty-five? Jackson suspected that even for all that not feeling good that he was talking about, Don hadn't exactly hoed a hard road. At the same time, there was Don's strong neck, the cords of muscle that sloped down to his shoulders. Let him have his little misery. "So, what happened?" he asked.

The lake was invisible from here, and Jackson imagined that they were somewhere else entirely, and that Don had brought him here on a date. The only dates he'd ever had were at Eric's table for twelve, set for two. The little dance of what was and wasn't real.

"Eliza, I suppose," Don said. "I had a year at Montana State and then we got together. We just – it wasn't her, exactly. I don't know. Ten years of shit and things get a little murky."

This, Jackson thought, was not exactly the turn that a date should take.

"I've been terrible to her," Don said. "She was a drinker. I was a drinker. We were drunks together. You know. We'd drive anywhere, drinking. That was the point. Go from one bar to another, and then we'd just drink and scream at each other."

It didn't sound that terrible to Jackson. It sounded like his parents at their worst and best. Romantic and ugly, the fights that could go either way and you didn't know if they'd all be eating take-out and laughing or packing the car for a motel. Besides, all the drinkers he had known were alone with their microwave dinners, their sagging faces and cancer coughs. None of them were young and beautiful and coltish. None of them had their boots up on his lap when there were a hundred other places to be.

Don picked up a handful of gravel and pitched it underhand, a little hailstorm. "We stopped. We don't drink together anymore. But maybe that was all we had in the first place."

"Maybe."

They sat in quiet for a while, and then Don said, "So, you've done this before."

"What, slept with my boss?" Jackson said, just to be a smart-ass, but Don shot him a wounded look and he felt bad. He thought about telling Don about Eric, but he imagined how Don would see him – the little hooker boy, turning tricks. Jackson didn't have two cents' worth of guilt in him for Eric anymore. That had been better, Jackson thought, than Don's empty sex with Eliza. Better than his mother and father. Eric had helped him. It wasn't so terrible. But Don – how could Don not imagine that Jackson must be damaged beyond belief? How to explain that sometimes, in the island of Eric's bed, his mouth full of caviar and once-a-week champagne, he'd been ecstatic with his own ability to survive?

"Sort of," he said finally. "A little bit. There was a guy from my high school."

Don laughed. "Jesus, you're young. I forget that."

Jackson had zero desire to listen to Don comment on his age. *And you're fucking me*, he wanted to say. Instead, he cleared his throat. "What about you? Have you done this before?"

"Nah," Don said, in a way that made Jackson not believe him. "I mean, I don't know, I just – " He looked at Jackson helplessly. "It's hard. People don't like it."

"But you have to live the way you want to."

"Jack." Don took a long drink from the wine bottle. He looked for a long time toward the rusted blast furnace, its silhouette. "You know what that would mean for me. I'd have nothing." He sighed, drank again. "It's better this way. You know that. I'd have nothing."

You'd have me, Jackson thought, but he didn't say it. He understood fear, he understood being afraid of losing everything. But he didn't understand being ashamed. At the bottom – he smiled for a second at his own stupid pun, bottom – Jackson himself wasn't. Jackson wasn't ashamed of wanting men. Sex was equal parts beautiful and messy, slipping bodies, grotesque things that looked ugly, but felt good, no matter who was doing it. If he had pretended to be Good Jackson, Straight But Not Narrow Jack, it would have been just that – pretend. Not some other, problem-free life he could have gathered up around him and lounged in. What happiness was there in a pretend life? Only pretend happiness; pleasantries, secrecy, fear. Maybe he would have saved his father from angry humiliation, Chris from shame, his mother from bearing the brunt of his father's disgust at his not-son-enough son. But he'd still be trapped inside himself; he'd still be the same.

So, no, he couldn't believe Don when he said this was better. Easier in the short run, a tragedy in the long. Maybe this was his modern inheritance, to be able to think this way. He didn't care. He wasn't noble about it. He wasn't self-satisfied. He was just sure that he was who he was.

Suddenly he didn't want to be sitting with Don anymore. He felt stranded, beached in his squat plastic lawn chair, its aluminum legs planted in the dirt. He wished he wanted to tell Don about Eric. About Chris. About his father, or about what had happened that day. The moment he kept repeating, had been repeating in his mind for months now and each time it was worse, because all the better endings he imagined did not actually happen: His father goes to the Starlight Motel, Room 121, to retrieve his mother and sister. It is the morning after he has told his father where his mother is. All night he has stared hard at his own reflection, his own ghost in the window. And now it is afternoon, and his mother and Lydia are back. They are the same, but not. They are duller, harder versions of themselves. Even Lydia is just across some invisible line. This happens for a week. He wakes up each morning with his blood pounding in his ears.

Then it is Saturday, a week after he told his father. His mother has spoken to him about school, about dinner, about a dress pattern. The Starlight Motel, the moment when his father showed up, have not been mentioned. His mother asks him to take Lydia to the mall, to buy a gift for a birthday party. "Take her on the bus after school," she says. "I have to finish some things around here."

On the bus he thinks of asking Lydia about the night his father showed up, about whether his mother is angry. He thinks of telling her he's sorry. At the mall he asks her what she wants to buy but she doesn't know; she just wants to wander, and pick things up, and ask him what he likes. They are in one of those tacky New Age stores, and Lydia is looking at a bonsai tree kit because she read *The Little Prince* last year. He tries to tell her it won't work, that no kid is going to want a tree on his or her thirteenth birthday. She is reluctant, and picks up a tiny package of herbs. He reads it to her – she can read just fine, but this is still a kind of game they play, where she is younger than she is, and he thinks of her that way, and it cuts at him, now – it is a Chinese herb, a tiny little caterpillar fungus, with a handmade tag that reads Winter Worm Summer Grass. The salesman is a white guy wearing a shirt that looks like it's made of hemp, and even though Jackson usually has a sad little hard-on for these kinds of pathetic men, he doesn't this time. The man explains that the little caterpillar root is called cordyceps, and when it grows in the wild it looks like a worm in the winter, and a piece of grass in the summer, and that it heals things, when it is cut and dried and eaten. That he himself has made a soup for his brother with this herb, and that he once spent two years teaching English in a remote Chinese village – he is adding this to show why he is such an expert – and this man has Lydia in the palm of his hand, which makes Jackson angry. "Like magic," she says, and the man says, "Exactly," and Lydia is following him to the counter and spending the birthday present money that their mother has given her on this little dry worm.

They spend some time walking past the shops, the Sunglass Hut, the Frederick's of Hollywood, the arcade, and Lydia keeps asking about the time, and he keeps trying to ask her about this birthday party, and the pathetic son of a bitch kid – *Boy or girl*, and she hesitates and says, "Boy," though he hasn't known her to hang out with any boys – who is going to get this little magic herb for a birthday present. The tiny dry worm in the pile of CDs and game cartridges, the requisite basketball.

And then when he tells her it is four o'clock and asks her if she wants to head home, she says she needs the bathroom, and he points to it, and she pushes the little plastic bag into his hands and sprints toward it, and turns back once. He paces around, and just when he wonders if she's okay in there he looks up and she is out the double doors, running, looking back at him once guiltily, and he is after her before he can even think of what's happening, running fast but she has a hell of a head start.

Outside the door he sees them pulling out of the parking lot, Lydia turned around in her seat and looking at him, waving sadly, his mother looking at him and then straight ahead, the car filled with garbage bags. They are leaving without him, running without him – from him – and he keeps holding the little root that was for him all along, and for the first time it is completely clear what he has done. And this will be the last he sees of her, and it is still winter, months before he will go to Silver, and even then, when it is summer, the Winter Worm will stay the same, dark and still beside his bed, the flower hidden deep within it.

Suddenly he felt Don's hand on his arm. "Jack," Don was saying. "Earth to Jack. Come in, Jack."

Jackson shook his head and laughed. "Sorry," he said, and shrugged. The sun was setting now, the June heat just fading away, and Don passed him the wine bottle. That day, when his mother and sister left without him, Jackson took the bus to the bottom of Firetrail and hitched the rest of the way home. By the time he made it to the house, it was dark, and from the porch he could see the yellow light falling out of the windows and onto the dark lawn, and through the foggy glass the figure of his father drunk at the kitchen table. Seeing his father there was like being relieved of a temporary amnesia. His father had only ever hated him, Jackson thought. And hated his mother, and his sister. There wasn't a day Jackson could remember that he hadn't been afraid, that he hadn't known how worthless his father believed him to be. What, Jackson kept thinking, have I done? It wasn't a question he could answer. By the end of the week he had moved into Randy's basement, and by the end of the month he was in Portland, living on the street. They had all escaped his father after all, but with no help from him.

Now, in Silver, Don was squeezing his arm, and drinking again from the bottle, and slowly the present moment settled back down around him. He pulled Don forward, across the space between the shitty plastic chairs, and then they were kissing, and he was willing Lydia away from him. Here was Don, the rough scrape of his cheeks, his eager mouth, and it was that easy, Jackson thought. You remember someone so you can forget someone else.

Lydia

Fannin, Texas, 2010

ON HACKBERRY STREET, AT THE BACK OF THE WOODEN house she grew up in, my mother and I shared a yellow bedroom. "Maybe we'll get our own place," she said, "when things settle down." She smoothed the pink roses on the bedspread with the palm of her hand, back and forth. "For now, we just need to get used to our new lives."

Our new lives. The yellow bedroom, the Purple Heart on the wall, the floor that drove a splinter into my heel. A window with dotted curtains, and through it the bare yard. There were twenty-three steps between the front porch and street. I sat on the porch in the dry air. I watched the sun sink into the scrub grass. The day slipped by, and then another after it.

"Don't you love this blue sky?" my mother asked. "Don't you love the sun, the river, this blue?" She kept asking, but it didn't matter. I was busy remembering, making a list in my mind of the things I didn't want to forget. The things I *did* want to forget, but knew I needed to remember, though I couldn't say exactly why.

In Washington, I told myself, we lived on Firetrail Hill. It was a mile to the mailbox and a half-hour's drive to town. It was a mess of gravel potholes and pasture grown over. The trees were sewn to the sky.

In Washington, the house was a double-wide mobile with off-white siding that arrived in halves on the bed of a truck, when my mother was just eighteen and still believed that my father was a good man. It was set on the edge of a slope and below was the creek, and the old rowboat, and every fort I ever built. I remember that I sometimes thought of following that creek off our land, to the ocean, to a lake or the sea, and how if I went missing police dogs would drag their noses along the creek bed; the lit windows of the house would glow like searchlights.

And the small things, too, I listed: The stacks of firewood swaying in the woodshed. The pits dropping from the cherry tree, and how they split with frost. The hiss of spit on the woodstove, the way the window glass shattered around my mother before we left for the Starlight Motel, my father's boot on her back. The way, when my father yelled, no one but us and the sinking ground could hear.

Even as I hung my clothes in my new closet, even as my grandmother said, "You're home now," even as my mother and I walked to town and stood at the front desk of the Fannin Junior High and my mother signed the papers with my new name, I was thinking of Washington.

And if they forget, I thought – if my mother slips out of that old life so completely that I am the only thing she recognizes from it, if Jackson lives as though he never knew us at all – it doesn't matter. I'll remember it for us, I thought; I will remember all of it; I will leave nothing out. I didn't know why it was important, but it was. I knew that even as my mother and I went out the front doors of my new school and started the walk back to the wooden Fannin house under the silver threads of telephone wire and the hard bright springtime sun.

Amy
Tulalip, Washington, 2008

IT WAS THE FIRST TRULY BRAVE THING SHE FELT SHE had ever done, to get the train to Seattle. She'd seen the ad for the rally in the paper the month before, and the plans she made were elaborately constructed, a wedding of caution and necessity. She invented a series of tests at the Everett Clinic, something to do with a cyst that was likely benign. A return visit in the afternoon. There was no reason to come home in between, she explained. She would go to the library, and perhaps to the grocery store. It would be a tiresome day, eaten up completely by things that couldn't be helped. She sighed when she brought it up, but her heart was pounding.

It was the end of May; Jackson and Lydia were in school. Jackson's sophomore year, Lydia in the fifth grade. Gary was at a construction job. That morning she parked the car on Pacific Avenue and walked to the Amtrak station. She'd been saving small amounts of money in the pointed, witchy toes of a pair of old heels; the round trip ticket was less than twenty dollars. It was worth the trouble of the train, knowing that Gary might check the odometer on the shitty Geo. Seattle was twice as far as Everett, and Gary was meticulous in his policing. Even if he didn't notice, there might be a problem with the car, and how would she explain where she was? Besides, she liked the vaulted, echoing station, the old world feeling of purchasing her ticket at the glass booth and waiting on the platform for the train to churn to a stop. It was a cool day, breezy and full of light, the best that spring could offer in this part of the country. She watched the old houses in south Everett flip by and thin out, giving way to the newer developments and the mall. From King Street station she climbed on a rattling city bus bound for Capitol Hill. When she got out, near Seattle Central Community College, the crowd was already bigger than she would have imagined.

A boy with a camera on a strap around his neck was leaning out of a sidewalk tree, snapping photographs. Amy had expected everyone to be young, younger than her at least, but now here was everyone – the very old and very young; teenagers with shocks of pink and blue hair, rainbow buttons, intricate torn stockings; women shivering with electrical tape Xed over their nipples; people in modest sweaters and slacks wearing buttons splashed with slogans. And the signs – *Gay marriage is a civil right. Love will win. Jesus had two dads.* It felt like a different world from the one she lived in. Where, in Fannin, Texas, was the place for two women or two men who wanted to be together, who did not want to wear the too-tight tie of the Baptist church? In Washington, just fifty miles from here, in the little house beside the dark creek, beneath those trees, what need was there for questions of rights?

There were tables set up in the brick courtyard outside of the college, and she walked past each of them slowly. She tried not to look too closely at anyone. She didn't want anyone to see how new it all was. Still, a woman at a table reached out and touched her arm. "Welcome," she said. "Take anything, please."

The stacks of fliers were for events, counseling, *How to Support Your Gay, Lesbian, or Transgendered Child*, one said, and she reached for it. The woman smiled at her. "Do you have a queer child?" she asked, and Amy flinched at the word. She had heard that word flung at kids at her own high school. Had she used it, even? She was terrified, now, that people were throwing it at her own son.

"I think," Amy said, "my son is gay. He's sixteen. I think." She took a breath. "That he's gay, I mean."

The woman smiled at her again. "Well, we have lots of information on how to talk to your son. How to support him." She collated a stack of pamphlets and offered it to Amy. "Your son is lucky," the woman said, "to have a mother who cares so much."

Amy felt a thick ache in the back of her throat, behind her eyes, a rush of gratitude. She glanced at the papers in her hand. "Say 'I love you,'" she read. "Let your child know you are there for him/her." She blinked hard and nodded at the woman. "Thank you," she said.

She stood in the crowd and listened to speeches from a congressman, a teacher, a man who had been born a woman. People were cheering. This is the right world, she thought. This is the way it should be. There were so many dark things she feared for Jackson, ways she imagined him hurt, his flawless body marred, his fierce heart stung, and here they began to burn away like early fog under sunlight: he would not be alone.

She ducked into one of the bars and ordered a gin and tonic. She took it to the back corner, sitting in the dim light and watching people through the open door with their signs, their dazzling, scrapped-together outfits. They looked happy. They were electric and shouting. She felt a breathless relief, an almost painful happiness, and at the same time it was the farthest she'd ever felt from the world, from history. She had been outside of everything, all of her life. However small her life in Fannin had been, her life now was smaller.

Always she had imagined that each person had a life that was coming for them, the life that was already in motion and would grab them up if they did nothing to change it. Her Fannin life, that she had walked away from. And then the lives they might choose instead – her life in Washington or the life she might have had if she'd gone to take classes in Seguin. They were infinite, these lives. But for a gay man, she thought, for my gay son, there are fewer lives, and more divided: a secret life, a non-life, a denial. Or the fear-life, a life that tasted of blood and dirt and smelled of prickling sweat and sounded like a boot to the ribs. For Jackson she wanted something else. She wanted every promise that lit from these hopeful tongues, the warm and waiting streets they marched on. She wanted him to have what was owed him, for the world to crack open for him. She wanted to give it all to him like a gift. She did not want for him to feel the poor, small life that was already around him for a minute longer, when all of this was here, waiting.

SHE PULLED UP at the house at five. Gary looked her up and down. "Well?" he asked. She imagined that the day had written itself on her, that the luminous world was on her skin.

"It's benign," she said. "Everything is fine; it's benign." She turned away from him and filled a pot at the sink, concentrating on how the water streamed bright as stars, the lick of flame at the stove, all the tiny miracles.

She lay beside Lydia first that night, stroking her hair until she fell asleep. Gary was still in the kitchen, slowly filling the ashtray in front of him. She knocked lightly on Jackson's door until she heard him call her in. He was in bed, the desk lamp casting a yellow light across his book, shining off his soft brown hair, and she sat on the edge of the bed. "Hi," she said.

"Hi, Mom."

"I went to the city today, Jackie," she whispered.

"Marysville?"

"Seattle."

He looked at her quickly, surprised. "What for?"

"They were having a rally. I wanted to see it. For people's rights, gay people." She wasn't going to say gay but then she did. What was so terrifying about letting him know she knew, she wondered. What was so big?

Jackson didn't ask why she had gone. "Oh," he said. He put his book down.

"There were so many people out there, Jackie. Everyone was so excited, marching. Giving speeches. I couldn't believe how many people."

He looked at her with interest. "One day," she said. "You should try living in a city like that." She was choosing her words carefully, afraid that he might retreat from her. She wanted him to understand. "It would be so good for you, to go wherever you want. You can be anyone in a place like that, a city like that." Where it's safer, she thought. Where everyone will welcome you, and who you are can be the same person who walks down the street.

He busied himself with tucking the bedspread in around him. It was an ugly bedspread, cheap cotton over batting. "Maybe after Lydia graduates," he said, slowly. "Maybe we'll move to the city."

She looked at him, tucked into his bed. He was sixteen, indisputably beautiful, impossibly older than his years. "That's seven years from now, baby," she said. "You'll need your life, too."

He looked at her, not unkindly, but as though their roles were reversed, and she was full of silly, childlike plans. And wasn't it silly, she thought, to pretend that they lived in a normal way, to pretend that Jackson wasn't already seeing too much, and worrying too much, and taking too much care of her and Lydia? A ragged pain tore through her; she breathed slow to stop it, reached up and touched his hair, swept it out of his eyes.

Two weeks later, she tried to leave for the first time. Gary was still doing contract work in Sedro-Woolley, which meant he was gone for long hours, and the kids were out of school. "Jackie," she said, "Go pack a bag with clothes, and anything else you absolutely need. And your wallet, and your bathroom things. And then help your sister do the same thing, please."

Jackson asked her nothing. He moved quickly, and whatever he said to Lydia kept her satisfied; she carried her pink backpack sweetly and with purpose. They packed the car with only what they needed. She was doing a last sweep of the house, checking for anything they'd forgotten, when she heard the rattle of the truck down the gravel road.

Gary took everything back inside quietly, systematically, almost bemused. The anger would come later, and until then they would wait. The taste of smallness and fear was a bitter lump in Amy's throat. Gary offered no explanation for how he had known, and she didn't ask. He was smart in that way only, but it was enough to keep him in a family.

Jackson

Missoula, Montana, 2010

DON DROVE THE TWO HOURS FROM SILVER TO MISSOULA while Jackson slept. They'd worked all week; it was Friday afternoon, and even though it was still early Jackson's whole body ached. A hundred miles or so through dirty snow, occasional breathtaking scarps of rock and pine. Little towns like Silver, old mining towns set off I-90, dirty bars that he wished they would stop at. A bar for anyone, Jackson thought, except for two men who are fucking each other.

The trip had been Don's idea. "For the Fourth of July," he said. "I want to show you Missoula. We'll get a hotel, go out on the river. Say yes." Later Jackson would think of a hundred questions, starting with what it all meant, but he said nothing. He felt still inside. He said yes.

Don pulled off at one of the first exits, before the town had even shown itself. A truck stop exit. There was a bar, a spaceship of a convenience store, a strip club, and a motel, which Don pulled into. Jackson had imagined that Don would want a fancier place, at least a Holiday Inn, someplace mildly astringent, and he felt briefly pleased and then disappointed. This was on Don's dime. Some shameful part of himself wanted the kind of vicarious luxury he'd had at Eric's. Instead, they had a dirty little room that smelled of smoke.

It was, in fact, the dirtiest motel he'd ever seen. Worse than the Starlight. There were cigarette burns on the plasticized spread and the walls were stained; Jackson tried not to imagine what had made those hazy continents. Don took the backpack from Jackson's hands and tossed it on the single chair, then pushed Jackson down on the bed with its sinkhole center and jizz stains. Jackson didn't care about the bed; Don was stretching his long body on top of Jackson's, kissing him, and every inch of Jackson's skin felt electric, alert. Jackson grabbed Don's ass with his hands, then dragged his palms up over his muscled back. They lay still that way for a moment, and then Jackson pushed Don onto his back and kneeled above him. He unbuttoned Don's jeans and took his cock in his mouth. Don's hands were tightening in his hair. "Oh, God," he kept saying. "Oh, God, Jackson." It sounded like he was crying. When he came, he put both hands around Jackson's ears until Jackson could hear a ringing. Jackson fell onto the bed beside Don, turning toward him, wrapping their limbs together.

Don's arms were tight around Jackson, and he could hear Don's heart pounding, feel it against him. The beat drove a quick, delicious pain into Jackson's heart. Don's wedding ring was a narrow belt cutting into his fourth finger, worn so long that there was no way to slip it off.

IN THE MORNING, Don drove him slowly through town. Jackson was watching him to see if he was nervous. What if they ran into someone Don knew? He wanted it to happen, just to know what Don would say. But the truck passed unnoticed through the streets while Don pointed to the bridges, the way to the college, the Wilma Theater, the Clark Fork River running high through the center of town. Don came through here all the time, Jackson knew; Don had told him this much. He would leave Silver late at night, then arrive in mid-morning the next day with supplies. Jackson couldn't bring himself to ask, but he knew what that meant – a few hours stolen with his wife in the middle of the night. Now, beside Don in the truck, he allowed himself the fact that he had hoped that this trip meant something – that Don was acknowledging their *thing*, that Don's wife didn't mean much to Don anymore. Jackson allowed himself the fact that he'd hoped for proof of it. That some kind of moment in town, some interaction with Don's *real* life, would prove that Jackson himself might be a part of it, now or one day.

They drove east, and just out of town Don pulled off at an old dance hall. "Harold's Club," Don said. "It's an institution. They've got a ram's head in a plastic bubble in there." Don went in and bought some whiskey and they parked near the river. Don pulled his fly rod and tackle box out of the back of the truck. Montana was beautiful, somehow more majestic than Idaho. The cottonwoods flicked their arms over the dark green of the river. Jackson had never gone anywhere with someone he was fucking. Or dating, though he'd never dated. It gave him a little thrill. My *boyfriend*. Don looked even easier and more coltish by the river, his big palms on his knees, and Jackson felt his cock twitch, that deep ache in his balls. Here they were, in this place that was Don's. The Clark Fork winding past, slow and green. Houses on stilts, the tumble of gravel into the river. He imagined them doing manly Montana things together – more fishing, Don with a line of silver trout. Jackson on a horse, picking his way up in the hills. He liked this kind of tableau, even if he'd never held a fishing pole in his life. The only time he'd ridden a horse had been in the sawdust arena at the Puyallup Fair; they'd put him on a fat old mare that farted loudly and embarrassed him.

Jackson took off his shirt and lay back on the warm rocks watching Don sort through his tackle. "Let me show you a cast," Don said, but Jackson shook his head.

"You go on," he called. The sun was on him. He wanted to stay there forever.

Don picked up the bottle and opened it and took a drink. He looked at Jackson's bare stomach, reached out and touched it with his fingertips. "You make me feel old," Don said. "You make me feel like an old man."

Jackson concentrated on the feeling of Don's fingers on his skin. "And all of this time I thought I made you feel young again," he said. Don laughed. That deep, easy laugh that made people like him. Everyone liked Don. He was a man's man – Jackson had said that to him once, lying in A-frame B, the airy crosshatch of beams above them, and Don had laughed, and Jackson pinned him down on the cool wood floor.

Don moved his hand and Jackson wished for it back. "Best trout rivers in the world," Don said. He held out a handful of shimmering tufts, pierced with wire. "This is a dry fly," he said. "It skims the top of the water. This one is elk hair – it's a natural imitator. This one is a nymph – it drifts down by the bottom." Jackson nodded. "If there's nothing up top, then we go nymphing, but there's hatch right now, so we try the flies first."

Jackson didn't care about the fishing, but he liked listening to Don's low voice, watching him throw the line, standing in the water in his jeans. Missoula was in a deep valley, and the brown hills rose up all around it. He felt held, tucked safe in this bowl of the earth. It seemed as though the things that separated the human world from the natural one were missing, as though you could walk from the road right up into the bare, unfenced hills and keep walking forever.

They spent most of the day at the river, then ate at a gas station café near Harold's Club. When it grew dark, Don drove them up above town. "This is the Rattlesnake," Don said. "The best seats in the house."

They hiked up the brown scrub until Don stopped and they nested down in the dirt. He had his face buried in Don's jacket when the fireworks started. The buttons against his cheek, the warm smell of sweat and struck matches. "Hey," Don said, and touched his hair. He slipped his fingers under Jackson's chin and tilted his face toward the sky. "Hey, Jack, you're missing it."

The hill was a silvery stage for the half-hearted displays down in town, dusty Roman candles and the smell of sulfur. Don lifted Jackson's cheek from his jacket and toward the sky, the colored sparks and smoke. "You and me," Don said. They had a bottle of cheap wine that Don tipped up to his mouth. A shower of sparks lit his face in carnival pinks and blues.

Don handed the bottle to Jackson. "A sweet little boy and a bottle of wine," Don said. "That's what it takes to make a honky-tonk time."

"Is that what it takes?" Jackson pushed his face against Don's neck.

"George Strait," said Don. "One of the greats."

It wasn't George Strait. It was Dwight Yoakam. Originally Johnny Horton, but Jackson let it go. Don's neck smelled like aftershave and cigarettes. It was the worst fireworks display Jackson had seen in his life. Three or four wilting rockets gave off an uneven spray of sparks. He remembered watching the fireworks in Everett last year, sitting down by the water with Randy and a stolen fifth of gin. That all seemed very far away now.

Don kissed the palm of his hand, held his lips there. Jackson watched the smoke fall, drifting down like streamers from a party. It was beautiful, he thought. All of it was beautiful because here they were, together. That old trick – love makes the world new. Trite conceits, sugary lies – and still. Always he had thought of his life as if it was waiting somewhere else, a party that he might finally arrive at, late, breathless, taking off his coat. It nagged at him, that maybe no one was waiting anywhere at all. But now – Don pushed Jackson's hand up under his shirt and held it there, against the broad plane of Don's chest. Down the hill Jackson could see shadowy figures and sparklers dripping bright, brief rain.

When the last stray fireworks had faded to smoke hanging over the valley they made their way back to the truck, walking gingerly in the dark. Don drove them back to the motel.

JACKSON WAS ASLEEP, deep asleep, and when he woke up it took him a long time to remember where he was. The springs of the bed creaking, the dark like a heavy fabric over him. The cheap, slick feeling of the motel blanket. Don was moving around in the room. Jackson reached for the light.

Don was dressed, pulling on his coat. "What are you doing?"

Jackson asked. The coarse sheets and the smell of cigarettes were all around him.

Don walked over to him, switched the light back off. "You're tired," he said. "Listen, you just get some sleep, okay? I'll be back." He was out the door before Jackson realized exactly what had happened, or maybe he was too surprised to say anything.

He lay in the dark, not sleeping, a sick feeling coming over him about what he suspected Don was doing, and how, in the moment when Don walked out the door, Jackson had let him go. Like a dirty little callboy, he thought. Like a nobody, and now Don was probably unlocking the door to his house, probably fucking his wife – what other explanation was there? And Jackson had let him go without saying a word. It felt familiar. All of his life, he thought, he'd wanted the people around him to feel good. He'd not wanted to start a fight. And where had that gotten him, the not speaking? The not fighting? He thought of his father: Still-drunk mornings, when he would roar around the house. Sheets sweated through. Lydia on his shoulders, shrieking and giggling, happiness and fear.

The first time he'd seen his father beat his mother, his father had come home late. Carpenters were being laid off. They were coming for him, he said. In two weeks his job would end, and who knew how long it would take until he found a new project? He had a drink in his hand by the time he'd crossed the kitchen from the back door, and by eight he was reading the same page of the newspaper again and again, talking to himself. He said something to Jackson's mother that Jackson didn't hear, and she was crying, covering her face with both hands. A murky little memory, just his father trying to lift her up from her chair, but she would not stand. "This is my home!" he cried suddenly. "You are my wife! This is my son!" He looked at Jackson while he shook her. "Stand up!" he cried. "You are my wife! This is my chair!"

Because he was seven, because he knew the power of possessions, it did not occur to him to wonder what it all meant. He was scared, only, and he understood that his father's ownership over them, over even grief itself, was absolute.

His mother did not stand. He lifted his hand and struck her across the face. Her lip split and she stopped crying but she did not say a word. She would not look at him. In the back of the house, Lydia started to cry.

His father put down his hands. He pressed his face to Amy's breastbone for a long time, and then he stood and led Jackson to the truck and together they went out to town. And so, Jackson thought, he had been complicit all of his life. He couldn't explain why, but he had the same feeling now.

He drifted through a light and restless sleep, sick to his stomach, the clock blinking through two o'clock, three o'clock, four. He was half-angry, and half-hating himself. His heart darted around in his chest. When he finally heard steps outside the door, the fumble of the key card in the door, he kept his eyes closed and his face turned into the pillow. Jackson heard Don come into the room, but he didn't say anything. It was four thirty? Five? The light was just this side of dark. "Jack?" Don whispered.

Jackson didn't want to talk, or ask, or know anything. He heard a bottle smash out in the parking lot. What had he told his wife to get away so soon, at such a dead hour? A supply run? Had he told her nothing, just slipped back out again?

Jackson thought of the Garth Brooks song, the famous one, where the woman is pacing in her flannel gown, waiting for her cheating husband to come home. He'd put Eliza in the gown since he'd first learned of her, and now it was him, had maybe been him all along.

Don sat lightly on the edge of the bed and was touching his back, lay down beside him and Jackson could feel Don's cock hard against the backs of his bare thighs. He let Don kiss his neck, his back. He didn't turn around.

Finally, he rolled over, suddenly and onto his knees. He pulled Don over onto his stomach and undid his jeans, pulled them down, sucked his own fingers and pushed them slowly into

Don's ass. Don groaned and pushed back against him and Jackson pulled his hand back, pushed his own hard cock in. Was he angry? He didn't know. He was hard, his whole body ached; he wanted Don, but he didn't know why or how, wanted him like this, down on his knees. Don was touching himself, groaning. The window blinds let in only small gray swatches of daylight, and Jackson pushed himself in and out slowly, holding Don's hips. He wanted to cry and at the same time he just let it wash over him, the sweetness of being wanted, that warm, wanting body beneath him. Don groaned again and shot off against that terrible plastic comforter, and then Jackson was coming, deep inside Don, and the whole room was still – a place, Jackson thought, built for stillness, for secrets, a place alone, for those parts of your life that could just as easily be beautiful or shamed.

Amy
Tulalip, Washington, 2009

SOMETIMES SHE WOULD DO SOMETHING ON PURPOSE TO make him angry. She could stand whatever Gary did more easily than the anticipation of it, the way the air hummed tight as a wire. When he had done it – broken the window, or pushed her down in the dirt, or kicked her until her ribs felt splintered – there were weeks or even months of respite, of his remorse. She could imagine they were any family. Always, though, the rooms grew close again. They began to walk more softly.

She put Jackson and Lydia on the bus for camp at the end of May. It was a weeklong program for the middle school and high school, an approximated summer camp during the school year. Leadership games, night hikes, teachers patrolling the cabins, keeping the high school students in their own bunks. In the school parking lot that morning, she watched Lydia climb the bus steps with both arms around her sleeping bag. Lydia turned and looked back at her and Amy waved, smiling as wide as she could. One of the other mothers stood beside Amy, waving at a face in one of the bus windows. "I just worry," she said to Amy. "I'm just a mom, I worry. What if they get homesick? What if something happens?" She rubbed her folded arms against the chill; it was a gray morning, ruthlessly cold.

Amy wondered what it might be like to be that woman. To sink into a week of occasional worry for her children and relief at the time alone. Amy did feel relief but for a different reason. Things had been building for weeks and now that the kids were gone, she knew. The wave would break over her at any moment, but then it would be over. Jackson and Lydia would come home and it would be over, for a while. She smiled pleasantly and nodded at the woman, watching the bus pull slow as a barge out of the school parking lot. *Take me with you,* she'd wanted to say. At the same time she wanted to run after the bus, knock on the windows, remind them: *Be children. For five days and four nights, be children.*

Jackson was hardly a child. He was seventeen; beautiful, moody, defensive. He was still easy with her, kind and caring, always looking out. In the moments when he did lash out at her, it was worse than any physical pain Gary could have inflicted. Lydia was twelve, and Amy worried about her. She was quiet, vastly internal, smarter than she let on. Amy worried that Gary might turn on her. With Jackson, it was different; the things that put him in danger in the outside world kept him safe at home. He'd come home one day with a broken cheekbone that he wouldn't explain, but it was as clear to her as if she'd been there – someone wanted to teach him a lesson, for being the way that he was. For the same reason, Gary wouldn't touch him, talk to him. Jackson existed in a cold and separate circle from her husband, and for that she was grateful.

That night, browning hamburger over the stove, she asked Gary how work had been.

"Fucking Lou is talking about layoffs again," Gary said that night, pouring four fingers of whiskey into a glass. Without the kids, he would be hiding his drinking even less than usual.

"Layoffs," she said slowly. "What does that mean?" She knew what it meant, and what it meant on top of the lost job, the tight money – long weeks of Gary at home, pacing the house, watching her.

"What the hell do you think it means?" He wrenched open the refrigerator and took out a can of beer. "No fucking work."

"There'll be something else."

Gary didn't say anything. He pulled the tab off of his beer and flicked it hard against the wall. It clicked on the linoleum.

She breathed slow and deep. *Get it over with,* she told herself.

Just let it be done. She took another breath, and said quietly, "Why can't you even take care of your family?"

If there was a moment between her words and his response, she didn't hear it. The pain was red, with blue edges behind her closed eyes. She let it roll over her. She pictured herself running, far out of reach – branches and wet leaves slapping her face, plummeting between trees, rock, the dark of the sky against the darker leaves. The explosions of silver sparks seemed to come from somewhere deep inside of her.

It was the clavicle, the doctor said. He'd wrapped her tightly in a sling while the nurse looked on. She was waiting for her prescription when the nurse slid the linen curtain back open. She was young and blonde with a square jaw and a nervous look. They'd given Amy a shot of something and there were shivering halos around the lights, around the nurse's yellow head.

"Listen," the nurse said. Her voice was unsteady. "If someone did this to you – you, you should call the police."

She knew it was the drugs that made it seem funny, but she wanted to laugh. The police? They were so far from town. The time between dialing the number and the police showing up on the gravel road – what could happen in that much time? But more than that, she understood – she had always understood – that if anyone else was involved, if she said anything, then all deals were off. Gary had never touched the children, but she knew, without him ever saying, that they were a card up his sleeve; if she gave him reason enough, she was certain that he was capable of hurting them to destroy her.

"Has it been happening for a long time?" the nurse asked, high and pleading. How could Amy even answer that question? It had happened so slowly at first that it had taken her a while to notice. Why would they need friends, especially out here, where everyone was gun toting and paranoid? Her parents would only be sad that they couldn't afford to visit; why call them? Even the play dates – those other children were only setting bad examples. The walls shifted closer.

Other small things – the pig Gary had brought home that hoofed desperate ruts in the pasture and tried to break the fence; the steer that whiled away its miserable hours licking a cube of salt. The work kept her away from town, and with a freezer full of meat there was no need to go, anyway. "Plant a garden," he said. "We have all this land." It seemed idyllic from the outside – back to the land, back to nature. Instead, her ties to the outside world grew more and more tenuous. Amy imagined that woman from the school parking lot. "I dream of a garden," that woman would sigh. How could Amy explain that each of these things moved her a step farther from town, from the everyday reasons to leave their land?

"If– " The nurse was blinking fast, running her thumb back and forth over the prescription. "You can take him to court for this," she said. "Send him to jail. You don't have to live like this. You don't deserve it."

The halos of light were waxing and waning and Amy concentrated on them until the nurse's voice seemed to shrink. She made it sound so simple. Amy watched a medical chart on the opposite wall, a figure latticed with pink muscles. An empty urine specimen cup on the clean white counter. Stainless steel tools on a stainless steel tray.

"Listen," the nurse said. "I'm just going to say this. I can't help it." Her mouth was shaking around her words, her thumb rubbing the paper faster. "There was a woman, last spring. Maybe you heard about it." She took a breath. "Her boyfriend shot her kids. In front of her. He made her watch." She looked at Amy and Amy looked away. "Take him to court," the woman said. She put one hand on Amy's cold arm. "Please."

Her skin prickled. This woman didn't know her, and didn't know her husband. She took the prescription and eased herself off the table. She didn't look at the nurse. She concentrated on the glow of the green arrows pulling her toward the waiting room.

THAT NIGHT, AFTER Gary was asleep, she went to the kitchen and poured some of his whiskey into a glass. She sat in the dim light of the kitchen stove, looking out the dark window, listening to the steady thump of rain. *Right in front of her.* She drank quickly, letting the liquor erode the edges of the pain. *He made her watch.* She imagined the other women out there, in their own dark houses, living the way that she was.

She knew it as clearly as she knew her children's faces: if she called the police, if she took him to court, if she fought him, that is when he would do something irreversible, something to hurt her more than any physical pain ever could. That is when she had to be truly afraid. This way the pain was dull but it was over, she thought. He wouldn't touch her again for a while.

She watched her own face waver in the slick black glass, the beads of water running down it, dividing her reflection. "The Devil is beating his wife," her mother would always say, holding her palms up to catch the rain. All of those wives, the constellation of lights from their midnight windows. All of them making their own bargains with God, all of them wide awake.

Lydia

Tulalip, Washington, 2009

THE SCHOOL SENT JACKSON AND ME TO CAMP FOR A week. He was with the high school, but I was with the sixth grade, on the other side of the field, under a stand of trees. "You need anything," he said, "I'll be in cabin two, okay? Just ask someone to come find me."

I nodded. Marta liked me that week. She was standing beside me and she looked at Jackson and put her hands on her hips. "Cabin two?" she asked, smiling her school picture smile. I elbowed her.

Jackson smiled. "Don't get into any trouble," he said. "At least not too much." I watched him walk back to join the rest of his group.

That night Marta and I stood at the steel sink in the corner of the cook shelter, brushing our teeth. I balanced the butt of a flashlight next to the soap dish. The water tasted like rust and smelled like tinfoil. The beams up above us were lacy with spider webs.

In the cabin, Marta showed me a picture of her boyfriend, who went to the high school and played the guitar for her youth group. The rubber mattress made our legs sweat even in the cold. The boy in the picture was tall, wearing a Yankees cap over hair gone dark with grease. "He's going to be a mechanic," she said. "He already rebuilt a car. A Cadillac. He got it from his grandfather."

"Oh," I said.

"Your brother's cute," she said. I didn't say anything. I didn't want to think about Marta liking my brother.

"Have you ever been kissed?" Marta asked.

I thought about walking away but that would be worse; then Marta would know that I hadn't. Finally I said, "Oh, sure."

"Who was it?"

I wanted to cry. "Oh, just some guy," I said. "It was no big deal. A couple guys, actually."

The flashlight lit Marta's face from underneath. The shadow of one eyebrow was raised. "Must not have been very good then," she said. She went to her bed and spread her sleeping bag out. "I'll probably have dreams about him tonight," she said. "Your brother, that is."

In the cabin that night I couldn't stand it. Rain on the roof; Marta's face in the cook shelter. I imagined Marta with the boy in the baseball cap, her hand in his, his thumb rubbing a circle into her wrist. There was an ache in my chest that felt rock hard, like it might never go away. I thought of the boyfriend leaning over the hood of the Cadillac. Of Marta, pulling the burnt skin from a marshmallow, holding the raw center back in the flames until it was just a coal-black lump. From outside, I could hear a dog barking, far off. I thought of home and in that second I knew: *if I don't get home right now, something will happen.* It was a weight on me, holding me down, and I pushed against it and put on my shoes. I have to go home, I thought. I have to get Jackson, and we need to go home. Something is wrong.

I left the cabin in the dark and no one saw me go. I had my flashlight and I followed its yellow path toward the high school cabins pushing through the sword fern and salal and into the field. The flagpole was a long silvery arrow pointing to the sky. "I'll be right here waiting," my mother had said, and when I turned and she smiled at me it was like a stone sunk inside me. Something bad was coming.

My light from my flashlight touched the top of the cabins and they were colorless, all the same. Which one was cabin two? I wanted to cry. Where was he? That morning, eating our eggs in the little dining hall, he'd said, "Have fun with your friends, Lydia.

Don't worry about home. Don't worry about anything." I stopped at the fire circle. It was piled with charred logs and there were empty cans in the ash. I sat on one of the benches beside it and looked down at the flashlight. I couldn't go back to my cabin. I couldn't go anywhere.

I heard the branches cracking; there was a tunnel of light, a weak yellow beam. I shut off the flashlight. Don't look at me, I thought, but already someone was moving toward me from out of the woods.

"Who's there–?" I knew that voice, I thought, and there was Randy, with his flashlight lighting up his face. I wanted to run to him but I stayed on the bench.

"Randy," I whispered.

"Lydia? What are you doing out here?"

"What are *you* doing out there?" I asked.

"Just checking out some stuff," he said, shrugging.

"Ghosts?" I asked. Randy looked like a ghost himself, in his long black coat, his face floating, big and wide as a balloon. He smiled and I didn't mean to but I started to cry.

"Hey!" Randy said. "Lydia–hey, it's okay. There's no sign of ghosts out here, I promise. I would know if there was."

"It's not that," I said. "I need to go home. I can't stay here, Randy."

"Hey," he said again. "Come here." He sat on the bench beside me and put his arm around me. I put my head against his coat. I imagined it was a curtain I could crawl behind and stay.

"Please," I said. "I want to go home."

"Do you know what I do?" he asked. "When my dad is drunk and I'm afraid I won't be able to wake him up?"

I looked up at him. I had never thought of Randy's dad before, of where he lived, and why he lived in the basement alone.

"I think of what my own house is going to look like one day. What I would put in each room."

"Like what?"

"Like in one corner there's going to be a chair. A recliner. It'll be by the window, and my radio will be next to it."

"How come?"

"I like it. I want to sit there and watch TV and listen to the radio. Now you do one. What do you want?"

I thought of the things I wanted, but none of them seemed important. "A dog," I said finally. It would sleep on my bed, which would be so soft. It would bark if anyone came near.

"You're funny," he said. "You'll grow up and you can have anything. A dog or a mansion or anything."

I felt bad for Randy. He was thinking about a chair and a radio. At least I had Jackson, and my mother. "Randy," I said, "you'll get those things." He put his arm around me and we kept sitting there in the dark. I made a determination right there to see the week through.

On Friday afternoon, Jackson and I stood in the school parking lot waiting for my mother to pick us up. There was a rash on my legs and bracelets of nettle sting on my ankles. My father's truck pulled up and my stomach hurt. I knew something was wrong. I tried not to think of it. My father didn't ask how the camp was, and I didn't ask where my mother was, but the question beat hard inside me. Jackson's hand was on the back of my neck so tight and I tried to concentrate on it, to think *She's okay. She is waiting at home for us. Smiling.*

It was only May, but it felt like we were driving away from summer. I thought of the lake where I could see the reeds moved slowly underwater, and the grace rolling down from the mess hall. *Back of the bread is the flour, back of the flour is the mill.* I would not look at my father. *Back of the mill is the wind and the rain and the Father's will.* He stopped the truck in the driveway. I thought of the creek down there, how dark it was, and moving fast. For a minute there was no sound, just the press of the house against the slope, and whatever was waiting inside.

Jackson

Silver, Idaho, 2010

THE WEEKS AFTER MONTANA. THE OVER-THE-WATERFALL rush of bright dry July into brown scorched August. He'd never done this before. Nothing he ever felt for someone else had ever picked up weight and speed like this. The infatuation with Chris had been dead in the water, no pun intended. Eric–that was a business agreement, and anything Jackson felt he set carefully aside, filed away as a blunder, a consequence of intimacy. Now the days were hot and vivid, streaming like movie clips. Something was scaring him. One half elation, one half desperation. The scenes upon scenes:

Late July. Don at the job site, dusted up like a chimney sweep. A pocketful of nails, a tool belt, Don's throbbing cock–even though Jackson couldn't see it through Don's coveralls, he knew it in his mind, in his mouth. There were more and more nights in A-frame B, nights when Don pulled from a handle of vodka, hungrily, slurping. On those nights, they drank until the night was a soapy lens to squint through, and when Don fell asleep, a desperate ache would begin in Jackson's chest and throat. Don would sleep with his mouth open, the snoring drunk. Wake up, Jackson would think again and again. Wake up.

A night in early August. It was late, more morning than night, and in the eerie purple dawn Jackson began to talk about Lydia. He did not tell Don that what happened was his fault. He told him that they left him, Lydia and his mother, and that his father didn't want him. His mother was wearing an old coat, he told Don, and Lydia was carrying her little green change purse when she ran away from him at the mall. When he went back to the house, he found that his mother had left him twenty dollars and no note. Don was sympathetic, sweet. Don kissed his eyes and said the right things, which were wrong. Jackson thought about the moon-shaped scar on Lydia's left temple, left there during a night they spent on Firetrail Hill. Twenty dollars, an old coat, a green purse. He wanted a drink. He wanted summer to be over.

Another morning and he was ill again, nauseous and impatient and angry. Whose darkness was it that was dogging him? He had the feeling that he was in his own shadow, that it moved across him.

And then it was August twenty-second, his birthday, though he didn't tell Don or anyone. He was nineteen. He should have just graduated high school, in some other life. The collage of possibilities that seemed equally impossible: carrying boxes up to some jailhouse college dorm, or moving into an apartment with a scrapped-together group of friends from high school, or setting out to some new city. Or, he was here, the lake a cool silver coin, and Don was somewhere just out of his reach.

The night before, he had dreamt of Lydia, and in the dream she was crying, calling his name. He woke up sweating and furious at himself. How he wasn't there for her. He met Don that afternoon, down on the old riverbed where no one went. Walking through town, he still felt angry, a bitter stinging anger toward all of it, the kids in town running their bikes up and down the mounds of dirt outside the job sites, his birthday, and what kind of life did he have? He was fucking a married man, and somewhere his baby sister was calling for him.

The old riverbed was a dirty swampland with no clear edges. Mosquitoes were everywhere. Jackson had a hard time imagining that it would ever grow over and become the promised forest, the boreal sketch on the new construction plans. Just about the time the riverbed dried up in the August and September heat, the snow would settle and everything would be condemned again.

"I need a cigarette," Jackson said. "Where'd you put them?" He felt quietly furious. He hated it all.

Don handed him a cigarette. He pulled out the pint of Rich & Rare and opened it, took a loud smacking drink. He elbowed Jackson and handed him the plastic bottle. Jackson could feel his aggressive cheer in the face of what was Jackson's obvious irritation. "C'mon, Jack," Don said. "Let's get drunk."

"Everything's dead," Jackson said. "And the new things will never grow right."

"What is up with you?" Don asked. "You pissed off about something?"

Jackson didn't say anything.

"Jackson," Don said. "I just need a little more time."

"Please," Jackson said. He looked out at the pitted trench. "Can we talk about something else, please?" He didn't want to think about the pathetic little hope he had that Don had left Eliza back in Missoula. That he had left in the middle of the night to break her heart and then come back and fucked Jackson out of victory and courage and a good righteous hard-on. There was a rusted out old car sunk in the mud, and he concentrated on looking at it until he noticed something caught in the wheel well. Jackson looked at it hard and made out a dark mat of fur. He felt a wave of nausea. Everything was ragged and matted and dead.

He thought again about that long-ago memory, his mother in the dress, the revolver in her hand. It had been a game – at least that's how he thought of it now, a construction all for him. They were going to shoot a bobcat. Jackson had imagined it in the dark shades beneath trees, the upside-down skirts of roots from where the pasture had been cleared and then gone again to seed. She'd packed them sandwiches, and they'd walked through the woods for what felt like hours. There were slips of movement everywhere. The blinking underside of a leaf was the bobcat's steely eye; a moth was the terrible white claw. He'd believed in the bobcat as completely as he believed in the furniture of that forest – the snaking brambles, fireweed seeded out in purple. They sat to eat their sandwiches, quiet with their chewing, and Jackson threw the crusts of his bread into the dirt and backed away, hoping the bobcat would smell them.

Time had passed, and he was hungry again; the shine seemed to wear off the day as the bobcat was nowhere. He whined for the house and dinner and his father. And then, just as he'd said, "There's no bobcat. We'll never find it," his mother had stopped. She showed him the gun, and made him sit away from her. She lifted the revolver with both hands, pointed it at a tree – had she ever really shot a gun in her life? – and fired it. And a bird had dropped to the ground. He understood now that she'd killed the bird, but in his memory it fluttered up again, and flew. She had knocked it out of the sky and lifted it back up as though her hands were making and remaking the world it in front of him.

He couldn't explain it to Don, though he wanted to. He knew that anything he said wouldn't make the sense he wanted it to and that depressed him. He picked up the whiskey bottle and held it to his mouth.

SITTING THERE IN the late afternoon light getting drunk again, an idea was nagging at Jackson that he was his mother. Not his mother when she had lifted the gun like a Wild West queen or a high forest priestess, but his mother at her weakest, most tractable, and easily convinced: "Never again," he had heard his father sob raggedly in the aftermath of nearly every beating he'd ever given his mother. "You're everything to me." And Jackson understood that his mother had wanted to believe him – had needed to believe him. Because how else to live with yourself, to allow the person you want most in the world not to deceive you to do it, again and again? His skin was twitchy and sparking with the heat, the corona of drunkenness fuzzing the edges of his sight.

"Let's go back," Jackson said. He didn't want to try to talk, didn't want to hear Don get cheerfully drunk. "I'm tired."

Don obliged, tossing the bottle into his truck and fiddling with the radio on the way back around the lake. Jackson stared out the open window all the way back to the semi cab. Don pulled in and turned to him. "Jack," he said. "we're not going to do this forever. I'm going to leave her."

Jackson looked at Don. He was half-smiling, the dark hair in his eyes again. His arm was draped over the back of the seat. He looked loose and easy and oblivious. The anger chewed at Jackson's stomach again. "It's fine," he said. "You'll leave her, and we'll be happy." He climbed out of the truck and shut the door behind him. He didn't look back until he was inside his little semi cab with the summer air tight around him.

HE LAY IN the semi cab until seven or eight, until he couldn't stand to think of any of it anymore, his mother or Don or Lydia, and then he walked to town with loose arms and legs, stumbling a little. The café in town was full; between the soda signs and taped-up notices on the windows he could see the crowded backs of families, the movement of the waitresses like bees over the flowers of the tables. The Longhorn parking lot was full with the drinkers who hadn't gone home to dinner yet and the ones who had come early for the night rush. The air of the bar hit him, a hot breath of liquor and cigarette smoke. He didn't go to bars often, mostly because of his age but also because the people who tended to hang out at bars seemed to be able to see it on him, his queerness. In a little bar in Everett, his junior year, he'd managed to get a drink, but in the first half an hour someone had called him a faggot and he'd had to leave out the back. Here, no one gave him a second glance.

He looked different these days. He looked like part of the work crew, and he had some muscles for the first time since the season he spent running cross-country, which he'd done mostly to get out of the house and because then he was still doing anything he could to fill his days, to pack whatever he could around the dull, creeping sense that there was something about him that was different. He remembered an unreasonable fear of the clammy, tiled locker room. He sometimes thought of the years in Tulalip, in his parents' house, as a series of grisly snapshots: Jackson at sixteen, deeply shy, caught with a porn magazine. His father throwing a glass that shattered beside his mother's head. A senior at the high school fractured Jackson's cheekbone in the empty locker room because Jackson was rumored to have been watching him change. His father drank too much and threw his mother down in the drive outside the house; the gravel made a pattern on her cheek. During those months, Jackson shoved enough coke up his nose to start sneezing a buckshot pattern of blood into his own hands. He chewed his lips until they bled, and started missing school. He remembered his father pulling him aside at home and saying, "You can't buck city hall, son. Don't try to buck city hall."

The Longhorn bartender brought over a beer before he asked, bought for him by someone he recognized vaguely from the work crew. He picked it up and tilted it briefly toward the man at the bar. A birthday drink, he thought to himself. There were still three or four hours of his birthday left, and he pretended for a minute that the man had bought him the beer for that occasion.

He drank and started to feel better, evening back out to his early drunk. He needed to remember to get groceries soon. He had money now, yet he was still living like he was homeless. He thought of Ida, the social worker – Mike Leary's kind, plain daughter. "Get food stamps," she'd told him, back when he was living on the street. "No matter where you are, if you have no money, apply for food stamps. You don't have to tell anyone anything. You don't have to owe anyone." A quick rush of gratitude – his life might be fucked up still, but it was fucked up in a less obvious way. He finished that beer and ordered another.

He felt boozy and warm in the dim light. The table was a round of wood on top of a barrel. The surface was pocked and scarred: *Hott Girlz; Bills a pussy; I Luv Rick 4Ever 4Realz.* He was feeling a kinship to everything around him, to this little town where he'd landed. The drying lakebed to the west, studded with lost things. The new lake to the east, clean and full of promise. The bar, with its fans humming, its sweet-faced waitress. He fished around in the pockets of his winter coat with the halfway hope of digging up an old baggie that he could scrape a line out of. He knew the pockets were empty but he checked anyway. Nothing. The lining had worn through and his hand slipped into the batting. He ordered another beer.

The Longhorn was a half a mile from Don's trailer, and when he paid up at the bar he started walking there. It was ten, and he'd had three beers; he felt better. He liked the idea of watching Don from a distance, of seeing him for the first time. The way you might enter a party and see the person you love lit up from across the room, completely absorbed in everyone but you. He had the feeling that if he could see Don, just watch him for a while without being noticed, that he might answer a question. He might know what was going to happen between them. And he felt sorry for the way he'd been earlier. For not trusting Don, for pushing at him like a teenager. Like a child. Part of him wanted to see Don to apologize, to make it right.

The worker's trailer camp. Chili pepper lights, beer cans, dirty floor mats reading *Go Away, Just Wipe It, Oh Shit Not You Again*. He'd never been inside Don's trailer, but he'd walked past it enough. Someone had used silver reflective tape to spell out "Newlon" on the siding beside the door. It was nicer than most of the trailers, bigger, and Don's truck was parked in behind it. The back windows – the bedroom, he thought – were dark when he walked up, but he could see a glow around the side and he hung back in the underbrush, making sure that he wasn't in the light.

He walked quietly around to the front of the house, where the kitchen and living room lights, in a neat row of windows, were blazing. He hung around the shadows, just beyond where the squares of light were falling on the grass. He could see into the kitchen. It was bright and empty, the counters bare except for an open wine bottle. Jackson liked that about Don, the wine thing. One of those faggy details that reminded him of how different their lives were and inexplicably turned him on. Food in the fridge. Landscaping. The carefully wound garden hose, the ball games on the weekends, chain restaurants. The strange asexuality of all of it–but it drove an ache down deep in Jackson's stomach to imagine Don in the forest glen of cul-de-sac he'd grown up in, a suburban wood nymph, thirteen and his cock pressing up against the slick and expensive sheets.

The living room window was a shade dimmer than the kitchen; he could see the outline of a table lamp, hear the faint sound of music. He stood just outside of the line of light. There was a stand of weeds and he tripped for a minute, then caught his balance and moved closer.

Don was on the couch, a glass in front of him. He was watching television, blue ghost shapes flickering across his face. God, Jackson thought, he was handsome. Just sitting there, and he was still the most beautiful man Jackson had ever seen. He watched Don for a long minute or two, leaning back, lifting the glass to his mouth, rubbing his forehead. Jackson must have moved. He must have turned his head or fumbled in the grass, because Don looked up and caught his eye.

Don stood up quickly and went to the door. For a minute, Jackson imagined that he would come inside. They would sit together. They would go to bed. Don craned his head toward Jackson. "What are you doing here?" he hissed. His voice was cold and sharp, and he put his foot in the doorframe, as if Jackson might try to push his way inside.

Jackson felt too drunk, suddenly. "I–" He looked at Don, pleading with him. "I just thought–"

"This isn't a good idea," Don said. "What if someone saw you? Are you drunk?"

Jackson felt like he'd been slapped, that same old feelings of anger and sorrow fighting each other for which would rise to the surface. "Jack," Don whispered, "you have to be more careful."

"Forget it," Jackson said. He wished he could take it all back. The bar, the walk, the bushes. His stupid stumbling feet. "Sorry." He turned and left, his whole body blazing with humiliation. It was still his birthday. He was nineteen. The moon pale and graceful above him in a way that made him want to punch it, to black it out.

HE WENT DOWN on Tuesday morning to burn the pits. A-frame A. There was construction material blowing all over the place – enough to build a whole house, he thought. The house up in Tulalip – his parents' mobile home – had it even had a quarter of all of this shit? And now he was supposed to burn it.

He was still standing there looking at the city of trash that ringed that new house when he heard the sound of Don's truck. There was something wrong with the U-joint – that was what Don had said – and when it stopped and started there was a shudder, a heave of metal. He felt it in his balls first. Was that what love was? He turned around and there Don was, his dark hair darker with sweat, hanging half out the window. "Fire ban," Don called. "You can't burn today."

"What do you mean?" Jackson called back. He'd imagined his whole day ahead of him, the hot breath of the fire surging in front of him.

"Go sweep sawdust or something. They probably need a handyman on the East side. You have to wait till it's cool and then you'll need a permit." Don looked him up and down. *Fuck*, Jackson thought. He felt like a brute and a little bitch at the same time.

"The ban's on," Don said again, grinning at him. Jackson's erection was almost painful against his jeans, and he could see Don looking at his crotch. Fuck you, he thought.

In that moment, Don had everything and he had nothing and Jackson hated it and it turned him on. The truck made that shuddering noise and lurched into gear, and Don was gone, with just his hand – that tight, smooth hand – trailing out the window, leaving him there.

Lydia

Fannin, Texas, 2010

THE HALLS AT THE FANNIN JUNIOR HIGH SCHOOL WERE long and beige, and the things we'd rehearsed I said easily, but they meant nothing. I was nothing. I kept thinking I saw my father slipping behind the library shelves, kicking a ball across a field. I wanted to be erased. A chalkboard smudge. I pulled my coat tighter.

In the gym we sat on the cold floor and waited to be chosen for sides. When the girls came to sit beside me and ask me questions, I told them: I am Lena Harris. I am in the seventh grade. "You talk like a Yankee," one of the girls said.

"Well, I'm not," I said. Their faces were blank and blinking. I hated them all.

"You look like a Yankee."

"What does that mean?" I asked. The eyes were a row of window shades, drawing closed, open, closed. The teacher called a name and when one ran off the rest scattered like a pack of dogs.

The classes were the same: a page of spidery numbers, of snaking words. I pretended I didn't understand. I could see what the Fannin teachers thought, and it didn't matter how I acted. They knew enough of our story to know that we weren't who we said we were. "You're going to be safe," my mother said. "I promise that I will keep you safe, and so will all your teachers." When I turned in my math test with rows of numbers that I'd invented, no one said a word.

In the cafeteria I heard them, from two tables away. "Fag," one of the boys said to another.

In a second, I was above him.

"Shut the fuck up," I said.

They looked at me. The milk cartons and trays shrank to points. One of them started to laugh. "Oooh," he said. "Who's this?"

I didn't wait for what they would say next. I smashed my fist into his sandwich. "You go to hell," I said. I didn't wait to see what he would say. I went out to the front steps of the school. The opposite of life isn't death, I thought. It was this. The sun was orange, burning through the sky, and I looked at it until I could see the burning of it on the back of my eyelids, the same color as I was inside.

The assistant principal caught me by the arm and spun me back inside. She steered me into the armchair in her office and gave me a square note with a line on the bottom for my mother to sign. I didn't care. Lena Harris was braver than Lydia Holland.

My mother was asleep, and I didn't want to tell her what I'd done. My grandmother was in the kitchen, pulling out the jars of flour and sweeping behind them with a rag. A cockroach shot past and was gone. "Shit," she was saying. "Shit shit shit."

"Grandmother," I said, and she turned. The note felt heavier than the paper it was on.

She laughed. "Stop that, please," she said. "Call me Grandma. Or Linda. Don't make me sound ancient."

"Here," I said. "Would you sign it?" I put the note on the counter.

I picked up a pencil from the table and poked the point into the palm of my hand. She put down the rag and unfolded the note. I held the pencil tighter.

"Why don't you tell me," she said, looking at me, "why you got in a fight?"

I shrugged. I concentrated on the point of the pencil, needle sharp. It left a gray mark deep in my palm.

"Why did you get in a fight?"

I felt angry all of a sudden. *Because I hate that school, and the people in it. Because I hate this place.* "Maybe I got it from my dad,"

I said, and I knew as I said it that I believed it. "You're your father's girl," he liked to say, dragging his palm across my hair. I remember it felt like a curse.

My grandmother's eyes snapped up at me. I dropped the pencil on the floor and started to walk away. I felt her move behind me and she reached out one hand and pulled me back. She held my shoulders. I looked past her at the wall. There was a picture of my mother, in a yellow dress, when she was eight or nine, and I wished she'd never left this town. I would have been born as someone else, maybe a boy, or maybe a girl who was more beautiful, who never smashed a sandwich in her life.

"Listen to me," she said. "You didn't get anything from him."

"It was after I was born," I said. "It started then." I'd never said it out loud before. If I hadn't been born, it would have been different. Whatever changed in my father would not have changed, and now I wouldn't have to know that his anger could be inside me, ticking like a bomb.

"No," she said. "It started in your father a long time before that. It was him, not you."

"Still," I said.

"Not still," she said. "It was him."

"Once," I told her, "I tried to kill him." The glint of glass lit the worst of my dreams, cutting through the dark, a bright and warning knife. How I couldn't do it. How I was too afraid.

She looked at me for a long time. "You need a little place," she said.

"What kind of place?"

"A place of your own," she said. "Follow me."

She led me out of the house, down the gravel road, out toward the river. Against the bank was a little shelter, a lean-to of wood, bleached from the sun. It looked like bones, like a house of ribs. I thought of the fires Jackson and I used to make in our little forts. We tended them so carefully, but in the wet forest they would never take for long.

I looked at her. She didn't look like my mother. I wondered if she looked like me. "Did you build it?" I asked.

"Oh, no," she said. "But someone did. Some kids, maybe. I can't remember a time when it wasn't here." She brushed her hair out of her eyes. "If you want it," she said, "it's here."

I climbed inside and she followed me, squatting on her heels like a bird on a nest. It was dark and cool inside. I picked up a stone and it felt good in my hand, round as an egg and heavy on my palm.

"You know, I thought about you every single day since you were born," my grandmother said. "I waited and waited to meet you. I wondered who you would be."

I felt a tightness in my chest like I might cry, but I wouldn't. If that was true, I thought, she would have come for us. She would have helped us. She would have come. I didn't say anything, just squeezed the egg stone tight in my hand.

"I *did*," she said. "I hope you'll believe that one day." She pointed across the river, where a tree dipped its branches low over the water. "I saw a cottonmouth right there once," she said. "It's why I don't swim. I hate snakes."

"Will you sign my note?" I asked. I watched the place where the snake had been and the hard shine of the water.

"If you don't fight anymore," she said. "Let's not tell your mother about the note this time. And I'm still going to call you Lydia," she said. "When it's just you and me. Is that okay?"

I nodded, but I didn't smile. I knew what she was trying to do. You should have come for us, I thought again.

"Your grandfather," she said. "He loved this river. He used to swim for hours." She sighed. "We would come here, when we were young. When we were first together. I'd sit here and watch him and be dumb and in love." She smiled.

I thought of him in the water, splashing, young as my brother.

"You know," she said, "your family doesn't begin or end with your father."

We sat in the slatted shadows for a while. I didn't ask her

any questions. I watched the spot where my grandfather had been, diving and surfacing like a fish, the water beading off of him, not knowing that one day I would be here, and I would think of him.

Jackson
Tulalip, Washington, 2009

HE REMEMBERED BEING SMALL AND HOW FIRETRAIL HILL had seemed impossibly long and treacherously steep, pulling cars like ants slowly skyward until they disappeared into the treetops. Now, standing in the ditch in the dusky light, it felt just as dangerous. Froth of wings in his stomach, vertigo. "Okay," Randy was saying. "This is base."

Jackson kept hold of Lydia's hand even though she was getting too old for that. She had wanted to come, and Randy insisted. "She's got a good sense," he said. "I can tell. She knows things."

They'd gone to Randy's after school and he'd borrowed his dad's car to drive them up here. Afterward, he'd take them home, but Jackson still felt a buzz of alarm when the cars drove by. It wasn't terrible, what they were doing, but he didn't want to explain to either of his parents why they were waiting in the underbrush for the sun to go down.

"If we want the Society to take us seriously, we have to make sure our methods are sound," Randy said. He spread out a tarp in the ditch and it rose up in peaks over the tall grass. He stepped on it to flatten it.

"What's that for?" Jackson asked.

"I'm making a base camp," Randy said. "For the equipment." Jackson tried not to laugh. The equipment was an old Sony tape deck, a bag of chips, two flashlights, and half a dozen Hostess cupcakes, but what the hell, he thought, wouldn't doubt spoil it? Besides, he liked it when Randy got serious.

"These guys are very experienced in case investigation," Randy said. "We're talking metaphysicians, engineers, researchers. And sensitives, of course."

Randy was hoping to gather data that would earn him entry into the Washington Ghost Society, which, from what Jackson could gather, was a bunch of pale and mentally unstable guys listening for poltergeists and wearing tinfoil hats.

"Sensitives?" Lydia asked.

"Psychics," Randy said. "Mediums. It's necessary. You do everything you can with science, and you combine that with the science we don't yet understand."

It was Jackson's father who first told him about the Firetrail ghost. "You'll be driving up the hill at night," his father had said, "just minding your own, and–*bam!*–he's beside you, running. Just running like hell, looking in the window of your car." Over the years kids at school had added to and amended the story: He was old, or he was young, he had a weathered face, he had sad eyes, he ran beside your car at night, or you'd look in the rearview mirror and he'd be sitting in the backseat. He was looking for the people who'd murdered him, or he was young and lonely. He'd torture and kill you, or he'd put one cold hand on your shoulder. He was good fortune, or death.

"So, what do we do?" Lydia asked, folding her arms. She was wearing a sweatshirt that was about six sizes too big for her, and she kept her hands tucked up in the sleeves, but her tone was all business. Jackson had the feeling that he was the tagalong here, that this was really about Lydia and Randy. Lydia was twelve, young enough to still believe in magic, and Randy saw UFOs in the glow of streetlights; the fog was a ghost whipping her hair.

The objective, Randy explained, was for the ghost to feel at home. To run with them. They would all take a turn, according to Randy, but Jackson had guessed from the start that Randy's bet was on Lydia, that he thought that she would be the one to see the ghost. She was small and wiry, and Jackson understood that in some ways she was braver than him. And it wasn't a stretch to imagine a ghost wanting to talk to her. She *did* know things, he thought. She didn't get good grades, but it wasn't because she wasn't smart; she just didn't care what people thought. She didn't have any friends, but she knew when things were going to swing good or bad, when to enter a room or when to hang back. She reminded him of a cat, every sense alert, skirting trouble, landing on quick and gentle paws.

"We run," Randy said. "We do what he does. You start when you press the tape, and if you see or feel anything, you say it. Shout it while you run. That way, we have a record of the time, a record of what you heard, and any noises from the ghost get recorded, too."

Even as stupid as this Society business sounded, standing on the hill Jackson started to feel the vertigo shift into a manic excitement. Chris had given him some pills and he'd taken one and it was making him feel full of air and also warm toward Randy. They could get Randy into the Society, and what would that mean to his only friend? Everything. More than everything. All those big dreams, and here they were running in the blue light on this nowhere hill. The poignancy of Randy was that he wanted so little.

"If we can get some raw data," Randy said, "they might get interested. And if they get interested then that's the go-ahead to start obtaining better equipment. I'd like to get a video camera and of course better sound equipment. But this is it for now." He stood on the tarp. "So, who wants to go first?" Randy said. He opened one of the packages of cupcakes and took a bite of one.

"Maybe you should show us?" Jackson asked. He really did want to see what Randy wanted, but he felt bad at the same time. Randy wasn't a runner. He was the perfect director of his own movie.

Randy nodded. "All right," he said. "But you guys don't laugh." He put down the half-eaten cupcake and shrugged out of his trench coat, dropping it on the tarp. He started toward the side of the road.

"Wait," Lydia said. She fumbled for the tape recorder, ejected the tape, and pressed it back down again. "Here."

"This is just to show you," Randy said, but he took the recorder. "You're going to run as fast as you can up the hill – press play when you start. And if anything happens – if you hear *anything* – then you should just say it. Shout or something – *Ghost!*" He grinned. "Or, *Now!* Anything that indicates that you've made contact. Got it?"

Jackson nodded. "Got it."

"Okay," Lydia said. "Show us."

"First," Randy said, "I think it's important that we invite him in."

"Invite him in?" The pill was softening the edges of everything. Jackson felt like he was watching something elaborate and silly. A puppet show. Invite him in. Have him over for a nice dinner.

"Tell him that you're good, you know. So he feels comfortable. If it's a he."

"How do you do that?" Lydia asked.

Randy arranged the tape recorder under his arm. "Just say – like, 'Okay, here I am. I'm here in peace. I'm here to run with you.'" He cleared his throat and looked straight ahead. "I'm here in peace. I'm here to run with you." He hunched down. "Ready – oh, shit," he said. "I forgot." He walked back to the base. "Okay, before you do it, you're going to mark the time." He held down the first two buttons of that old tape recorder and the tape started to turn. Would the Washington Ghost Society accept such archaic equipment? Randy's face looked a little distorted and Jackson wanted to laugh. Lydia was so serious. She'd tucked her hair behind her ears and she was frowning. She had eyes like their father's, deep-set, shadowy. Someday soon all those shitty commercials were going to start targeting her, trying to get her to buy shit for her under-eye circles. Jackson wondered a lot about what kind of grown-up she would be. It was hard to imagine her as some kind of femmey cheerleader, but she wasn't a complete tomboy either, and he was pretty sure she wasn't queer. She could stand there and be engrossed in Randy's ghost chase, but she wasn't the same kind of devoted dork. She seemed unformed, existing before all of that.

"Jackson," Randy said. "Are you even listening?"

"Sorry."

Randy held the tape recorder out again. "Okay, so one more time: you push Play and Record at the same time to get it to start recording. Then, you're going to mark the time." He pressed the buttons and droned, "Tuesday, September 23, 2009 6:53 PM, Firetrail Hill, Tulalip, Washington." He stopped the tape. "Got it?"

They nodded. "Okay," Randy said. "I'll demonstrate."

He ran a hundred feet up the hill, his T-shirt fluttering behind him like a flag, the tape recorder under one arm and the other in front of him, like a football player. A car driving down the hill honked and Jackson gave the driver the finger.

Jackson went next. It was chilly but bearable, the lukewarm edge of summer still in the air, and it hadn't rained in two days. He recited the day and time to the tape and started up the hill. It felt like he was running into a green tunnel, the trees knitting together over his head. He'd hadn't run much since his freshman year, but still he didn't expect to be as winded as he was, sprinting that stretch, the gravel spitting up under his shoes. He forgot to look for the ghost at all, and he supposed that made it a definitive non-sighting.

Jackson passed the tape recorder to Lydia and she wound herself tight, crouching low to the ground. "Time?" she asked, and they told her; she recited the date and time into the recorder and took off like she was built of pistons. She shot up the hill and jogged back down again. "Sorry, Randy," she said. "Nothing."

"Jack?" Randy asked. "You want to –"

"I want to go again," Lydia said. She shrugged out of her sweatshirt and went back to the side of the road. "Time?" She ran again, tirelessly, hardly panting.

"*Damn,*" Randy said. "She's *fast.*"

The light was fading. "Stay off the road!" Jackson called, but she kept going, two hundred feet up, loping back down, crouching on the shoulder.

"If this doesn't work, it's not because we didn't try," Randy said, sticking his lower lip out and blowing his bangs off his face. "Jesus."

Jackson stopped paying attention at some point. It was like watching Chris swim; sometimes ten or fifteen minutes would pass with nothing to mark it, just the lap of the water against the sides of the pool, the silver beads of water raining from Chris's fingertips as they surfaced and dipped. Lydia lighting up the hill, shrinking into the dim light, the trees, pivoting, descending. There weren't many cars. He was watching the twin paths of headlights starting toward them from below when he heard her scream.

He was running before he realized it. He had been standing on the tarp in the ditch, and now he scrabbled and tripped his way up onto the shoulder, stepping on the bag of chips and exploding it under his boot, pounding up the hill toward her dim form. She had flown from the shoulder and into the overgrown ditch, almost a straight line from where he'd been standing, and the sound of that scream rang in his ears still, loud and ragged–was she hurt? He tripped back down into the ditch; she was on her knees in the long grass with her head in her hands. He leaned over her.

"Lydia!" he took her by the arm. "What is it? What is it?" She kept her face buried in her hands. "*Lydia!*" He was yelling but fear was all over him like he'd been splashed with it. His skin was cold and clammy. Randy came up behind them, breathing hard.

"What happened?" Randy asked. "Was it the ghost?"

Lydia took her hands away from her face and there was a shallow gash on her temple. There was gravel in it. "It wasn't the ghost," she said. "I just fell."

"Shit, Lyds," Randy said. "Oh, shit, her head."

"Lydia," Jackson said, "what happened? Are you okay?" He took her face in his hands and tilted her head to get a look at the cut. It didn't look deep but it was bleeding.

"I fell," she said.

"It was like something pushed her," Randy muttered.

"Come on," Jackson said. "Let's go." He helped her up. "Randy, will you take us home?"

They folded the cupcakes, the chips, and the flashlights into the tarp and pushed it all into the backseat of the car. Randy had the tape recorder and Jackson knew he would be up all night, running over Lydia's scream, listening for the ghost, for a hidden message. Fucking werewolves and spirits. Lydia's banshee scream. Jesus Christ. He sat in the backseat with her while Randy drove them over the hill, through the lightless corridor of trees, turning down the gravel road that would lead eventually to the little trailer, the squares of light spilling out on the sunken grass.

"Bye, Randy," Lydia said. "Sorry we didn't see the ghost."

Randy smiled. "You're a hell of a runner," he said, and she grinned. She looked eerie, with the blood on her face. It made Jackson think of a horror movie.

THERE WAS A fire in the woodstove and Lyle Lovett was playing. It was such a relief, the pure physical comfort, after the dark stretch of Firetrail Hill. There was chicken in the oven, and Jackson could tell it was going to be an easy night. He would get Lydia to the bathroom, help her clean the cut, and nothing would need to be said. Before they were completely inside, though, his father was in the kitchen. "Whoa," he said. "What happened here?"

"What is it?" his mother called.

His mother cleaned the cut and his father bandaged it. "Kids will be kids," his father sighed. It was strange, Jackson thought, that when he said she'd fallen, no one asked for more information. The excuse was accepted so easily. It gave him a sick feeling. So many times that his mother had been hurt and no one had said a word about what they all knew. If Lydia was his kid, he thought, he'd want every detail.

"Hell," Gary said. "When I was a kid, if I wasn't in a cast, I had a rusty nail in my foot. Kids will be kids." Jackson wished he'd stop talking. The conversation was giving him a bad feeling.

When Lydia's cut was bandaged and they'd eaten, Gary pushed back his plate. "We need some dance music, Amy," he said. He looked like any father, any happy man. His beer was propped beside him on the windowsill, but he wasn't drunk; he was smiling his big, easy smile, cuffing Lydia lightly on the shoulder, calling her fierce. Jackson looked at him. What would it be like if his father was this person all of the time? If he'd chosen to be a dad, a husband?

His mother had changed the music – Garth Brooks, Randy Travis, George Strait. "The Fireman," which always made Jackson think about some hot older man, a bear, maybe, wearing a fireman's hat and slicker, carrying a big hose. Original, he thought. A big hose. His mother was laughing, doing a quick two-step with his father. Lydia was dancing a little, weirdly, but he knew that just to dance was probably a big deal for her. They weren't exactly living in a haven of approval. He went to her, and spun her, dipped her. He wanted, one day, to be able to say, "We were good sometimes. It wasn't all bad. We danced."

His father whistled at them, and Lydia smiled. The corner of the bandage was dipping over her eye. His mother cut in and danced with Lydia, and then with him. She looked happy. They were all flushed from the warmth, from the dancing. Even when he felt tired, Jackson kept dancing; he wanted to hold it, to keep it exactly as it was.

He remembered a night when he was four or five, sitting next to his father, patting his dark hair, telling him how much he loved him. "I love you," he said over and over, and his father would say, "You, too, son." Every time his father said it, Jackson would start again. "I love you." Even then it seemed like the answer might change at any moment. The only thing he could do was to keep vigil. "I love you," he said again, stroking his father's hair in the lamplight, a deep sadness in him, as though even this moment was already lost.

Lydia
Tulalip, Washington, 2009

MARTA KEPT ASKING ABOUT JACKSON. IF MY FATHER WAS working in the neighborhood, I rode the bus with her until he picked me up. Jackson stayed after school. "Working on the paper," he said, but I knew it wasn't true.

Since the week we went to camp, Marta wouldn't stop. "Does he have a girlfriend? Have you, like, seen him naked?" she asked. We sat in her pink room across from Jennings Park and she tried on all of her clothes and read out loud from magazines. I looked at myself in the mirror. Marta used a flat iron to make her hair fall straight and smooth. It was movie star hair. My hair was still short. It looked the same as it did when I was seven.

"No way," I told her. "Gross."

"I want to have sex with him."

I didn't want to talk about sex. It felt like it should be secret. "Stop," I said. I felt dizzy.

"Whatever," she said. "He's cute."

I knew she was right. Jackson had shaggy hair that looked perfect, like a boy in the pictures that Marta tacked on her wall. His eyes were big and he had long eyelashes, while mine were stubby and pale. "Your brother is a rogue," Marta announced, the copy of Teen open in front of her. "'This bad boy is nothing but trouble! Unfortunately, that makes him extra hot! Enjoy listening to his band practice, or sitting around a fire on the beach, but don't expect him to come over for dinner with the parentals – it's not his style!'"

I tried to imagine Jackson in a band, or with his arm around a girl at the beach. It didn't seem fair, I thought. Jackson didn't even like girls, and girls liked him so much. No boys liked me. Randy was the only boy I knew.

Marta stood up and went to the closet mirror. She pushed out her chest. "What do you think?" she asked. "Am I hot enough to date a junior?"

MY FATHER PICKED me up at six. He reached across the front seat and unlocked my door. He put his big hand on my shoulder and squeezed it. "'Lydia, oh Lydia, say, have you met Lydia?'" he sang.

"Hi, Dad," I said. He was smiling and his eyes looked shiny. It was a day when we were being happy.

"'Lydia the tattooed lady. She has eyes that men adore so, and a torso even more so ...'"

It was already getting dark. Marta's house in the truck's mirror was a fire burning far off on that beach, where boys put their arms around girls and the sand was a blanket to lie on. It faded out. My father was still humming, tapping the steering wheel. "I thought we'd get pizza," he said, wagging his eyebrows. "Let your mother have the night off from cooking."

I nodded. The school parking lot was empty. Under the streetlights there were rainbows of oil in the puddles. I fixed my eyes on the double doors. I waited. I had this idea that if I could concentrate hard enough, I might be able to catch Jackson coming out and see him as a stranger. I might be able to see him as a person who wasn't my brother, and it might tell me something about me, whether or not I was beautiful, too.

The truck idled. He was late, and I watched my father out of the corner of my eye. Hurry, Jackson, I thought. He's singing. And pizza.

I saw Jackson across the parking lot. He was coming from the pool, though, not through the double doors at the front of the school. He didn't see us at first and I felt a hot jealousy. His face was open like a flower, like the sun.

The truck idled. Jackson was walking toward the car in the six o'clock gray and his face was light and faraway. He had been somewhere that didn't include me, where he was beautiful as ever and someone else knew it. If my father saw, he didn't say. I climbed over the front seat to the little bench in the back. I wished that Jackson and I were connected for different reasons. I wished that we'd chosen to be friends, that it wasn't because he was my brother. That it wasn't just because of my father that Jackson wanted to look out for me.

Driving back home, I watched the breaks in the trees where there was still white daylight. My father told a joke about a man from work. Jackson smiled. But like a dark hot fire, the anger was in me. I looked for the Firetrail ghost, but there was nothing. My chest was a nest of bees. It was two months now, since that night on Firetrail Hill when Randy, Jackson, and I tried to find the ghost.

That night, I was running so fast, hurtling through the dark. I had the tape recorder under one arm, and I could see the headlights of a car coming over the hill. I was just slipping through the dark, and then the anger came out of me, at nothing, at everything, as if the night around me was choppy water. I told Jackson and Randy that I tripped that night, but it wasn't that I fell. It was pounding inside of me, my hands were fists. I wanted to smash something. I wanted to hurt someone. The anger burst in me again and again and I had to give something to it, and then the gravel was slipping under my feet, and I was down in the ditch. And when the pain started, when I was down in the wet grass and I felt the blood warm on my cheek, it did stop.

I felt it coming back now, an edge of that same feeling. Jackson in the front seat, and even his ears were pretty. I made fists so tight they hurt. "You have your father's eyes," my mother would say, and I wanted to ask, "What else of his do I have?" Once, when I was seven or eight, he had turned to me. "You're just like me,

Lydia," he said. "You'll see. You're your father's girl." The words shivered over me. They hung in the air.

I couldn't tell anyone, but that night, in the moments before I fell, I wanted to burn the forest down. I never wanted to stop running. I wanted to run until I was someone else, until I knew I would never become like my father. My heart was pounding, and there was a mean and angry voice inside of me, gripping me until I stabbed it out.

Jackson

Silver, Idaho, 2010

THE AIR IN THE TRUCK WAS STALE. JACKSON KICKED aside fast food bags and empty cigarette packs. His back was wet with sweat.

Don didn't say anything until they were out of sight of the crew, then he reached over and squeezed the back of Jackson's neck. He angled the truck down a spur road off toward the ironworks. No one went out that way, since the flood sent creeping red rust over everything. Even before then the ironworks must have felt dangerous; the year before, Jackson had heard, a boy from town climbed the old blast furnace and fell.

"They don't need me on the West side?" Jackson asked.

"I'm leaving Eliza," Don said. "She's coming tonight. She's coming tonight and I'll tell her. Then you can come stay. Or hell, we'll rent a room. Together." He put one hand on Jackson's thigh.

"You're going to tell her about me?" Jackson pictured a blonde woman, dark alleys of mascara, suitcases. The specters of everyday destruction.

Don nodded. He looked away. "I want to do this right for you, Jack," he said. "You deserve it." He looked over at Jackson and smiled. His front teeth had a tiny gap in them. He was thirty-four years old, but that gap made him look like a little boy.

Jackson smiled back. He wanted to laugh, to open the car windows, to shout something. *This is my boyfriend*. What was he, twelve? He took a breath. Slow, he thought. Go slowly. "Are you okay?" he asked. He understood that this was tricky. That you couldn't leap from one person to another, from one life to another, so easily. Sometimes, he still woke up feeling dread like a heavy blanket, hearing the spray from the lawn sprinkler hitting the window, and down the hall his mother crying, his father shouting. Time could slip that way.

"I'm fine," Don said. He slid one hand from Jackson's shoulder down his back, into the waistband of his jeans. His warm hand on Jackson's ass. "You and me, Jack?"

"You and me," Jackson said. A flash, just a flash, of what it would be like: asleep on the sofa together at night, the television blinking blue, Don's head on his chest.

"I'll find you soon," Don said. He leaned across the front seat and kissed Jackson hard, pulled him close for a minute and breathed into his hair. Then Jackson slid back over to his side of the cab and they drove back to the job site in silence.

HE COULDN'T SLEEP that night. All he could think about was what was happening in Don's trailer. He lit his cigarettes off of the ends of the ones that came before. Even worse, he had the next day off; a shipment of something had been forgotten. Mike Leary had announced it like a great surprise, this wonderful day of rest, but what did Jackson have to do? He decided to go the next morning to Mary's, to buy a real breakfast and stop acting like he was still homeless. The leaves were just starting to turn. On the muddy lawn in front of Mary's someone had erected plastic gravestones and littered small plastic skeletal feet and hands in the dead garden mulch. A cloud of dirty cotton was stretched like a spider web across one window. Halloween. It was only September. Jackson had loved Halloween as a child, but Lydia hated it. There had been that urban legend about the syringes, and she wouldn't eat the candy. Jackson felt kingly and cruel, sitting in her pile of colored wrappers, eating them alone.

There were a few cars outside of Mary's – Mike Leary's F-150 and a dirty little roadster he recognized. He thought he'd get coffee and read one of the terrible county papers. The sad little ads: "Wanted: Old Buttons for Serius Collector"; "Clean Gutters 4 Cheap"; "Photographs in Your Home for Family or Glamour." Jackson imagined that before the construction jobs started everyone in Silver subsisted on these tiny trades. Remember how I fed you, remember the pig I gave you when yours was lost, remember the time you slept with my wife. Everyone survives, Jackson thought.

The bell over the door rang a dumb little tune. Inside it was warm and Mary was holding the coffeepot. Her husband had tied an apron over his belly and was sweating in front of the grill. Mike Leary waved from one of the barstools, where he had a generous breakfast in front of him, and Jackson sat next to him gratefully.

"How's it?" Leary asked.

"Fucking great." Jackson tried a toothy grin.

Leary looked at him. He was a smart man. Jackson guessed Leary probably had some idea about him. If Ida hadn't told him, he would have guessed anyway. He wondered how Ida was, but he didn't ask. It seemed like to ask would be breaking some kind of code; he didn't want to remind Leary that he'd been some street kid, a charity case.

Mary poured him a cup of dishwater coffee and he drank it black. He took the entertainment section of the paper from where Leary had pushed it aside and read the comics, which weren't funny. Had they ever been? There was an AA meeting on Thursday and a high school dance on Friday. If he was back in Marysville he might have gone to a dance. Or might have been eligible to go, more like. He would have stayed at Randy's smoking pot and listening to ghostchaser radio.

In hindsight, Jackson had come there to see them. Even not in hindsight. He'd come there just for that. And then they were through the door, and he didn't even need to look up from Dear Abby, who had long since been replaced by someone else. If there was a way to feel someone across the room, he could feel Don, Eliza, the whole damn breakfast crowd at Mary's pushing in all around him. He turned a little. His heart was smashing around in his chest. Did he breathe? He reached for his coffee and just rattled it in the saucer. It spilled a half moon around the rim.

Eliza was nothing. She was a negative of a picture of someone's wife, the pretty girl in high school who got good grades but didn't put out, the one with a neat list of colleges lined up against the checklist for Letters of Reference and Application Due Dates. She had two small shiny dimples where her glasses sat, but now they were pushed up on her head, and she was wearing jeans and a nice sweater. She didn't look like someone who got drunk and screamed outside of bars. She looked nice. Respectable. Not the kind of woman who'd ever be cheated on, not the kind of woman who'd cheat, but not too churchy, either. Someone who waited for movies to come out on video, who made pancakes late at night and could sometimes loosen up and have a good old honky-tonk time. She was walking toward him, smiling.

And Don! Don looked, Jackson thought, like the worst kind of sweaty, clammy fear. He remembered the first night he'd gone to Eric's house, before he knew that Eric was just fat and rich and lonely. Before dinner, before the first – okay, the third, counting the drinks Jackson had alone in the parking lot – drink, before Jackson understood that Eric was a good decision and not the last bad decision he'd ever make, he'd felt like Don looked now, gray and sick.

If Leary wasn't there they might have just pretended not to notice each other, and suffered through a sick and sour breakfast, and then he would have figured out what to do from there. But Leary knew Eliza. He knew Don. He knew them all, and Eliza said, "Mike!" and then they were there. He could smell fishy sweat on Don, which made him think of fucking Don, and he reached for the coffee again and tipped it over. He reached for the napkins and coughed. Graceful. Perfect.

"Mike," Eliza said again. "How are you?" Her voice was sweet and kind and she reminded him a little of Ida, a little of his mother – even a little of Lydia, the way that Lydia would be one day.

"Liza!" Leary said, and stood up from his stool. Jackson felt a surge of relief as Leary's wide back shielded him. He mopped up the coffee mess with shreds of napkin that didn't seem to work at all. "You look beautiful," Leary said.

"Oh, Mike," Eliza said, and squeezed his arm. "It's looking great out here. I keep telling Don that it's only a few more months – but to see it! I love the layout. All of it."

Leary grinned and nodded at Don. "A long hot summer. I should just pay these boys with beer." He stepped back and leaned on his barstool, leaving Jackson in the empty, gaping space that separated him from Don. Don's face was a tiny point. A sweaty, terrified point. *I'm leaving her. We'll get a place of our own*. Don's terrible face, those eyes. "Have you met Jackson?" Leary asked.

"Jackson!" Eliza said. It was a kind tone. He couldn't be scared, because nothing had happened yet, and it was all in slow motion – she held out her hand with its diamond ring and he took it and he held it while she squeezed his own.

"So nice to meet you," she said. "Donny has told me so much about you."

And then, slowly, he realized. His vision seemed to tunnel in, to sweep the table, closing in on the sugar decanter, the constellation of spilled salt, the ketchup packets in their tidy little lodging and he thought, she doesn't know. She pumped his arm once, twice. "He's had a good time showing you the ropes, I think."

The ropes. Don was looking at him with a hard stare. He'd never seen it before. Half warning, half pleading. Jackson could not figure out for the life of him what to do with his mouth. He half-smiled. Leary, he realized, was also staring at him, and it was clearer what he meant: go on, just do it, what you have to do, and then this will be over and we can all go back to breakfast.

Jackson looked up at Eliza. "Good to meet you, too," he said, and she smiled widely, like he'd said something truly wonderful. Her lipstick was on her teeth but not in a trashy way. More than anything he felt sorry for her. "I've heard a lot about you," he said.

"Oh!" she smiled, pleased. "Good things, I hope!" Her enthusiasm wasn't to cover anything, he realized. It was just being shy, being hopeful. A godforsaken kitten. A Christmas pageant angel. He was the worst piece of shit that ever lived.

Eliza had her hands up around her face, picking at something that wasn't there. "You're so young," she said, and for a moment his stomach lurched with fear, with excitement – maybe, maybe she did know – but then he thought better of it, again; her face was open to him, she was looking at him like he was a child; she was earnest and happy and he was nothing, he was no one to her. "It seems like you should be in school, not out here."

"I'm alright," Jackson said. New voice, new man-voice, curt and quick. Alright. Justfine. Grababeer. Or twelve, and then a handful of Randy's prescription painkillers. Sleep for a week. Sleep until spider webs stitch over his mouth. He nodded at Eliza, took a drink of his coffee, nodded at Don. And somewhere after the nod, in the static cotton air, they were gone, following Mary to a table by the window, pulling out their chairs, settling themselves. The bell was ringing at the door; a family walked in, the clatter of plates and the chatter all around him. They were six, ten feet away, opening their menus. He thought he might throw up. Mike Leary shook his shoulder once, like *Hey*.

Jackson didn't explain it to Leary, just left a handful of dollar bills on the counter and left, the bell on the door ringing again as he went out into the wet wind. He made sure not to look at Don and Eliza sitting together at their table.

And now, he thought – what now? He didn't want to think about Don's face, about any of it. He studied the cracked pavement, the dark leaves beneath his boots. He hadn't imagined what would happen today because he knew – somehow, somewhere – that it might not. That he might spend the day alone in the cab drinking hotplate coffee, reading the mystery books he'd taken out of the library. But even then, he had believed, stupidly, that Eliza might fight Don, that she might refuse to leave, but that he would tell her. That eventually she would leave town, weeping but resolved. Jackson concentrated on the street in front of him. The shuttered up businesses, the cafes, the bars with fogged windows. There was a pay phone outside of the gas station and he made his way there, used the creased phone card from his wallet to call his dead cell phone and check his messages.

Randy was the only one who had the number. Jackson had bought the phone the day before he hitched to Portland, and Jackson had called him, figuring someone should know where he was; now there was a single message from his one friend: "Hey, man, just wondering how you are, where you are, give me a call, worried about you but you're not missing much." Jackson knew it didn't make sense but he couldn't help a stinging disappointment – some hope that his mother or Lydia had somehow tracked him down. That he might dial up his voicemail and hear one of them, tentative – "Jackson? Are you there?" But there was just Randy, good old Randy.

Randy was his only real friend since they both took the long bus ride around Lake Goodwin, down Firetrail Hill, into Marysville and Marshall Elementary. Pots of paste, the rubber letterpress, a tiny bathroom in the classroom he'd been terrified to use because the other kids might hear him pee. The same class of assholes from kindergarten through the year he'd left high school. Jacob, Megan, Brianna, Alyssa, Ryan. Andrew with the fucked up legs. Mariah, who lived in a trailer on Firetrail, too, and hers was worse, but her dad didn't hit anyone. Randy. He was weird all the time, even as a kid, but you can be weird for a while when you're a boy. Ham radios and aliens. In the sixth grade, Randy wore a long black duster, and rain boots, and tinfoil bracelets. He built his own radio from a gem kit or something. Maybe it was just that he had a rock tumbler and the radio came later. Jackson rode the bus home with Randy and they sat in his dad's pickup with the CB turned on, listening to any snatches of conversation they could pick up. Randy would send out words he'd picked up somewhere and wait for a response. "Going double nickels, boys!" Jackson liked to watch Randy get so excited, the trembling way he waited, adjusting the dial. There was a world full of intrigue out there, according to Randy, and even though Jackson didn't give two shits about the far-off grunt of a trucker over the radio, he cared that Randy cared. Details like that killed Jackson. He found so much sorrow in the tiny joys that people had – they seemed so small, so unambitious.

Standing outside of the Silver gas station now, Jackson thought about calling home – but it wasn't his home, not anymore. His father's house. What did he want to know? If someone else, some other woman, would answer the phone?

Instead he hung up, pocketed the phone card. There were dark clouds like tall buildings assembling to the east, and he hoped it wouldn't rain. It meant he could burn as much as he wanted to, but it also meant slogging through the mud, rainwater filling the holes that he would need to refill, the trash sodden and the damp seeping through the cracked soles of his boots. He knew it was true without knowing it – his father, in the arms of some smoky, tattered barroom girl. His father was nothing alone, worse than nothing. He propped himself up with anyone who would have him. Maybe he'd never seen it firsthand, but Jackson could picture it. He knew it without evidence. Another girl would be swept in, probably already had, until his father ruined it all, until she was sent out into the world of caseworkers, garbage bags, the Starlight. Even now, he thought of domestic violence as a cheap motel.

He bought a bottle of tequila at the package store. No one gave him two looks about his age there, but Eliza thought he should still be in high school. He walked with the bottle back to the semi cab, had it open before he was even at the door. It was one in the afternoon and he didn't care. His little home – the narrow bed that had only known Don that one time, that quick fumble one afternoon when they'd wrestled around and Jackson had felt his own cock pushing up against the waistband of his underwear and then they'd gone out and sat watching the sun over the ironworks. He lay back on the hard little pillow and drank.

He thought about Randy's message again. "Hey, man. Worried about you." Randy was lonely; that had been his big shtick, his main quality all through middle and high school, and there was a time when Jackson had liked to imagine Supermanning his way right into Randy's lonely little world, whisking him away from his drunk dad and his damp basement hovel. Some nursemaid fantasy; harmless, really. The smell of pencil shavings and moldy textbooks came rushing back at him, thinking of school. A brief regret, for not having finished, just to say that he did.

But here he was, mad at Don, lonely as hell. He kept thinking about calling Randy. He'd never had a friend like that, someone you could call, ask for something – company! How sad was that? He didn't know if Randy would even come out to Silver.

He thought of his father. Jackson had revered him as a child, even though his father had been always stern and often cruel to him. He remembered his father calling him names, calling him a girl, a fag, a little prick, and how Jackson had ached for approval. When his father occasionally paid him attention, warmth would spread through Jackson; it was like he was standing in sunlight.

Right now Tulalip would be the same as Idaho: summer being driven steadily out by the cold, wet wind. The mildew creeping up the edges of the mobile home. The dense green underbrush. The Northwest. What had brought his father there except to secret them away where only the sinking ground and deep wet woods could see or hear? The corner of Tulalip where Gary had set down his tiny demagogue's empire, his kingdom. Gary had known from the start, Jackson thought now. From the moment he had left Texas, he had known what a misery he was going to make of his wife's and children's lives. Jackson looked around the cab of the old truck.

He was getting drunk.

He thought now of the summer when he was thirteen, when there had been a chill between his parents, worse than usual, an eggshell frost. It was the burning fuse, the long wait. Something was coming, and he wanted to be far away when it did. Lydia was eight and full of the world. She liked to play detective, to know every secret. He devoted that whole summer – the summer before Randy, when things were still not just about his own pitiful heart – to Lydia. He gave her the forest and all of its attendants: the abandoned rowboat. The narrow creek. Stands of huckleberry, each branch dotted with berries like hundreds of delicate pursed mouths. Seed pods helicoptering around them. It was all the world they'd needed.

At the same time, lying in bed drinking in the middle of the day, sick at Don, at himself, at the world – he could see now how it was – how pathetic, and wrong. Everything they'd done then had been because of his father. He'd taken Lydia to the forest because his father had forced them there, pushed them out of the house with the force of his own selfishness, his cruelty. Everything they'd done had only had the illusion of freedom. The moments that they had thought they were in control were the same moments when his father had truly succeeded.

He was sure of it, and he promised himself then, in the truck cab, and in his deepest heart, that he would never see his father again.

HE CALLED RANDY the next morning from the phone at Mary's. He was full of a gray feeling from the tequila. He was *sick* – but inside; he wanted to peel off his own skin. He couldn't smoke a cigarette if he tried, even though he thought it might make him feel better.

He ordered toast and asked about the phone; Mary brought the whole receiver and cradle out to him on a long cord. He was missing work. Was he going to be in trouble? Did Mike Leary know? He tried to imagine Don leaning in toward Mike Leary, his voice low. "Kid's a little upset. You see, I told him I was going to leave Eliza, you know, but Christ, Mike, you know how it is." Leary, keeper of the secrets of men. More likely, Don had told it so Jackson was the sad little fag: "He got a crush. I mean, I'm not going to give him a hard time about it, I could, you know, but I'm not that way. Poor little guy. Let him lick his wounds for a day or two."

Randy's phone rang six, seven times – "'Ello?" Randy had something in his mouth. Or he was very, very stoned.

"Randy?"

"Who's this?" Randy's dopey voice. Jackson felt better.

"It's Jack," he said. "Hey, man."

The cook had mixed up an order, and Mary flipped it down the counter to Jackson. "Eat," she mouthed at him. He smiled gratefully.

"Jack? Hey!" Randy's voice was high and excited. It was his ghostchaser voice: *Listen, they're gonna play that tape and no one was in the house, but do you hear those clicks those are Morse code, if you ignore that first minute* – "Oh, man, you've missed some lame shit. Graduation, all of it – finally! The worst years of your life. Where the hell have you been? I tried your phone – "

Jackson hadn't spoken to Randy since calling him once from Eric's, lying in that pretty wedding cake of a bed one morning while Eric ran out – to go to the cash machine, Jackson knew. "Portland, just hanging out, staying with some friends," he'd said. Randy had wanted to visit then, but Jackson had put him off.

"I'm in Silver, Idaho," he said. "South of Coeur d'Alene. Close to Montana."

"Is that where the old silver mines are?" Of course Randy would know about the old silver mines.

"Sure," said Jackson. "I got a job on a construction crew. Building houses on a little manmade lake."

"No shit." Randy giggled. He sounded like a baby. Randy even looked like a baby, he thought – chubby and soft with short arms and a child's haircut. Thinking about that bad haircut made Jackson miss him.

"So what are you doing now that you're a free man?"

A weedy cough from Randy. "Oh, my God," he said. "I'm leaving here soon. I don't know where for. I saved some money. I want to check out some places, man." Jackson imagined the Stonehenge of Texas, Midwestern haunted houses, footprints in the butter. Randy on a trail chasing them up and down the little roads between the highways. "Hey, I want to come visit!" Randy said. A rush of relief – why had he been so afraid to call? What was the big deal about having a friend? "What's it like out there?"

Jackson looked around Mary's. There was an elderly couple in one of the three booths, eating hard-boiled eggs out of little silver eggcups. There was a man alone at the other end of the bar drinking coffee with the same shaking hands that Jackson had this morning. Down at the lake, the crews would be well into the day. Would he even be missed? His stomach was sour. "It's okay," Jackson said. "I'm living in the cab of an old truck. I work five days a week. It's a bunch of guys ... " Did that sound the way he thought it did? "It's up in the mountains, kind of. You'd like it." He took a bite of the abandoned breakfast and it was good. "You should visit."

"Hey, man, I could come through Idaho on my way out of town," Randy said. "Seriously, you should come with me. You're already out there seeing the world."

"When are you leaving Marysville?" Jackson asked. He felt a little disappointed that Randy couldn't just come now. He didn't want to be alone.

"I don't know. A few weeks. I'll call you. Can I call you?"

"I'll call you. Or use this number. The woman – Mary – will take a message." How many shamed men had been dogged by their wives here? Mary's wasn't even a booze joint, but you could see the booze joints across the street. If you were at the Longhorn the bartender would lie for you, but Mary might just spot you through the glass.

"All right," Randy said. "Hey, man, this'll be great!"

"Yeah," Jackson said, and he *did* feel that way, because there was a life out there, someone who knew him who would still know him in a different town, and who did not know Don. How easy it was to let your world get tiny. "Hey," he said, and his voice sounded ridiculous. "Have you seen my dad or anything?"

Randy paused. "Once in a while," he said.

"Randy. Lydia's not there, is she?" God, if she was – !

"No, no." Randy was quiet again. Jackson breathed out through his nose, pushed some egg around on his plate. "They're not here. I've seen your dad around once or twice. Nothing seemed different."

Meaning, Jackson thought, same old asshole. Probably the same old asshole with a new girlfriend. But still – they weren't there. As much as he wanted to know where they were, he wanted even more for them to be gone. "Thanks, Randy," he said.

"Hey, talk soon," Randy said, and they hung up, and Jackson passed the phone across the counter again to Mary, and she didn't charge him for his toast or the breakfast, and he walked out feeling better.

He would go to work, he thought, and see if he still had a job. As he made his way toward the work site it happened again – he thought he saw his mother. This time it was a woman, an older woman in sweatpants and a dark coat buttoned high around her throat, and as soon as it happened it was over; it wasn't her. There was no pattern to these moments, except that he had come to expect them, even to welcome them, and at the same time this did not diminish the surprise in it. It embarrassed him, the simplicity of what it represented – a simple, forgiving reunion – and afterward he would feel hurt and angry at himself, at the way that he could dream for such a clear impossibility.

He would be walking from the work site, or past the row of new houses, and a dog might run between the trees, or a carpenter would be stooping in a pile of useful debris, picking out nails or reclaiming his scattered tools. However unlikely, these ordinary articles would assemble themselves into the form of his mother – his mother at her most gallant and admirable, wearing a dress that he had seen only in the occasional photograph that surfaced from the early days of his parents' marriage. It was his mother as he had never known her, picking her way over sawdust and twisted lengths of orange construction tape, walking toward him. His mother as she would have looked down at some roadhouse in Texas, where the plank boards were treated with beer to a dark shine. His mother with none of the stiffness or disappointment of his mother now. She would approach him near one of the work trucks, elbow on the rusted bed. "Oh," she would say, "Oh, Jackson, it's all been fine, you know, it's been just fine."

He would grasp, then, when he shook his head a little and the dog became a rangy mutt or the carpenter straightened with his arms full of tools, just what exactly he was going to lose – his mother's past, her present, all of it. The times that had so captivated him as a child – the times before he existed at all – were even farther from him. Somewhere far from him, she was going to grow old. He wanted so badly for her to materialize, to come out of the woods in that old dress, the one he remembered from when he was young, the one he had maybe even created in his mind. He would tell her, he thought, that he had been wrong, more wrong than he could have ever imagined, and instead of acknowledging that he had done her in, had not treated her as a son should treat his mother, but more like an enemy, and she would just lean against that truck and smile.

"Oh, well," she would say, "we go on, don't we?"

The woman kept walking; the wind picked up. He kicked through the leaves to the work site, to the day that was waiting for him. The day he was late to. He tried to imagine, for a minute, that Don didn't exist at all.

Amy

Fannin, Texas, 2010

AMY STOOD OUTSIDE ON A GRAY TUESDAY HANGING LAUNDRY on the frayed line. The back door of the little Fannin house opened onto the same thatch of grass, the gravel road leading out to the same sparse field. Had anything changed in the years since she'd left and come back? There was a line strung from an eyehook above the door to a narrow, anemic tree just over the wall. It was cutting through the bark, bleeding a weak sap down the trunk. Slips the color of flesh; her mottled, threadbare bathrobe; Lydia's shirts housed the wind, arms lifting and dropping. The wind was pinning leaves to the siding. The smell of hot stone in the air, a match struck – somewhere a neighbor was burning leaves. When she turned, her mother was standing in the doorway.

"Will you come in here?" her mother asked. "I need to talk to you."

Her mother was the same and different. She seemed content, Amy thought. At peace, in a way that Amy had never seen her before. She had welcomed them home, brought them in as though it had only been days since Amy left. Amy put the clothespins down in the grass and followed her mother. Inside, there was a stack of old spiral notebooks.

"I want to give you these," her mother said. "They were your father's."

Her father's old notebooks, the pages marked in even lines, fading pencil: "500 yd dash, 2 mile run, short sprints to Pancake House. Build new fence, 5′ × 12′. Stop smoking. Become a better person." He must have been what, she thought, nineteen? All of these tiny wants, these good intentions.

Her father. The storied boy. "He was brave, very brave," her mother had told her when she was a little girl. She imagined him, swinging like Tarzan through the jungles, the tangled vines. And when that war started to assemble in her mind, she imagined blood, and noise – noise everywhere, even the silence growing loud, weighted with what might be coming. They were lucky, everyone said, to have him home. Only later did Amy start to wonder what it must have meant for her mother. To spend thirty years shaving your husband's face with a straight razor in Fannin, Texas, far from the cities where people stood and waved signs against LBJ and Vietnam, and then against the next war, and the next, and to look your neighbors in the eye when they called your husband a hero, to wave and smile when they went back to their own homes, far from the shaving cream and straight razor and everything else that waited for you.

"You never showed me these before," Amy said.

There were so many other things she meant to say: I'm sorry. I love you. I loved him, and I'm sorry I wasn't here.

"Amy," her mother said. "You need to make a life again."

She thought of her mother's life, how small it had been. Did her mother wish she could have done it differently?

"Do you wish you'd left Daddy?" she asked.

"No," she said. "He kept his promises to me. I did the best I could. I don't wish that any different, but I wish I'd come for you."

"I wasn't here," she said. "When Daddy died."

"You have to forgive yourself," her mother said. "Start with this."

"I don't deserve to be forgiven," she said.

"You didn't invent feeling that way," her mother said. "Did you think you invented it?" It didn't sound angry, just a question. *Did you think you invented it?*

Amy lay on her back on the floor and looked at the ceiling. She thought maybe she had.

She went the next week to see Jennifer. "You should go see her," her mother had said. "She lives in Lockhart. I'm sure she's in the phone book." She drove her mother's car. She still needed to trade their old car – she couldn't believe she hadn't done it yet. There was something safe about being in Fannin that she hadn't counted on. All of this time, she had thought it was the last place she should go.

Lockhart was the same as she remembered it – barbecue joints, the ornate buildings like Viennese cakes facing the square. Jennifer's little apartment was across from a city park with a gazebo. There were kids on a patch of concrete shooting baskets. It was nice, Amy thought. She tried not to be nervous.

The door swung open before Amy could knock. "Holy fucking shit," Jennifer said. She'd gotten heavier but she was still pretty. Her hair was still big, Amy noted. She still smelled like lilies, like cheap perfume. "Let me look at you!" Jennifer put her hands on Amy's shoulders. "You're so thin, you bitch," she said, leading Amy inside.

The house was compulsively sunny – the kitchen was painted yellow, bordered with a parade of sunflowers – and it smelled like burnt coffee. There were photographs everywhere, on the walls, framed and propped on the counters. The mirror in the living room was wedged full of snapshots. Amy walked around the room, picking out things she'd forgotten: she and Jennifer at homecoming, when they'd worn matching dresses patterned with black and white triangles and pinned three-pound mum corsages to their waists to stop the mums from dragging down their décolletages; Jennifer drunk at the Watermelon Thump in Luling giving the finger to a parade float. There were wedding pictures of Jennifer in a waterfall of white lace, Scott in a blue suit with a pink carnation in the buttonhole. I should have been there, Amy thought.

"Janie's in her room," Jennifer said, gesturing down the narrow, wood-paneled hall. "Janie! Come meet my best and oldest friend."

The door opened and the girl flounced down the hall. She

was Jackson's age, Amy thought, maybe a year or two younger, sixteen or seventeen. Her dark hair was chopped short on one side and she'd lined her eyes with black liquid that was smudged at the corners. She was beautiful, Amy thought. She looked like Jennifer. It was like looking at her old friend, twenty years ago.

"Hey," Janie said. "Nice to meet you. Mom, I'm going out."

"What, you're not even going to ask?" Jennifer said. She tilted her head toward Amy. "You see what kind of a mother *I* am," she said. "She just does whatever she likes."

Amy smiled. She watched Janie pick up a little beaded purse from the counter. "Be back later," she said, and went out the screen.

Jennifer went to the pantry. "Well, now that she's gone," she said, pulling out a bottle of wine, "let's stop being old." She pulled down two coffee mugs from the cabinet. "Take a seat," she said, waving one hand at the kitchen table with its sunflower placemats. She opened the wine and tipped it into the mugs.

"Where's Scott?" Amy asked, taking one of the mugs from Jennifer.

"Oh, God, don't even say his name!" she said. "I just call him The Motherfucker. He doesn't even call Janie." She sipped from her cup and winked at Amy. "I told you I'd have a girl and name her Jane. You would not believe some of the shitty names people come up with these days. Not me." She picked up the ends of her hair and assessed them for split ends. "That bastard ran off with some skank in Luling. Whatever. He called and wanted me back, but there's no way I'm going near that, especially after where it's been. But I'm sleeping with two guys now." She leaned forward. "And one of them has a horse dick, hand to God."

Amy laughed. She felt a pull toward Jennifer, the easiness of it, as though no time had passed. At the same time, her other life, what she thought of as her whole life now, was still there, heavy inside of her.

She tried, as best she could, to tell Jennifer what had happened. She couldn't, though, not completely, but she tried. It felt good, Amy thought. Never, in all those years, had she talked to anyone about Gary.

"I worried about you," Jennifer said, holding her coffee mug between her palms. "I told myself: Amy is either very happy or she is in trouble out there, but I'm going to say she's happy, because what the hell else can you do?"

"I don't know," she said. "I don't even know where Jackson is, and Lydia is so sad, Jennifer. I can just see it on her. What all this has done to her."

"The best thing you can do for your daughter is to get yourself a life, girl. You're a good mama," she said. "But get a life!" Jennifer laughed. "For God's sake."

Amy laughed. Nothing was right, she thought, but in that moment, across from Jennifer in the butter yellow kitchen, it seemed like she might be able to make something of what she had and start to try to live.

IT WAS ALREADY dark when she pulled up; she was later than she'd meant to be. "Mom?" she called. "Lena?" The house was too quiet. "Lydia?" Maybe they'd gone out to dinner. She went to the kitchen and turned on the light.

There was a note. "L. didn't come home–DO NOT WORRY, I've gone to look for her in town. Wait here in case she calls or comes home."

Somehow she made it to the sink before she started to retch, the pounding behind her eyes just *No. No. No. No.* She ran out onto porch and looked out at the field. She was dying, she couldn't breathe, she was *dying*. If he had come back. If he had come back. She was dying. She retched again. She knelt on the ground with her hands in the dirt.

Lydia

Fannin, Texas, 2010

I HAD THE FEELING AGAIN THAT MY FATHER WAS THERE. The page in front of me, the smell of chalk. I bit the eraser of my pencil and tasted the old taste, the house back around us, the sounds rising up. Go, I thought. Go now, and it was easier than I'd imagined. I followed the halls, and the lockers were soldiers with cold eyes. The gym was empty, and then I was out those heavy double doors.

It was worse outside.Every car on the main street was his car. Every corner was a corner he would know. When my father was drunk he would sometimes tell the story of how he met my mother. "The ranch where I lived was just a stone's throw from the town where your mother lived." His eyes would be glassy, and I knew that at any moment his smile might turn mean. "A ranch hand and a small-town girl, what do you think of that," he would say, and in my mind the ranch was a dark place because it had made him. And now it was a stone's throw from where I stood outside–was that a mile? Ten? I imagined the ranch was calling my father back. It was whispering to him that we had come back, that we were nearby for the finding.

I closed my eyes as tight as I could and wished for Jackson. Jackson, who knew the rest of everything that happened to us, the parts that belonged to him. I opened them again and the cars were dragging past, heavy as train cars.

I started toward home but thought, They'll send me back. Once I watched Jackson stick out his thumb like it was a long rope that pulled a car right to him, just for a ride down the road. But where would I go? The cars were loud and grinding, and in each one was another face that might recognize me.

In the end, I went to the river. I walked up and down the shore. I dragged my hands along the ground and picked up as many rocks as I could, and I waited there. I don't know how long I waited. The sky turned pink, and then it turned red. I was waiting for him. If he came, I thought, I would kill him before he killed me.

MY GRANDMOTHER WOKE me. My mouth tasted like aluminum foil. I was in the fort, and the rocks were still in my hands. She had a flashlight and she shone it across me. I had not dreamed of him. That was something.

She pulled me up against her, the flashlight in my eyes. I was so tired. She shook me. "You're all right," she kept saying, "You're fine–you're fine–"

"I thought he was here," I said.

"Who, baby?"

"My father."

Her arms were looser around me now. "No," she said. "No, I promise you, no." She was colorless in the flashlight. It seemed like I could see the veins running through her. "I looked for you everywhere," she said, and her voice was quiet and slow. "I looked all around town. I looked and I looked, and then suddenly I knew–you'd be right here, so close to home." I leaned against her. "When you're older," she said, "you'll be able to go wherever you want, and no one will stop you. No one will hurt you. And if they try, you'll have people around to protect you, just like you do now."

"What if he finds me?"

She put her arm around me. "He's haunting you like a ghost," she said. "But you're safe here. And one day, he'll be nothing but ashes and dust. He'll be gone for good."

"None of it was your fault," she said. "And everything you felt, she feels it to." She sighed. "She needs you. Lydia–she is a person, too. She isn't just your mother."

I was so tired, and she was warm against me. I followed her. I let her take my hand and lead me back up the gravel road from the river.

The light from the house looked warm and safe and I felt sorry. How long had I been gone? My mother was at the kitchen table crying. She was crying and her makeup was running down her face, and she held me so tightly that my ribs felt like they were breaking beneath her arms. Finally, she let me go. She pressed her cheek to her knee. She didn't ask me where I had been. "I'm sorry," she said, again and again. "I'm so, so sorry."

She tried to wipe her eyes but she just sobbed again. "You do these things," she said, "you do these things you think you'll never do because you think you have to – " I left my arms around her and they weren't my arms, they were someone else's. Through the screen, the prairie was dark and it did not end. "And there is another answer, I'm sure, but you don't know it," she said. "And then it's done – " She was crying again, and I let my arms drop. She was gasping, hardly breathing.

And it was Texas fall, still hot, and I wanted to tell her I understood and I couldn't. I couldn't say anything. I wanted to tell her that I knew, that her life had been before us and would still be after, and what should she have done? I wanted to say it but I didn't, and she said "I'm sorry, Lydia. I'm so sorry," and she stood and left me on the porch and went out the screen door and onto the road.

I wanted to run after her, but I just kept sitting. I wanted to tell her I knew. I pressed my cheek to the porch screen. I thought of my father beating my mother, the broken glass, and Jackson, with his hands reaching out to me as I left him behind. My mother was nowhere in sight, and I wanted to call after her. You do these things because you have to. I knew what my grandmother had said was wrong. It's not that you are still yourself. You are never yourself again. Your heart will break and break, and your children may be lost to you, but in the end you are still a mother.

Amy

Fannin, Texas, 2010

"YOU DO THESE THINGS," SHE SAID TO LYDIA, "YOU DO these things you think you'll never do because you think you have to–" I'm sorry, she thought. I'm sorry for all of this, because I knew. Somewhere in me I *knew*.

It is a Sunday afternoon, and she is searching the house. It has been less than a week since Gary came to the Starlight, since he brought them back home again. He is sweet and attentive, but she imagines a calm surface of water, the fish darting and frantic underneath. She is full of a terrible pain for her son, for what he has done, for the way she understands that Gary has that power, to hurt Jackson, to draw out of him such anger that he would do what he did, would tell Gary what he wanted to know. She is searching deep into the backs of the closets, under the heating grates, behind the washer and dryer. Somewhere Gary has hidden the children's birth certificates, and though she has long given up on finding them, it makes her feel like she is doing something, *anything. She imagines herself as someone else might see her, pulling things from dark shelves, shaking out the winter coats, sweeping the dust from the corners. Someone who doesn't know her, who might just see a simple effort, a small happiness: the search for a misplaced glove, a spring cleaning.*

When she has turned every stone inside, she moves out to the shed. It smells stale, and it's full of junk–appliances they meant to fix, scrap metal, dusty canning jars. There were always mice. It would make a good hiding place, she thinks.

It's dark in the shed and she pulls box after box into the light, watching the time, flipping through old papers and junk, scattering mouse droppings, looking for anything he might have hidden, anything that might help them when they go.

Beneath stacks of old paper, receipts, a broken answering machine, she sees it. The leather is old and smooth in her hands, and the sickness starts to come over her before she can say why but she knows. It has been eighteen years since she has seen Sam. She would know that collar anywhere.

"I'm sorry," she kept saying. "I'm so sorry." A shard of glass, a fingerprint bruise. Afternoons when Jackson and Lydia hid in the back of the closet with winter coats around their heads so that they wouldn't hear. She'd known. But there was this other side of their father, too – his hand on Lydia's bicycle seat when he taught her how to ride, the galloping cant of his shoulders. Once, he ran backwards across the lawn to make them all laugh.

For as long as she can remember she has been saying to her daughter, "You have to keep dreaming your life. You have to keep dreaming the life you want."

She left Lydia on the porch and went down the road. Her feet were bare and the stones were warm beneath them. If she could dream her children's lives, they would think only of the days that were coming, open curtains, bright streets.

She already said goodbye, long ago. The soup bone, buried in the front yard, the flowers she lay beside it. The night that Gary came to dinner and walked off into the warm night and Sam did not come home. The darkness in her husband had not begun the night of the Legion or after the car accident. It wasn't because they'd had children or because they were getting old. It was not about sex, or housework, or the weather. It was not about her. She holds the collar, weighing her husband's terrible heart. She understands for the first time that all of this was set in motion long ago. What other decisions, she thinks, what other pieces of her life are not hers? What truth is left?

She lays it back in the box. Okay, she thinks. So it is. She calls the New Mexico shelter the next day. She makes the decision to leave her son. To give him his life, just beginning, and to believe he will know how to use it. But here is her ugliest, most unforgiveable truth: the collar does not surprise her. In some small and secret way, she always suspected. Her Sam, her dog, her one love after her parents and before her own family, had gotten in the way of what Gary wanted, and she had allowed herself to pretend it was otherwise.

She knew her way to the river even in the dark, and when she was there she stopped, standing in the warm dark, breathing, the same air she had breathed twenty years before, when everything was still ahead of her. When she had ignored the voice inside of her that told her to pause, that told her something wasn't right, and instead gone on. For that she felt responsible: she had gone on.

She turned and looked back toward the house, the yellow glow of it in the dark. And you go on now, she thought.

Lydia was still on the porch when she walked back up from the river, and Amy felt the air go out of her, all of it, the guilt, the sorrow. She sat beside her daughter, and Lydia held her.

Jackson

Silver, Idaho, 2010

IN THE DAYS THAT FOLLOWED, AFTER HE HAD MET ELIZA, certain dreams he woke from had the same kind of sadness – nothing he could mourn, not really, because it was already gone. It had never existed in the first place. He worked with a focus. It felt good, to put things in order.

Don avoided the job site for three or four days. Jackson wondered if he was coming back at all, and then, that Friday, the pickup pulled up and Don climbed out. He wandered through, talking to the rest of the crew, shuffling papers on his plastic clipboard. Jackson felt an ache somewhere in the bottom of his stomach.

Don walked toward him. Those hands, with their long fingers and broad nails, the deep creases in the palms. The lines around his eyes. The first night that they had slept together, on the floor of A-frame B, the lake had reflected trails of light on the bare wood floor. Jackson had woken with his heart pounding and the taste of old bourbon in his mouth, a cold fear in his stomach at what they'd done, what it meant for his job and his life, but Don had just pulled him closer and touched his face, kissed his hair.

"Jack," Don said. He smelled like good sweat and new wood. "How are things?" The boom of his work voice. It used to make Jackson want badly to fuck him, to stand there talking about work orders and storm windows. To know that in a few hours those long hands would be on his cock, his teeth on the olive skin of Don's shoulder.

"Jackson," Don said. "You've been doing some good work here."

"Fuck you."

"Jack," he said. He looked at Jackson. He held his arm out as though he was going to reach out and touch him, then let it drop. "Jack," he said, softly this time.

"What do you want?"

"Let me buy you a beer or something," Don said.

His mouth. His hands, with the rounds of callous on the pad of each finger. At night Jackson could hear the whine of his teeth grinding, feel the muscles in his calves twitching. All of those things that had made Don so alive, so real – and that had been the miracle, that there was someone who he wanted so badly who was *real*. "You see, I would ... " Jackson said. He hated how his voice sounded, so high and bitter.

"So, do," said Don. There was an edge of authority in his voice. Jackson was aware of how everyone around him saw them: contractor and laborer. They probably imagined that Jackson had fucked up, of course he had. Late one too many times, some calamity of bent nails and sawdust. If they knew, he thought, they wouldn't see any of the real things – not Don turning in the cage of his arms, not the slow lap of the new lake against the dock pilings, not the spill of light through the frame of the house in the mornings. Just cheap, he thought. Cheap labor, cheap trick. Sleeping with the help.

Don cleared his throat. "Please?" he said.

Jackson looked at him. "No," he said. "I have to do something."

"Don't walk away from me, Jackson." Don's voice was low. His hands were deep in the pockets of his work jacket and his eyes flashed a warning. His stupid face, Jackson thought. His stupid hands.

"I could ruin you," Jackson said. "I could ruin you and your life would never be the same." He looked at Don, looked him right in the eyes. Don's face was blank, his eyes flat, his face a frozen half-smirk. He looked weak, Jackson thought, and the fight went out of him. It was useless, he thought. He'd only wanted something back–some sliver of power, of knowing that they had existed together, that he had meant something–*anything*–to Don. It didn't matter, Jackson thought now. It didn't change anything. Instead, he turned and walked toward the edge of the lake, the dark line where the fresh dirt ended and the forest resumed. He tried to walk as though he really had something to do–*like what?* he thought. Gather berries and skip rocks? Sit in the dirt and jerk off? He could feel Don watching him as he walked, faster and faster, the dust making small clouds behind him.

His throat ached and he knew he might cry. He hated it. He lit a cigarette and walked down to the edge of the lake to look at the houses going up. He stood at the edge of the water and looked at the houses, the planes of glass still marked with storm tape. The old town and the old river were gone, and this would take their place. He wanted to remember it like this. It seemed rare, to be able to see the moment when something changed.

IN THE AFTERNOON, they moved concrete on the biggest house. Big blocks of it, reinforced with wire and rebar, that were going to be sunk into the hill and then backfilled with gravel and dirt to make a terraced garden, a little Idaho Tuscany. It looked to Jackson like a shoddy set-up. The concrete retaining walls would have to be somehow fronted with stone or brick to make them look all right, but what did he know? This whole project was an exercise in fabrication, of creating beauty where there was none, patching it together and hoping the money would follow. One of the guys that Jackson didn't know well, a burly looking guy who used to drive pile in Oregon, was moving the blocks with a forklift. The whole crew was out since they were waiting on electric in some of the newer frames, and besides it was kind of a party. They would sink the retaining walls and start putting in the drainage system. There was piss beer and it wasn't too hot, for once. Don was there and Jackson was careful not to look at him too closely. He had the feeling that if he could do something right – if he only knew what that was – he would be able to make things go the right way, for Don to leave Eliza, for a letter from Lydia to somehow turn up pinned beneath the windshield wiper of his semi cab, for the things he'd done wrong to become obsolete, erased from his history.

He could feel Don all around him. The whole site seemed to have collapsed to contain only the points between them, the small orbits they made around the site. The sounds around him were light, fly buzz, a hive of bees. "Lift that up – you know, she's working the closing shift, I might just stop by, see if she needs a ride home – Where the hell is Dave? – Hell if I'll be here when the freeze starts, I'm going up to the oil sands, there's better money, get on it while it's early." Don was helping with the forklift, directing, "A little to the left, that's it." Jackson kept pausing to watch and then catching himself. A blizzard of panic would blur his eyes and he'd look away.

The pile driver had another block hovering in the air. It was five feet by six feet by one foot, part of the first and tallest level of the terrace. Don was crouched down where the block would be set vertically on edge, measuring with his hands. One day, Jackson promised himself, there would be other hands, more beautiful, that would touch him.

He paused again, watching, and Don looked up at him, and then the concrete was sliding from the metal tusks of the forklift, and the vertical end slammed to the ground and the whole block toppled forward. How much did it weigh? Four hundred pounds? A half ton? More? There was a strange quiet, a drawn-out silence, and then noise, but it seemed like things were out of sync – like the sound happened after the block fell, or maybe he could only notice one thing at a time, and his mind put them together later, the sounds he remembered, the sounds he invented: the shriek of metal on metal. A terrible crunching. Bone against rock.

The picture took a minute to come together, and then a minute for the rest of the crew to understand. Don was in the dirt. One of his legs was trapped under the concrete block. There was Don's face, and his torso, and then the wide flat block flush against the ground as though the leg had just been obliterated, had disappeared. His face was ashy. His eyes weren't focused, and Jackson heard himself cry out, a strangled little yelp. And then Don was looking at him. Someone was screaming. Was it Don? Don was looking at him. He was holding out his hand, reaching toward Jackson.

In front of God and every man on the site, that hand. Don's face was the closest to – and even now he knew it was obscene, all of it, the leg, the screaming – the closest to his face in sex, in orgasm. The hand still reaching for him – No, he thought, and he heard birds, passing overhead, his mother – "Listen," she'd say, "listen, you can hear the birds going somewhere warm for the winter." Jackson shut his eyes.

And then they were wedging up the block and hauling him up, his limp leg dragging in the dust, a dark stain coming through his jeans. They heaped him into the truck and sped off to the clinic or farther on to the hospital in Kellogg. The tires kicked up dust and then they were gone.

Don's hand, reaching.

When the truck sped off there was a crescent shape left in the dirt where Don had been. The concrete beside it, like an ancient relic. There was a fog of dust that the truck had kicked up, and Jackson could feel something dark inside him, like a poison in his blood. He wished, more than anything, to be sitting in the rowboat, against the warm, worn wood. He wished he could put his hand out and feel Lydia's small bones, her bird shoulder. There was just the awful smooth coin of the new lake. Don's face in a grimace, his hand reaching up like Jackson could save him.

Lydia in the rowboat, warm soda, the nicked and dusty bottom of the boat. There was a game Lydia liked to play. "How much for your arm?" she would ask. "A million dollars? How much for your leg? What if you had a baby, how much would you sell it for?" Seedpods twirled past them. Jackson would catch them and present them to her. "That won't even buy you my big toe," Lydia would say. The men had come to Don, clustering, moving to move the rock, that terrible mountain, and Don had looked at him, pleading. Jackson hadn't moved. He had not gone to him. He felt cold. The September sky was closing around him. It might as well be winter. Lies.

Someone was saying his name.

"Jackson," Mike Leary said again.

Jackson didn't move. His throat felt raw and he could imagine nothing worse than crying now.

"We're going to be needing you over at the West house," he said. That was all. Leary knew, and for whatever reason Leary didn't blame him.

"I'm going," Jackson said, and he stepped over the concrete blocks and toward the truck that would carry him around the rim of the lake. "I think a million dollars for my heart," Lydia would always say finally. "Yes, I think maybe a million." His own heart was pounding. The lake was in his eyes. He couldn't see anything.

HE LAY IN the cab that night with his hands pressed against his chest, against the ache that had settled there. Don would be in the hospital right now, in Kellogg, or Missoula, or maybe lifted to Seattle. Eliza would be beside him, and when he woke, she would lean over him. She would hold him. And even if it had been different – even if Don had left Eliza ... what then? Fuck you, he thought. Fuck you, fuck you, fuck you, and he meant it at Don and not at Don, at everything, at himself, at some stupid small hope he must have always had that it would be easy – that it would be possible – to live his life and to be happy.

In his dream that night, Don's face was hopeful, shining. He was radiant, Jackson thought. He closed his eyes and listened to Don's breathing. Be quiet, he thought. He didn't want to think of anything. He felt himself sleeping, but he pushed it back.

"I love you," Don said. Jackson reached forward and pulled Don's belt open. He pushed Don's jeans down, careful over the ruined leg, all those scars.

Jackson kept his eyes closed against the leg. Then they were in A-frame B, Don facedown on the pallet, the layers of blankets, the dark crown of his hair. Don pushed against him, and he reached for him, and where the leg should be there was nothing, just a hard knot, like a knot in a tree, and he knew that outside the cabin was a clean white corridor that led to a hospital waiting room, and he knew that Eliza was there, *but she doesn't know the way here*, Jackson kept thinking, and Don's cock was pushing against Jackson's belt. *I have never loved anyone*, Jackson thought, *as much as I love you*, and Jackson could hear the click of shoes, and he knew that Eliza was coming, that in moments she would see them, and he was wild with fear – he was trying to get away before she saw him and before Don could tell her that it was Jackson who didn't belong.

He woke up and it was dark in the cab. He was sweating and he could see even in the dark that a cluster of insects was beating against the screen, crawling up and down.

He pushed out the screen, let the moths and beetles fly free, took gulps of air. I never loved anyone as much, Jackson thought. Even then he knew how fleeting it was, and how no part of it was a lie.

Amy
Tulalip, Washington, 1996

THE LAND IN WASHINGTON WAS NOTHING SHE HAD known before, nothing she could have imagined. The outside came in on their shoes and in their coats. A black mildew knit up the corners of the window glass and clots of wet leaves marked the carpet. And the woods – when she walked there she had the feeling that she was being swallowed by something alive, alive in a dark way, wet and fecund and powerful. She would slip under the trees behind the little mobile home and stand in the shadows there, the trees keeping the rain out, the moss thick under her feet, the light all but squeezed out. And then, occasionally, a day like this one: Amy woke up that morning and the sun was burning through the fog, already spilling across her bed, lighting the corners of the room. She stood up and looked out at the yard, early summer overgrown, and then went to the closet and reached behind the ticking water heater.

It was a beautiful gun. A .38 Special with a four-inch barrel and walnut grips. Her father had bought it for her mother before he left for Vietnam, and when Amy was fifteen her father's old friend Lawrence had taken her out to his ranch and taught her how to shoot. When she left for Seattle her mother gave it to her with a box of bullets buried in a bag of sanitary napkins. She'd never told Gary about it. It sat cradled in that nest of maxi pads for years, and it seemed stranger and stranger to mention as time went on. But this morning she wanted to teach Jackson something. She also wanted to shoot it again, if she admitted it. She remembered how it had felt in her hands.

She left the bag with the gun in the closet for now and pulled on old jeans and a sweater. Jackson was waiting in the hall for her when she came out. He was five now, and she was five months pregnant. He put his hands on her belly. "I can feel it," he announced. "It's swimming." She laughed and bent down and kissed him. Her beautiful boy. Gary had been different lately, tired from work, tense. She avoided his gaze and turned to Jackson instead, so ready to accept her love, to love her back. It would pass, she thought. When there was more money, and when the baby was born. Gary would come back to her.

"Breakfast time, Jackie," she said, and led him to the kitchen.

"Breakfast," he echoed, and she poured him a bowl of cereal.

"Do you want to have an adventure today?" she asked him. She took the gallon of milk from the refrigerator.

"I hate milk," Jackson said.

"No milk," she said, and put it back. She turned on the radio that sat on the kitchen counter. When she and Jackson were alone she played the old country station. "So, do you want to go out in the woods with me?"

It was June. There was the whole long summer before Jackson would have to start taking the bus to kindergarten. She couldn't stand to think about it, the creaking bus that would take over an hour each way. It didn't seem right to make him ride that long for a few hours of coloring.

"Can we go to the creek?" Jackson asked.

"We can do that," she said. "Or we can go up on the hill. I want to show you something."

"Show me something," Jackson said. "I want to go up on the hill." His pajamas had airplanes on them, and his face was still marked from his pillow. She kissed the top of his head.

"Finish your breakfast," she said. "And then we'll get you dressed."

Their plot of gnarled roots and underbrush was hemmed by

forty steep acres that sloped down toward farmland on the opposite side and seemed to belong to no one. Because it was untended there were occasionally families who set up camp there, picking chanterelles or just waiting out hard luck. They sank trailers into the loam and their trucks made deep ruts through the woods that filled with rainwater and dark leaves. Mostly, though, it was abandoned, and she thought of it as belonging to her and Gary and Jackson.

She wrapped the gun in a sweater and put it at the bottom of Jackson's little green backpack, then added the bullets, two pairs of earplugs from the bureau, an old Coke bottle full of water, and two sandwiches. She picked out jeans and a sweater for Jackson and helped him into his yellow rubber boots.

There was an old logging road that ran up into the back forty and they walked it until it was rutted and overgrown, and then they cut into the underbrush and started up. It was all mud, held together with a skein of roots and somewhere, underneath, a crag of rock. She lifted long arms of blackberry out of the way, careful to keep Jackson in front of her, steadying him with one hand.

They stopped to drink water and eat the sandwiches, sitting on a stump thick with moss.

"Jackson," she asked as they walked. "Have you ever seen a gun before?"

"Like in the movies?"

"Yes," she said. "Like in the movies. But the movies aren't real. Guns are very, very dangerous. I want to show you a real gun so that you know what it looks like. That way, if any of your friends, the kids you meet when you go to school, or *anyone*, ever has one, you will know not to touch it."

She reached into the bag and pulled out the bundle. It was a six-shot revolver with a heavy bull barrel. She held it out toward him. "Whoa," Jackson said. "Whoa." He was breathing heavily like he wasn't sure if he was scared or excited. She let him look at it, to touch the smooth walnut. She clicked out the cylinder and let him spin it.

"This is very serious, Jackie," she said. "I want you to see this so you will always recognize a gun. I want you to promise me that you will never, *ever* touch one. This is special because I'm here with you, and I can keep you safe." There had been so many stories lately on the news, and a boy in town had shot a friend in the face, playing with a gun he thought was unloaded.

"Can we shoot it?" Jackson asked.

"When we go up on the hill," she said. "I'll show you. I want you to see how powerful it is. You should never just play with something like this."

He nodded. "We should shoot the bobcat," he said. There had been bobcat sightings out this way; someone had lost a dog.

"This gun belonged to my daddy," she said. "Like Gary is your daddy, this was my daddy's."

"Where is your daddy?" Jackson asked.

She fought a stinging guilt. "He's in Texas," she said. "Far from here. And my mama is, too. Like I'm your mama, she's mine. You'll meet them one day. Your grandparents." One day soon, she promised herself, after the baby was born, they would go back to visit her parents. And Gary's too, maybe. Whatever was between Gary and his parents, she thought, whatever drove them apart–it would be different now that they had children.

"Let's keep walking," Amy told him, and helped him over the fallen log. She knew Gary wouldn't approve of any of it. After the first few weeks of being sick the pregnancy had been easy, but still.

It wasn't far, but it was another half an hour before they cleared the hill. There was a break in the trees, and she was warm from the walk, panting. Jackson's cheeks were pink and his jeans were damp up to the knees from walking through the underbrush.

"Is it time?" he asked.

"Yes," she said. "I'll show you how it works. But first I'm going to give you these." She handed him a set of earplugs. "I want you to go sit on the stump over there, and then put one of these in each of your ears, like this–so that the sound doesn't hurt your ears." She pointed to a fallen tree, overgrown with huckleberry. When he was settled on it, his earplugs in, his hands folded in his lap, she lifted the gun. She pulled out the cylinder and held the gun carefully through the frame, putting the round into place. She clicked the cylinder latch and waved at Jackson. "Ready?" she called, and he nodded. "Put your hands over your ears!" she called, but he couldn't hear her.

She pulled back on the hammer and sighted. "Look straight down the barrel," Lawrence had said, standing beside her on the ranch. "You'll be fine. Your daddy could shoot the nut out of a squirrel's hands." She fired from the top of the hill, through the trees. There was a rustle of leaves. Fifty feet away, a bird fell, a pile of black feathers streaking toward the ground.

She dropped the gun. "Oh God," she whispered. She walked slowly backward, watching. Was it possible she had done that?

"Mama," Jackson said. "Mama, is it a bird?"

She turned and ran to him and covered his eyes. "Oh God," she whispered again. His tiny hands reached for hers, pulling them away, and she turned him toward her, pointing to the sky.

"Mama, is it dead?" he asked. His eyes were wide.

She pulled him to her, and lifted his chin up toward the sky. "Look," she said, "Do you see it?"

He looked hard. "Up there?"

"It flew, baby," she said. "It just flew right away."

He looked at her with wide, adoring eyes. "I saw it," he said. "It flew." He put his little arms around her legs and she touched his soft brown hair. He put his palms flat on her stomach again. "Did the gun scare the baby?"

"No, honey," she said. "Let's go home." She took his hand and they started down the hill. Tomorrow she would sell the gun, she thought. She didn't want it around her children.

3.
The Fish

Jackson
Silver, Idaho, 2010

"YOU DON'T EVEN KNOW HOW MUCH SHIT THERE IS OUT there. There's whole communities dedicated to this stuff. I mean, of course you don't know. You've been here for months and you haven't even been to Garnet Ghost Town yet." Randy opened his atlas on his lap and looked at it by the light of the fire they'd lit outside the semi cab. "Man, I'm so glad I got out of there. Marysville is shit and everything else is even worse. Skagit County is just a dump. Those guys, man – Ed, he fucking lost it on a turn. He's in a *wheelchair*, man."

Randy seemed elated by the semi cab. "This is exactly the kind of place I need to get. So I can sleep on the road. I'm going to hit all of these places and then write a book. *Haunted Highways* or something. An exposé."

Randy. Jackson felt so grateful for him as he sat there, pontificating in his ugly trench coat. That same old pocked face. He looked like a little kid when he was excited.

"And girls – there's no girls in Marysville, practically. But once I'm out there ..." He poked at the fire with the toe of his sneaker. "What are the girls like here?"

"Randy," Jackson said. His heart sped up a little. "I like guys."

"It's cool," Randy said. "I just thought, maybe, you didn't want to say yet."

The relief made him want to laugh. Jesus! All of that. He smiled in the dark. "I figured you knew," he said.

"So, you're seeing somebody here?" Randy said. "You got a boyfriend?" Jackson felt a little flush of pride. Never in his life had he been able to tell someone, yes, sure, that's my boyfriend. You couldn't exactly say that when you were jerking off the local swim star or fucking a man for money once a week. But on the back of the pride – the sting of it. The ache, which still hadn't gone away, even though it had been nearly a month now since Don's accident. Don would be back in Missoula now with Eliza. He didn't hate Don, but he never wanted to see him again.

"I did," Jackson said. "Not anymore." He kicked the fire with his own boot and watched the sparks fly up.

Randy nodded, as though he already knew the story.

"He was a fucker," Jackson said finally. The heat had worn off and he felt cold suddenly. He leaned toward the fire. He was glad Randy didn't ask what had happened. They sat in the quiet, ash settling on them.

"You ought to come with," Randy said after a while. "Tour the whole country. See some shit." He reached a broken stick into the fire and concentrated on burning its end to a glowing point. "You and me, we're alike, you know. Not the homo stuff, you know, but *alike*" – and even though Jackson felt embarrassed he also felt good and he let it be. It grew quiet. The fire was ebbing to coals, spread out and blinking like a city seen from high above.

"What do you think it would have been like if we were born somewhere else?" Jackson asked.

"You mean if we hadn't met?"

"No, just, if we'd had different lives. What we'd be like."

"Wish in one hand, dude."

"No really. What would you want your life to be?" Jackson felt silly but he didn't care. He didn't talk this much normally, but how long had it been since he'd seen anyone from his old life? The little hobo fire. Randy's tin-can car looking even smaller next to the semi cab, ready to take him out to all those waiting wingnuts. He'd probably marry some girl with a ghost fetish and they'd have little kids who wandered around tape recording the silverfish in the walls. Jackson felt so happy for Randy in that moment, the older, future Randy.

"You know, man. My weird shit. That's what I like. What do you want?"

He considered his own question. What did he want? A life without his father, where his father had never existed. But mostly he wanted Lydia. "My sister," he said. "I fucked up. Bigger than anything."

"You'll see her again."

"I don't know." He'd sold them out, and even if they wanted to find each other, how would they? And he'd done it all on purpose. All those days in the woods sitting between the seats of the wooden rowboat, the cool rough wood on their skin, pushing berries into Lydia's bow-shaped mouth. There was the truth – sometimes he'd dreamed a life without her. Sometimes he imagined the berries were poison and that when she died he would finally be free of her. That she was the thing holding him back.

"Listen, how hard is it to find someone? That's right up my alley, man. We can find them together."

"Randy, it's not that easy. I'm sure they changed their names. They could be anywhere."

"So we start with the people who've changed their names. There's records of all this shit. Don't you know anything about the Internet? Where do you think they would go?"

"If my dad hasn't found them yet, then they haven't left any records."

"Jack," Randy said. "Your dad is a stupid shit."

"I don't know," he said. "I don't know if they're still in Washington. Maybe Texas, but I doubt it. My dad would know to look there."

The best years he remembered were Lydia's baby years. A summer when she was one or two, just a baby, and his memory must have changed things, distorted them, or maybe it was because he was so small – that summer, he remembered lichen moths taking over, on the walls, on the grass, a thick blanket of them. He'd been rapturous and terrified, following the blizzard of their flight, afraid to touch them, to knock the dust off their wings, to hurt them. Long afternoons walking carefully through the snowy grass, the wings beating around him, Lydia bobbing behind him on a blanket. Another season, that year or the previous or the next, his mother had pointed to fine gray threads in the sky and showed him where it was raining far way. Even the ordinary wonders – powdered milk that transformed beneath the faucet, the tiny hole where a beetle had bored through a leaf – captivated him. What around him wasn't magic?

"Jackson," Randy said. "If you want me to find them, I will."

"I do," he said.

Jackson made Randy a bed on the dinette cushion with his head by Jackson's feet. "What's that?" Randy asked, pointing to the little Chinese herb, the Winter Worm, in its plastic packet on the counter.

"Nothing," Jackson said. It looked ugly to him now, mean and gnarled. There wasn't any life in it. Just Lydia, pushing it into his hand, her face closed to him. The last time they would touch, and he hadn't known. He pushed it into his pocket and finished making up the bed.

It was warm in the cab, and comfortable, Randy snoring lightly at his feet. It came back to Jackson then, just before he slept himself: ten years ago, twelve years. "And here I am, king of all this," his father says, coming into the kitchen where he and Lydia are on their hands and knees playing horses. "I work all my life and all I have to show for it is this shithole and you assholes." It hurts Jackson to hear him even then, at seven or eight, with his sister's pink hand – her hoof – in his own. This mountain is theirs, Firetrail Hill, stretching up into the dark night, and somewhere on it is at least the single light from this kitchen. Somewhere on it is all that Jackson knows.

"King of all of this," his father says again. He is probably drunk, though Jackson doesn't know it then. The tiny light from the kitchen barely leaking from the window onto the grass. His father is swaying above them, and he is waiting for them to look up and see how worthless they are, but Jackson keeps kneeling with his sister.

HE LEFT RANDY asleep in the morning and went down to the work site. He was early. There was the new terrace, the place where Don's accident happened. Over the last three weeks the project had gone on; the terrace hadn't been backfilled yet, but the stones were in place. Jackson could only pick out the concrete block that had fallen if he looked for it, and that surprised him, that it wasn't marked in some way. That it didn't jump out at him, blood-stained, foreboding. It was just one more rock.

The early morning light was gray. He lit a cigarette and stood there. He might just stay the winter, he thought. There would be work if he wanted it. This was no different than any other town, really. Just one more place that people gather on this earth. But then – he thought of Randy's offer. "If you want me to find them, I will. Come with me."

He looked out at the lake, at the rows of new buildings. In six months or a year, he thought, all of the sorrow of Don's life would still be stretched out before him, but around this lake, framed in these windows, would be a hundred different futures, all beginning. He understood, too, that he had been spared. In everything that had happened, he had been able to go on. He started walking around the edge of the lake. He didn't know how early he was, how much time he had, but it didn't seem to matter. He didn't want to look at the concrete block. He didn't want to think of Don anymore.

When he came to the dam, he crossed it, following the water to where it washed up against the old baseball diamond, the dusty lots where teenagers would have parked once, sliding damp hands into each other's shirts. It felt good to walk. He thought about the pits that needed burning, and his station by the skill saw where Dave Riley yelled down measurements for him. He kept walking. What if he did go with Randy? Was that crazy? He could hear a truck in the distance. He could hear all of them going to work. Since the accident he was careful, avoiding the eyes of the men who must know, or suspect. If he let himself think about it he was full of a cold fear. Don's hand reaching toward him was the reaper's scythe, the owl calling his name.

He stopped when he was as far from the work site as you could get. He stopped where he had a good view of the lake and sat down in the grass, the damp of the ground soaking through his jeans. The little herb was in his pocket, and he took it out. Whatever life was in it was so deep inside. He didn't want it. It was a consolation prize, a reminder of how he'd fucked everyone over. He could think about it all of his life, he thought, and he wouldn't understand why he had done it. He used one hand to make a cold little flat of grass, breaking and smoothing it. He opened the cellophane packet and spilled the Winter Worm into that nest, letting the grass fall back around it, hiding it. He could stay, he thought, or he could go. He could go with Randy. That was something his mother had given him – the ability to go where he wanted.

"So let's go," he said aloud. Why not? he thought. He couldn't think of a single reason why he shouldn't, and a hundred why he should. "Let's go," he said, and this time the words sounded electric and sweet, carrying across the water in the still of the morning.

The sun was breaking through the fog, the faintest warmth on his arms. He felt like laughing. He stood and stretched his legs. Even as he thought about leaving, it was as though it had already happened, and there was no way that it couldn't. He was shaking Mike Leary's hand. He was closing the door of the semi cab. The dashboard was glowing; Randy was drumming a beat on the wheel. Somewhere, Lydia and his mother were waiting for him, and he believed Randy when he said he could find them.

"Let's go," he said again. He pushed through the woods, catching branches on his bare arms, and thorns, but he was imagining the radio, the painted lines of the road slipping past, the signs for towns they'd find or forget, and he walked faster. Happiness was rising in him, he was running up out of the woods, and it felt like the future was just beyond the trees, shining. It was offering itself to him, he thought, and all he had to do was step forward. All he had to do was take it.

Amy
Watermelon Thump, Luling, Texas, 2010

SHE POINTED OUT LANDMARKS TO LYDIA AS SHE DROVE: the boarded up library where she used to take out books; the roadside stand that was miraculously still in business, selling pickled okra and chow-chow; the secret path down to the river. She parked the car in Luling in front of Andy's Lounge; the sky over them was dark, trapping the heat as though they were under a galvanized bucket. She was excited. It shouldn't have meant anything; it was just a fair, once a year when the streets were loud with Tejano music and shouting, singing, popcorn that stuck to the soles of your shoes, card tables with stacks of foil-wrapped burgers, fabric roses glued to safety pins, and whirligig carnival lights striping the streets. The Watermelon Thump. She'd been on a blind date here, long ago, and danced with different boys from Fannin High and Luling, and once she'd kissed Scott, even though he was with Jennifer. They had big bottles of wine weighing down their backpacks and nothing meant anything, it was all just sweet and damp; wet mouths, cheeks pressed to hers, her own hands between her hot legs.

She took Lydia's hand and they started toward the main drag, where the parade would be. Even with the thick dark clouds it was still summer and she was full of what she'd forgotten flooding back to her, even though she hadn't thought of these things in years: lantana, prickly pears, and the smell of cedar in the woods. A Luna moth beating its wings in her cupped hands. Pink crape myrtle, white, purple. The Dairy Queen and Stonewall peaches and

Mexia peaches and beggar's lice. Iced tea with Sweet'N Low in the pink packets, the pile of them beside a glass and spoon. Always she and Jennifer had said they were going to go to Mexico and drink mescal. They were going to float down the San Marcos every day with a keg strung between their inner tubes. They were going to get brave enough to go gigging frogs with their dates, but they both were going to scream before the boys could prong them. Why would the boys care when they were wearing dresses that would make every man in Fannin pause with a tender ache in his chest?

SHE LED LYDIA through corridors of people and lawn chairs. Half of the faces looked familiar – people she'd known, or their children. To stand on a crowded street – the simple indulgence of that – made her grateful. What terrified her in Washington, what had put her in danger, protected her here; everyone knew a scrap of her story. Gary's name hung around the town like a fog. Even if she'd been away for eighteen years, she belonged to Fannin, and he didn't. She doubted he even belonged to Geronimo, where the ranch had been. If she thought about it too long the fear would start to rise up – the suspicion that he was never who he said he was, that she might have married someone who was even more of a stranger than she could imagine, even after everything he'd already done. She didn't want to know. She thought instead of how, if he so much as turned down First Street, the news would pass from mouth to mouth and someone would help them.

She was sure that it wasn't all wonderful, that people must be talking about her. Women in the aisles of HEB lowering trays of gizzards into their carts after service at the Baptist Church. They'd say she was a saint for what she'd endured, they couldn't believe it, what a shame, but still – to leave a husband, that was wrong, wasn't it, and hadn't Amy gone to Seattle in the first place, practically dragged him out there, and Seattle, what kind of place was that, all kinds of liberal Yankee gays, fruits, and nuts, she must have done *something* to bring it on herself.

She and Lydia had just passed City Market Barbecue, one of

the big businesses in town – they were making money hand over fist this weekend – when she saw Scott. It was him, looking the same, just heavier, and jowly. His stomach pressed against his thin T-shirt. He saw her stop and looked at her. She could tell he was searching for who she was, and then lit on it. He smiled hugely. It was the same Scott, she thought. He could grow old forever and he'd still be a little boy.

"*Amy?*"

She smiled. "Here I am," she said.

"Well, shit," he said, and then bounded toward her, wrapping her in his arms, his sweat and barbecue smell. "Holy hell, you look exactly the same. You look real good, girl."

Amy held up her hand, joined with Lydia's. "And this is Lena," she said. "My daughter."

Scott looked from Amy to Lydia, and she wished for a minute she could see what he was seeing, what whispers of Gary could be found in her daughter's face, how much she herself had aged. "That's great, Amy," Scott said. He looked so happy to see her, as though he'd been waiting a long time.

"Actually," she said. "It's Ann, now. Ann Harris."

"Ann," he said, like he was thinking hard about the sound of it. "I guess you needed to do that, right?"

She felt heat rising up her face and neck. "Yes," she said. "I did."

"I heard he was trouble," Scott said. "I been feeling real guilty about that, Amy. Introducing you and all."

"Scott," she said. "You didn't know." It felt good to absolve other people of guilt for the things that she hadn't yet been able to absolve herself.

"Still," he shook his head. "Still."

"Just watch out for us," Amy said.

He nodded. He reached out a hand toward Lydia, lightly nipped at her shoulder with his fingers. "You're real pretty, Lena," he said. Lydia smiled.

"I saw Jennifer," Amy said. "I met Janie, she's so pretty, Scott."

"Aw," he said. "Janie's a doll. And Jennifer–" A sadness fell over his face. "You tell her, if you see her. Tell her I'm a broken son of a bitch without her."

Lydia was looking at Scott. Amy imagined her puzzling out these mysteries–who belonged to whom, who knew Gary and how, and why.

"I thought, man, I just thought, love me or leave me the hell alone," Scott said. "But I'm one broken son of a bitch without her." He slipped one hand up under his T-shirt and scratched his stomach.

"She'll come around," Amy said, and she believed it. Jennifer and Scott pressed close together in the front seat of Scott's beater truck on the banks of the San Marcos, against a row of gray lockers. It seemed like the two of them together held something important in balance, a tiny pivot point in the larger machinery of the world.

She hugged Scott again. "Don't be a stranger," he said. She shook her head, even though he had already passed by; she put one hand on Lydia's shoulder and they walked on through the sidewalk crowds. "Scott," she said to Lydia, shaking her head. "He's exactly the same."

"He's nice," Lydia said, "but he smelled like barbecue." They laughed. Amy was waiting for questions, wouldn't have minded them, but now her daughter was quiet, searching the crowd, her eyes skipping from the slumping carnival booths to the main stage and the trucks backed up on the grass. She seemed younger, Amy thought, or maybe Lydia had spent too long seeming way too old. Amy felt the same herself–too young, too old. She'd missed the '90s, nearly completely. She'd stayed home, raised her babies, ran from Gary, learned the ways to avoid him. Watched nothing but the nightly news. And now, on the Luling streets it was as though she'd aged unbelievably, and as though she was still eighteen, wearing a tight dress, weaving in and out of the crowd.

She and Lydia stood in line for the rides. On the Tilt-a-Whirl Lydia laughed, screaming, and clutched at Amy's shoulder. She looked like a child, Amy thought. She was glad that Lydia wasn't embarrassed by her, to be on the ride with her, and grateful to be able to appreciate something so trivial.

"There must have been good times, too," her mother had prompted her, a few nights before, looking so sad, and Amy said, "Yes, yes of course," not just to placate her mother but because there were. There were normal days, and terrible things, and then there were good ones, too. But the happy times, in hindsight, pained her. Not because she missed them but because they were *too* bright, full of sharp laughter and big-toothed smiles that seemed about to careen into something else. Like an alcoholic's happy times, she thought, reckless and lurching madly on a knife's edge.

Still, there were good moments that were quieter, between her and Jackson and Lydia, just the three of them. And this, she thought, pulling Lydia close against her, the two of them held still in the heart of the rolling ride, this was good. So what if people talked about her, she thought. Who gave a damn. She had her daughter, and somewhere her other baby was out in the world. It could have been the heat, or the disorienting, bucket-colored sky, the spin of the ride, but she felt like she could feel them both, as though she had one of them at the end of each arm.

She remembered a time when the three of them were down on the Sound digging for clams. It wasn't allowed that season, but they weren't keeping them, just shaping holes into the sand, sinking their arms to their elbows, reaching toward the dark sources of air bubbles. The tide was far out, and after a while they walked out to the water's edge. There was man there in a yellow rubber raincoat and tall black waders. He'd dug himself into the wet sand and he was pulling on a geoduck.

She'd heard jokes about geoducks before, about the long, flesh-colored proboscis. Still, she'd never expected them to look *that* obscene. Jackson was watching and she could tell he wanted to laugh, and Lydia was mesmerized because it was so unworldly–this man in a tug-of-war with a sea creature.

She met Jackson's eyes. "Hold your tongue," she said, and

Lydia said, "What is that?" and Jackson didn't laugh aloud but Amy was laughing with him, the joke danced between them, even as she crouched beside Lydia, wondering at the geoduck with her daughter. It was the same feeling she had now, even though Jackson was far from her. With Lydia warm against her spinning through the dark, she felt like she was suspended between the two worlds of her different children, a steady foot in each of those places, holding them both.

Lydia

Fannin, Texas, 2010

JANIE, JENNIFER'S DAUGHTER, DROVE ME TO GERONIMO, where my father's ranch once and maybe still was, on October 22nd, the day after my fourteenth birthday. It felt like we were just two friends, driving the dusty roads with the radio turned up. "An arrangement," my mother said, because of the time I ran away, and the time that Janie's mother caught Janie riding in a truck on the back road with a man who was much older than high school. Even though it was an arrangement, I didn't mind. I felt older with Janie, and more exciting. We'd dyed my hair, too. I liked how it looked. Reddish, darker. Glamorous, I thought. I wanted to feel different, like I wouldn't catch my father's eye. I imagined being face-to-face with him on the street and he wouldn't recognize me. I dreamed I walked right past him.

The fields we drove past were burnt brown. Here it was late fall and still hotter than any summer I remembered before. There were summers in Washington that passed so quickly I only remember the edge of the Sound pulling in and out, the water over my feet; the sun slanting through the thin curtains; an ice cream from the Lake Goodwin stand. A field that burned down the road, and the way my mother and father took the neighbor's call and drove the truck fast, kicking up a cloud of dust that mixed with smoke, and then beat the fire with blankets. Jackson and I ran after them, watching from the road, the smoking stinging my eyes, the rough taste of it in my throat.

"Wow, what a birthday present," Janie said, winding down

the window and letting the hot air rush in. I'd asked her to take me on a drive for my birthday. I said it was what I wanted, as long as it was secret. It took me a long time to find the address. There were two Hollands in Fannin, but that wasn't right. "Which city did my dad come from?" I asked my mother one day, as if I'd just forgotten. "I mean, which city was the ranch in?"

"Geronimo, don't worry, it's a ways from here," she'd said. There was only one Holland in the Geronimo phone book, which the Fannin library kept under the front counter.

It wasn't really a ways. Half an hour, maybe more. "Slow down," I said, when I knew we were getting closer, and I watched the empty dirt lots, the driveways, and the houses move past. When the numbers were close, I saw a sign on a fencepost painted *Holland*. My skin prickled. "Slow down," I said to Janie, touching her arm, and she looked at me but slowed the car. I knew what our moms were doing, making us watch each other, but just then I didn't mind.

The house was small, a trailer house like the house in Washington. There was a red truck parked out front. There was a chicken coop and a sign that said *Eggs 2 dollars*. There were three sheds, all leaning. They looked like our shed in Washington. I wondered if my father had built it, and the prickling came back over my skin. Once there were bees in the wall of our shed, so many that we could hardly get inside without being stung. My father stuffed the wall with fiberglass insulation that shredded their wings. After they were gone I would reach my hand into the dark space and bring out black honey on my fingers. It tasted sweet and rotten. I knew the bees couldn't stay there, but still I felt bad, the way it ended.

I hadn't known what I would do before the sign. "I need to get some eggs," I told Janie. "Can we stop?"

She pulled the car the rest of the way to the shoulder, then she looked at me and raised her eyebrows. "Eggs?" she asked.

I had a feeling that if I sounded certain enough she would agree to believe me. "Yes," I said, "Come on, Janie."

She looked at me again, then sighed. "I'm not going to regret this, am I?" She pulled the car out and made a U-turn, then turned into the driveway. She put the car into park next to the red truck and turned off the engine. She pulled her cigarettes out of her purse. She was smiling a little. "You're not going to run off with a boy or something?"

I smiled at her. "No way," I said.

She shrugged her shoulder. "Fine," she said. She slid her seat back and put her legs up on the dashboard. "I'll wait here." She tapped a cigarette out of the pack. "Don't tell," she said, waving the cigarette at me, and winked.

"You don't, either," I said.

There were flower pots on the porch, full of roots and dirt. A wind chime of rusted forks and spoons that knocked together but didn't make a noise. A plastic lawn chair with a broken back. My heart beat like it was trapped in a tiny cage, trying to burst out. I knocked on the screen door.

"Yes?" the woman asked. She had her gray hair up in a blue scarf. There was a television on loud behind her.

"I just–" I was looking at her, trying to decide if she looked like my father. If she looked like me. Her eyes were an icy blue, not like ours at all. "I wanted to buy some eggs."

The woman smiled. "Well!" she said. "Well, that's fine. What brings you all the way out here?"

"I saw your sign–" I said. The woman looked past me at Janie, who was sitting in the front seat with her cigarette hanging out the window. Janie held up a hand. "And–we stopped."

"Your sister shouldn't smoke," the woman said, but she was still smiling. "We don't get a lot of people buying our eggs, but we always have so many. It's a shame. So many go to waste." She held the screen open and I followed her in. There were roses on the wallpaper, big faded blooms. She went into the other room and turned the television off. "Anita Holland," she said when she came back in, holding out her hand. I shook it. "Janie," I said, because it was like I'd forgotten my own new name and even saying it would have seemed like telling too much. I could see Janie through the kitchen window and now with the lie in front of me I hoped she'd stay where she was, smoking and fiddling with the radio.

"Well, Janie, how many you want, you said a dozen?" The refrigerator was mostly empty, except for milk and orange juice, some casserole dishes, and four brown eggs in a shallow bowl. "You caught me being lazy." I started to say that four was enough, but then, I thought, she'll just send me on my way and I won't know a thing. "Come with me," she said. She pulled two empty cartons from a cupboard. "You got good shoes on?"

The coop was full of feathers and the sound of the chickens. "If we got more people coming out, I'd get them ready," she said. "But we don't."

"Do you need the money, though?"

She laughed and it sounded big and warm and it made me think of my father when he was good.

"Well, everybody needs money," she said, very serious, as though she was afraid I would think she was laughing at me. "But these eggs are just an extra thing."

She ducked into the coop, under the metal roof, and came back with a handful of eggs. "When I was a little girl," she said, "we would go to the railroad station for our chicks. They let you know when the chicks were coming and you would bring a flat box for your shipment."

"They came in on the train?"

"Yes," Anita said, wiping one of the eggs on her shirt and handing it to me. "We had a little shed with a light to keep the chicks warm, and chick feed, water, you had to watch them, before you turned around they'd start molting and the fluffiness would turn into feathers and pretty soon you'd have pullets and roosters. You only needed one rooster, so you'd use them up as they got good to eat. Then you'd get little pullet eggs, small like bird eggs. My mother would say, 'Oh, you're little, you get the little egg.' You could decorate teensy eggs at Easter and then as they got older, the eggs got bigger and bigger. They only really lay in the spring, summer, and fall months. Winter – they were getting older, we'd eat them."

"You ate them?" I asked.

"My mother would make such good chicken and noodles. You'd have broody hens, trying to keep their eggs, so you'd have to get the eggs out from under them. My grandmother, I'd follow her through the hedgerows and look for hens, try to bring them in. Sometimes the eggs would be good, other times they'd be so old and rotten. You'd find a hen that'd laid herself a big nest of eggs and you didn't know what would happen. Some would be fertilized, some would be pretty near hatched, some would be rotted."

I tried to hatch a bird's egg, once, under a light bulb in my closet. Jackson and I tried doing ESP, telling it to hatch, but it didn't. In secret, after three weeks, I cracked it open and a plain raw egg slid out, smaller but still with the same yellow yolk.

"What are you going to make with all these eggs?" Anita asked.

"I don't know," I said. "I haven't decided yet."

"Well, these eggs are a few days old, so they'd be good for an angel food cake," she said. "If you're going to make an angel food cake by hand, you need twelve eggs or so, and you need to keep them out. A fresh egg that's just laid will not beat up. They need to be three days old or so, then they'll beat." She pointed to the back of the coop, where the roof was low. "Would you go check around back there? They like to bury them, and I'm too darn old and fat to get back there."

I crouched down in the back of the coop and sifted through the sawdust until I turned up an egg with a mottled shell, and then another. "You're not old and fat," I said.

Anita laughed. "I sure feel it," she said. "How old are you, now? Just a baby."

"I just turned fourteen," I said, "two days ago." On the night of my birthday, my grandmother made tamales, wrapped in corn husks and foil, and my mother poured me a glass of wine thinned with 7-Up, and we kept toasting to nothing, to Fannin, to fourteen, to the best tamales this side of the San Marcos, to the San Marcos.

"Oh, these are the salad days," she said. "Don't ever get old."

I kept sifting through the sawdust, passing eggs to Anita. She was stooped under the chicken wire, puffing a little from the walk, and I felt brave. "Didn't you have any kids?" I asked.

"Ah," she said quickly. "No, no."

Lie, I thought. Anita looked flustered. She dropped an egg and crouched down to pick it up. "Ah, never mind me," she said. "Always clumsy." She had a dark face when she said it. She ducked out of the coop and brushed herself off. "That's about how many we need, isn't it? A dozen for you and a few for me."

I followed her back to the kitchen and she put the full crate into a grocery bag.

"How much are they?" I asked, and she shook her head.

"Oh, nothing," she said, waving her hand. "A birthday present. And for keeping an old woman company." She turned to the counter, where there was a bowl and a jar of mayonnaise. "I'm making a crab salad, if you and your sister are hungry."

"I said I'd be home for dinner." Another lie.

"You sure are pretty," Anita said. "You have those nice dark eyes. I've always loved dark eyes. I wanted a daughter."

"Why didn't you have one?" I asked. My mouth shook around the edges of the question.

"Oh, honey," Anita said. "Me and my husband–" She stopped for a minute, holding one of the eggs in her hands. "Me and my husband–he's out working now–a place like this will just work you to death. We did have a son–I don't know why I said that, just now, that I didn't–you just caught me off guard. He was the joy of my life, and then–he just went away from me. He and his father–they were just oil and water to each other, and as he got older he was so angry, just mad at the whole world. Something changed in him." She wasn't looking at me, just holding the egg. "It broke my heart."

I could see the kitchen fan pointed at me, its purring blade, but I couldn't hear a sound. Sweat ran down my back. "What happened?" I asked.

Anita looked tired. "I sure don't know, honey. I've asked myself that and I'll keep asking myself that every day that I walk this earth." She opened a drawer and shut it again. "The delight of my life, and then he turned thirteen, fourteen, and it was like he was gone from me." She looked at me and then away. "I'm talking too much," she said. "You don't need to hear an old lady's sob story." She shook her head.

I smiled. I wanted to say something important. I wished I could give her something but I didn't know what, and she was opening the drawer again, turning away, looking through the cupboards. "Thank you for the eggs," I said finally.

"You come back," Anita said. "And remember, keep your eggs three days old. People talk about putting them in the icebox, but don't listen."

It was in her voice, in the way she talked and talked. A sadness like that is as clear as your name.

"WHAT ON EARTH do you need a dozen eggs for?" my mother asked, but we made the cake that night, with a recipe from my grandmother's *Betty Crocker*. I felt happy. Lighter, even if I didn't know much more than I had before. My grandmother Linda had pulled out a cardboard box of old photographs and she was going through them while we baked, holding up one photo and another. "Just look at this," she would say. "Look at what a doll your mother was. And your grandfather! That was back when men were still handsome."

While the cake cooled, we sat at the table and looked close at the photos. When we lived in Washington, I thought of my parents as coming from nowhere, as though they had grown straight out of the woods, out of the little house, and their lives had not begun until Jackson and I were there to watch them. Now, in Texas, my mother's life before me was all there, in the photographs: My mother when she was a chubby baby, with her feet dangling in the river, held up by my grandmother. Sitting on her father's lap with her fingers in her mouth. I stared long at my grandfather's face with the carved out space in his jaw. He was my grandfather, but the scars on his face made him look like a monster, and I felt bad for the man he could have been. Pictures of my mother in her prom dress, her hair sprayed above her head and still in her face like a bride's tall veil.

I waited until my grandmother had gone back to take a shower, though I didn't know why. "What did Dad's parents look like?" I asked, and my mother leaned back in her chair.

"Would you believe I never met them?" she said. "He didn't like to talk about them. He said they weren't close, that they were always fighting. It probably seems crazy, that I never knew them, but it always seemed like talking about them made your dad angry, and I was so young–I let it go. I kept thinking that as you kids got older he'd make up with them and we'd all meet them together. It does seem crazy now. And then it was too late, and I didn't know if they were safe or not." She sighed. "We were married so quickly." She picked up a photo of herself as a baby lying on her back on a blanket and put it back down. "It does seem crazy now," she said again.

"I think they were safe," I said. I thought about Anita gathering the eggs, the look on her face when I asked her if she had children. It was the look that my father left behind, of something made dark and ruined. It was the way the honey tasted. The look of the field when the fire went out. One day, I thought, I'd tell my mother what I knew. Not yet, but one day.

"It's nice to think that, isn't it?" my mother said. She pulled out a roll of foil. "Let's go down to the river. We'll take the cake."

It wasn't dark yet, but there were clouds. The evening sun shot through them and made the leaves on the trees glow silver and bright. We sat on the rocks next to the river where my grandmother had told me that my grandfather used to swim before the war, before the scars, when they were young and in love. If you followed it, it would cross my little fort. My mother sat right in the rocks and scrubby grass. I wasn't angry at her anymore, just at my father. He was a sharp bead that I carried in my pocket, and I couldn't stop turning it over at the same time that I tried not to touch. It might always be that way, I thought, but I could also imagine it growing less sharp. I could imagine that one day I might not be afraid of turning into him.

"I love this river," my mother said. "When I hear the word river, this is what I think." She unwrapped the two ragged pieces of cake and handed one to me. A snow of crumbs fell down her wrist and onto the ground. Everyone belonged to a place, I thought. It didn't matter if you'd gone forever. You might never come home, but it was still inside of you. Texas was wound inside my mother like a tight bright string. And Washington was inside me, I thought. On the backside of my skin were the branches of trees. The darkness, the mountains hidden behind forest and silver sky.

"Do you know what I mean?" my mother asked.

The cake was sweet, light as clouds. I remembered being five or six, standing at the kitchen window in Washington and pointing to the place where I would put my own mobile home. I was so small and already I was aching for that place, even while I was still there, even with all of the bad things, or maybe because I knew that those things meant that one day it would all end. I will live here forever, I told myself then. At night I lay in the bunk bed built from two-by-fours, eyes clenched shut, my teeth against the pillow. *I will be here until I die*, I promised. I remember I touched my lips to my hand, to my ring finger.

"Yeah," I said, leaning against her. In the green of the river there were tiny fish scattering, streaming by like stars.

If you said it and kissed your left finger, it meant forever, if you said it until the promise inside you was loud as your heart, and I did.

Jackson
U.S. 30 East, 2010

THEY WENT TO THE DRY CREEK CEMETERY IN BOISE, FIRST, and stood on the edge of the canal, high on the cliff, listening for the sounds of a horse that was supposed to be running. The only sound was the wind, but Jackson tried; for Randy he leaned into the bitter cold air, trying to hear a whip, a clopping, and by the time they climbed back into the car and pressed their ice fingers to the lukewarm vents, he couldn't say for sure he hadn't.

They had a list: Kimama old town, where a woman sang whispery notes in Russian in the dark. Ammon Park in Pocatello, to find the ghost girl in a blue dress on the four-in-the-morning swings. Maybe they'd go down to Alcatraz, or east to Nebraska, where a man in Nebraska City had hung each of his sisters on the different hills outside of town, on to Ohio, the Athens Lunatic Asylum.

It seemed like Randy's world was bigger than his own, like Randy himself was bigger for all of the strings that tethered him to the world, filaments shooting from the Internet, mailing lists, letters he wrote. Randy was good at having friends, Jackson thought. Jackson didn't care much about any of the places they were going, but the sum of it was something. He had the feeling that it would mean more if Randy wasn't alone. If Randy wasn't the only one in the world this was important to.

They parked outside Pocatello as the sun was coming up. They'd been drinking in the park, waiting for the ghost girl in the blue dress, and now they lay side by side with the car seats jacked back, the bottle of whiskey wedged between the parking brake and Jackson's seat.

"An Easter dress," Randy said. "Baby blue, with white lace." He reached for the bottle. "God, I can't believe we didn't see her. Or hear the swings or anything." He took a drink and spluttered a little. Randy didn't drink much, but Jackson could tell it was a point of pride to make it seem like he did. "Brown hair," he said. "Shoulder length."

Maybe he was drunk, too, but Jackson was glad they hadn't seen anything. It was the brown hair, maybe: he kept imagining it was Lydia in that dress, and he didn't like to think about it. How strange, even imagining that if something happened to her he wouldn't know. No one in the world to tell him. Or no one for his mother to tell. He took the bottle from Randy. "So, what about what you said?" he asked. "About them?" He took a drink, held it in his mouth, swallowed. It burned. "I mean, finding them." He didn't want to bug Randy about it, but at the same time he didn't care.

"I'm working on it," Randy said. "I need the Internet, man. We'll need to stop the next time we can." He sighed. "Shit, though, I can't believe the swing didn't even move."

With his index finger, Jackson cut a line through the condensation that had gathered on the inside of the window. "Maybe she got scared off," Jackson said. "We smell like shit."

Randy laughed. "Maybe we should get a motel tomorrow," he said. "Or truck stops! They have showers there."

Jackson had the feeling that Randy had money but that in Randy's mind motels weren't part of all of this. The idea of a truck stop shower turned Jackson on, made him feel like a pervert. All those big dirty men soaping up next to each other, fumbling for quarters when the water went out.

"And they have waitresses," Randy said, and Jackson laughed. It was all the same and different. The truck stop was never just a truck stop.

"And truckers," Jackson said. Even with Don, he wouldn't

have said something like that. It occurred to him that he and Don hadn't said much to each other. Not really.

It was quiet for a while, and then Randy said, "I'll never get laid." Even though Jackson knew, of course he knew, that Randy was a virgin, it still surprised him to hear the words hanging in the damp, close air.

"No way," Jackson said finally. "There's going to be tons of girls."

Randy snorted. "Right," he said. "Who are you talking to, here? I'll never – be in love." He took another drink from the bottle. It was so dark in the car, but Jackson could see the faintest light on the bottle, hear the whiskey pour into Randy's mouth. It felt sexy, to be in the car, talking about love, the whiskey smell around them, Randy's mouth open, the liquor dripping in.

"I'll never be in love," Randy said again. "I mean, I'm sure I will, but – but, no girl will love me."

"Hey," Jackson said. He wanted badly, all of a sudden, to tell Randy that someone would love him. He believed it, too. He imagined that Randy would live alone, but that certain girls would love him terribly. "That's not true," he said.

They were quiet for a while. Jackson wasn't sure if Randy was asleep. "You will," he said after a while. "And they will." There wasn't an answer, but he said it one more time.

IN A LIBRARY in St. Louis, Randy turned up published lists of name changes, pages upon pages scrolling across the beige computer monitor, but nothing was right. He tried to find recent title transfers on cars that matched the one Jackson's mother had been driving. They stayed in St. Louis for three days, and Randy asked Jackson questions: "Would they go north? South? Warm or cold weather? How likely was the car to break down? How many miles did it have on it?"

"I don't know," Jackson kept saying. The country grew bigger. There were more and more corners that his mother and sister might have slipped around. More places they might have gone to become strangers.

They pulled out of St. Louis early on a Tuesday afternoon heading across the Mississippi and past the burnt-out edges of East St. Louis. What kept occurring to him was loneliness, how lonely it had been, and how it was only going to keep on; he had been without his family for months now, and it was still only the very beginning. It was that thought, the wish for someone in the world who knew his mother or Lydia well, that made it occur to him. There was one person, though he'd never met her. He imagined himself going to her and talking with her, and the possibility of it was such a relief; but her name, he thought – what is my grandmother's name? In a moment of grace, from somewhere deep in his mind, he remembered: Linda.

They had been driving silently, Randy defeated and Jackson fighting off the loneliness. "Linda Merrick," he said to Randy. "Can you find that name? Somewhere outside of San Antonio?"

Randy didn't take his eyes off the road. I-70 East unspooled in front of them. "Do you know how old she is?"

"I can guess," he said.

What did he know of his grandmother? He remembered being very young, and hearing his mother talk about her. Grandma was a shimmery idea in the back of his mind, someone kind and unformed, and absent – someone who hadn't come for them. Still, he thought. She might have tried and his father would have kept her away. And maybe she looked like his mother. Maybe she looked like him. It seemed like his best answer – to find her. She'd know something important that would lead him one day to his mother, or she would know him, somehow, in some secret blood way.

It was still humid in late fall, but the wind was picking up; it seemed like it might storm. The library they found in East St. Louis was surrounded by heaps of brick. People milled outside smoking. It took Randy twenty minutes on a desktop to find the number. 830-963-2314. "Landlines – listed landlines!" Randy shook his head and laughed. "It's like going back in time."

Jackson's shitty phone that he never used was dead again and stuffed somewhere in the back of the car, so he took a handful of sticky coins from the glove compartment and went to the payphone outside. His hands were shaking and it took too many quarters; it didn't work, and then it was ringing, and a voicemail picked up after two rings. He hadn't thought of that option, that no one would answer. Randy was leaning against the car and gave him a thumbs-up. The dumb sweetness of it calmed him down enough to speak, to say, "My name is Jackson, I think you're my grandmother," and he read off the number from the sticker on the phone box.

There was nothing to do then but wait. He realized how stupid it was, but he couldn't change it now. He stayed in the phone booth. Randy went into the library, and Jackson was left alone. An hour, he thought, or two; maybe he would leave another message with his cell number. There was a flattened pack of cigarettes in his jacket but he didn't have a lighter.

It was only twenty or thirty minutes. He hadn't thought it would happen, and when the phone rang it was shrill and he was suddenly afraid. He readied himself and reached for the receiver. It was cold on his ear and his voice hardly came out to say hello, but her voice was coming at him, the first voice he'd ever heard. It was his mother and she was crying. He leaned on the silver cord, his whole weight on this phone. Where were they? He was crying, suddenly. "I'm sorry," he said, and she said, "We're here, where are you?"

IT WAS LATE afternoon now, almost sundown. He walked back to the car, his body buzzing and electric. He must have told Randy, because Randy drove them back out of East St. Louis and then they were on I-44, heading southwest. Jackson stared straight ahead, the sound of the phone still ringing out to his fingers. Finally, Randy turned the radio dial with painstaking care, looking for his station. "Better get used to it," he said. "I have a printout that shows me the stations all the way from here to Texas."

Jackson laughed and rolled down the window and gulped

the fall air. Heat was still spreading through him. His eyes kept tearing up and he laughed again. He was suddenly unbearably thirsty and he reached for the half-empty jug of water in the backseat and drank it all the way down. He didn't know what to feel; happiness, he thought was too simple. There were regrets in him that would always be there, and small wonderful things, too. A small thing, to not be thirsty. He opened the glove compartment and took out the map. He unfolded it on his lap. Randy kept fiddling with the radio. Jackson kicked at his backpack at his feet. It was empty, except for the photograph, Eric's tie, the knife. He had nothing of Don's. Even the notes he'd drowned in the river. To think of how badly he'd hoped for their life together to be delivered and made real, while Don had been burning in shame.

But none of that mattered. There was the world before the phone rang, and the world after, and they were stepping into the new place, like driving into a dream. So this is what happens, he thought. We survived. His sister, shining, little star. She was a point in the sky, on the earth, that he could follow now.

They'd crossed back into Missouri and the sun was burning up the highway in orange sunset, and Randy kept twisting the dial and the station finally caught. He couldn't think straight to hear the voices on the ghostchaser station, but they rose up around him like a comforting crowd. It felt like all of the good in his life was there, in his hands and the things they passed – the road sign shining in the orange sun from the west was pointing them south, the handsome man thumbing a ride was every handsome man he might one day love. The hills all around them were burning with sunset. Randy was beside him, and maybe he could make things right again, now that they knew exactly where to go.

Amy

Fannin, Texas, 1990

SHE SAT ON THE FLOOR WITH THE TORN WRAPPING AND the gifts around her – a duffel bag, a wool coat, a Walkman – and thought, This could be my last Christmas with my father. The lump in her throat was a ball bearing, solid and metallic.

"I thought those things would be good for your trip," her mother said. She touched the sleeve of the coat. "It's cold in Seattle," she said.

Amy's father was dozing on the sofa. She watched his hands twitch in his lap.

"Thanks, Mom," she said.

They'd set the date to leave, and these small events paved the way: a dinner with her mother at City Market; dollar beers at the American Legion; Christmas. Then they'd be gone, and she could see how it was as good as done: you waited for something and then it was past, and it might as well have already happened, it all went that quickly. She swallowed hard against the lump.

"Amy – you can always come home," her mother said. "I know you need to go do this, have this adventure." She picked up a piece of wrapping paper and folded it in half. "I know that. Don't ask me to be happy – " She gave a choked little laugh. "But I know that. And I need you to know: you can always come home."

"Okay, Ma," she said. She looked away before she started to cry. She stood and went to the sofa, sat beside her father. She leaned against him, smelling his shirt.

It was six or seven when she heard Gary's truck pull up.

They didn't have plans to see each other until the next day, but she knew the sound of the truck and she slipped on her shoes and went outside.

Gary leaned out the window. He was drumming on the door, his face red, a cigarette burning in his other hand. "Please," he said. "I need to see you."

"But – my parents," she said.

"I just need to drive," he said. "I just need you with me." For a minute she felt angry – this was her last night with her parents, her last real night just for them, before they were half a country apart. But his face – he looked like he might cry, and it washed over her – this was the man she loved, and something was wrong.

"Give me a minute," she said, and went back in for her sweatshirt. Her mother nodded, as though she'd expected this, and looked away.

Gary drove the truck the length of Fannin and then out onto the highway, saying nothing. He put out his cigarette and gripped her hand tightly in his. She looked at him, brushed the hair from her face, waiting.

"Where are we going?" she asked finally.

"I don't know." He squeezed her hand. "I just had to get out of there."

"What happened?" she asked, but he shook his head. "Can't you tell me?"

He shook his head again, but then he started to talk, letting go of her hand, reaching for his cigarettes. "I just – can't take it!" he said. "I just can't fucking wait to be gone."

He was heading toward the ranch, she saw now. "They don't care what I want," he said. "If I don't work on that ranch, they don't want anything to do with me."

"What happened, Gary?" she asked. "Can you slow down for a minute and tell me what happened?"

He was pulling at his hair. "I've been working on this fucking shed all month," he said. "All fucking month. I work and I work.

It's like they don't even treat me like their son. It's like I'm just the fucking help."

"Okay," she said. "Okay. Did they say something? Are they upset about us? About us leaving?"

"Do you think I even told them?" he said. "Do you think I'm even going to give them the satisfaction?"

"Maybe if they met me – " They should want to meet her, she thought. They should want something.

"You don't get it," he said, looking at her. "You're mine. I don't want them to have any of that."

She couldn't decipher it, what was so terrible, what was making him so angry, but then she thought of his strong hands touching her, the curtain of his dark hair falling over her, containing her, the whisper of his mouth against her ear, her neck. Who could be cruel to him? Who could make him hurt this way?

"They treat me so badly," he said. "Don't ask me to talk about them. Don't ask me to even think about them."

"Okay," she said. "Okay."

They drove in silence to the ranch, and she imagined a scene with these parents. She imagined them with knotted faces, eyes like bullet holes, snarling mouths. But Gary turned the truck down the rutted road, far away from the house, toward a half-finished building, a frame and four walls – the building he'd been working on, she assumed. He parked in front of it and took three deep breaths. "God," he said. "God, I just want to be gone from here."

"I know," she said. "We will." She looked at him, trying to understand why they were here. He had that apartment. He didn't have to be out here if it was that bad. She was about to say so when he opened the truck door.

"There's something I have to do," he said. He climbed out and went around the back of the truck. It was getting dark and she could see him carrying something to the building, walking slowly around the perimeter. She could hear a splashing sound, but it took her a moment to understand. The smell of gasoline – but no, she thought, that doesn't make sense – but then she heard the scrape of the match, and a bright arrow sailed from his fingers.

She watched the fire spread, almost not breathing. Her mind felt slow. The bright flames were moving up the sides of the shed; they seemed to drip back down to the dirt, and even as she heard the sound of it, the heat radiating toward her, it was like she was watching from a distance. It was melting, she thought. Her hands felt cold, suddenly, and her body heavy, and she watched it as if she was watching a film. He came back to the truck and put his head in her lap. She held him, touched his beautiful face. He looked at her as the fire burned and the heat continued to blow toward them. She tried to make sense of it, tried to break the spell that seemed to have come over her – he was hurt; he was burning the shed because someone had hurt him; who would want to hurt him? Her mind was swimming and it welled inside her, his nameless sorrow.

They would go, she thought, far from where anyone could hurt him – could hurt them. They would leave, and they would protect each other. The moon was coming out, the fire was dying down, and it was beautiful. This night was lit up for them, she thought. The world was full of people who were terrible to each other, but it was full of beauty, too. They would find the beauty, she thought. They would spend it on each other.

Lydia

Fannin, Texas, 2010

WE WAITED. WE SAT TOGETHER ON THE FRONT PORCH and stared at the road and I didn't have to go to school. My mother cried for three days and said over and over, "I'm just so happy." The feeling was a song playing from far away, a line from a lullaby you hardly remember, "And I shall stay till my dying day with my whistling gypsy rover." I don't remember the night or if we sat through it. The day and the night were all the same in the middle, between, before, and after. Dust from the road settled on my skin.

I felt the car before I heard it, and then I heard it before I saw it. My heart punched my chest. The sun was in my eyes and I couldn't see them, but I knew it was Jackson, I knew it was Randy. My heart was still pounding but there they were, getting out of the car, and we were standing, we were moving toward them. And my mother was saying "My Jack, my Jack, my Jackson," and each time she said his name it was a late summer plum, it was like falling asleep in the sun in the afternoon. He stood in the light and looked at me. I'd thought my life was over, but now it was starting again. My mother was saying his name, and he was coming toward me, and I was his sister.

Epilogue
The Bird

STILL IT COMES TO AMY SOMETIMES, A DROWNING. THE darkness of the little house, the fear, the pounding of blood in her ears, behind her eyes. Nineteen years, she thinks. The length of time to know, to leave, to leave again for good, to slip his grip. The first promise she made to her children was to protect them. To bring them safely into the world. It swells in her, cold and swirling. What promises she broke. What it meant to be happy, and what was sorrow, the other lives she might have led, the feeling of her children's skin, their delicate faces, the tiny bones stringing them together, hunger of mouth, hunger of heart, loneliness, desire, the firmness of the earth, and memory, and belief in love, and belief in God – God, she thinks, and it seems so far from her, the only thing remaining her own dark song to Gary, pray for yourself. Pray for the rest of your terrible life. It washes her again and again: everything she had ever been was in those close rooms, trembling. Ruin was the lit window. Her skin was the shape of his hand.

And to stop it, she thinks of her children. It is always the same dream, and it is as real as if it is happening in front of her. She imagines them back in those dark forests, side by side, and she is somewhere nearby, watching. "Here," Jackson is saying, "is where our mother shot a bird down out of the sky and then made it fly again. Did I ever tell you that story?" Lydia shakes her head, and Jackson points to the trees. "Over there," he says, "Right over there. Did I never tell you that?" They are standing together in the stands of green pine, the rain hardly touching them. He is pointing for his sister and the bird is already lighting up from the wet ground, as though it has never been touched at all. And they are coming over the hills toward her, together. They are radiant, waiting to see.

Acknowledgements

I WISH THAT I COULD LIST EVERYONE WHO HAS GIVEN me love and support in writing this book – a thousand cups of coffee and hours talking over the same skipping Lucinda Williams album. There's not enough paper and never enough time, but I'll do my best.

Thank you to the faculty at Oberlin College who set me on my path, especially Dan Chaon, Ayse Papatya Bucak, and Sylvia Watanabe. In Portland, where the way was a little hazier, Evelyn Sharenov, Ariel Gore, and Kevin Sampsell shared their wisdom and friendship. I owe a debt of gratitude to many of the faculty and visiting writers at the University of Montana MFA program, including Kevin Canty, Deirdre McNamer, Judy Blunt, Beverly Lowry, and eileen myles. Thank you to Liz Gilbert, who, when I was twenty-one and lost in Wyoming, told me that the best thing I could do was to go out in the world and listen, and who gave freely of her time and kindness. Thanks to the advocates at VOA Home Free for allowing me, for a short while many years ago, to be part of their work and mission, and to everyone who continues to work in the movement to end violence against women and children. The Kimmel Harding Nelson Center in Nebraska and the New York Mills Regional Cultural Center in Minnesota provided weeks of uninterrupted time and support to write this book, and Brooke Warner's technical guidance brought everything together.

I owe a special thanks to some early readers and champions, including Cat, Rachel, Shahana, Anna and Chuck Kruse,

Elysia Mann, Mary Ann Bell, Oliver Butterfield, Molly, Lindsey, Lehua and Liz, Greg, Grey, Kala, Jenn, Chris, Sarah and Ash, Hank and Fred, Katie and Dave, Aylen, Marybeth, Ty, Dee, and so many others. Thank you to Emily, who was there through it all. Finally, thank you to Rhonda Hughes and the team at Hawthorne, who have been more incredible than I could have even hoped for.

Language has always been the way I hold on to the world. I will never stop being grateful for everyone who has been alongside me searching for the right words.